Always
Dr. Klein
Book III

Diana Scott
Published by Diana Scott
Copyright 2017 Diana Scott

Always
   Dr. Klein
   Book III
   Foreword
   Wake up
   New moons
   Don't look for me
   Truths
   With the scent of a woman
   A matter of luck
   Passions of Africa
   Hidden glances
   Run while you can
   Bargaining
   Caramel and beauty
   Alliances
   Learning to fly
   Hidden feelings
   Reality dawns
   Ghosts of the past
   Chained and released
   Of jealousy and truth
   I am this
   I am who I am
   Part II
   Clouds in paradise
   Perfect days
   Don't walk away from me
   Desperate solutions
   Let's write together
   Unresolved frontiers
   Saying goodbye

A not so distant future
Looking for you
Good, thank you
Don't listen to your heart
Back to
You and I
I want to be...
Epilogue

Other books by Diana Scott

Foreword

Her body was outlined in the wet sand of the beach under the glow of a moon that existed only to illuminate it. Her image nourished him like a starving man before the most delicate delicacy. Fingers numb with need tried to reach for her but her figure wandered away happy and laughing like the most mischievous of fairies. The smile on her full lips enticed him and he longed to join her but could not, she was his juicy forbidden fruit. No matter how much effort he made to hold her, she always left. Frustrated he cried out claiming to wait for her but the words would not come out. The rough, dry throat did not respond. Again and again his arms moved trying to hold her, but she fluttered around him like a butterfly, slipping through his fingers. The silky auburn hair vanished before him like a soft sigh and the scent of her sweet body marked a luminous path for him to follow. Once and a thousand times he tried, he wanted to stand up, to run to her side and claim what was his, but the harder he tried to get up, the harder he fell.

"No, no... don't leave me..." he pleaded desperately, but she continued to smile and move ever a little further away. Her seductive lips whispered for him to accompany her but his body did not respond. He tried, he wanted to run, he wanted to hold her, he stretched out his numb hands but she continued to blur in the distance. Desperate, he begged and cursed, but dense, lead-heavy legs crushed him to the ground again and again and again. "Wait...please wait..." he stammered choking as he felt himself losing her.

-No!" Her muffled cry echoed in the silent room.

-Come on, boy. Come back... It's time to wake up. We need you to wake up. This time the voice sounded a little more concerned and Akim felt covered by a thick cloud as she disappeared under his nose.

-No... no... -He gasped as he watched her body move farther and farther away. Brenda looked at him. He was no longer smiling now. Tears streamed down her delicious face and he wanted to scream with helplessness. Nervously he struggled to jump from the heights but his body refused. Don't cry.... I will not leave you... -He sentenced with superhuman strength struggling with the ropes that now tied him to a dark mattress. Tears bathed her delicate woman's face and Akim felt panic-stricken.

-No!

The roar of his own scream made him open his eyes, which, confused and drowned by sweat, searched for her in a room where she was no longer to be found.

Wake up

A man in a white robe insisted on dazzling him with a small flashlight and Akim felt increasingly confused. His head hurt like a thousand demons and the inability to understand what was happening there was upsetting what little consciousness he still retained.

Not far away he thought he recognized voices, maybe his father's and his best friend's, but his mental condition was not safe enough to guarantee anything, much less presences that sounded like ghosts from beyond the grave. Dazed, he tried to ask where he was but his voice was dead. With a superhuman effort he tried to move his arm but it would not obey either. Something was holding him back. Something hard and cold covered it from the elbow to the wrist, immobilizing it completely. Two weak, cramped fingers of his hand tried to free themselves, but even this simple task proved to be too tiring for a body as battered as his. Stunned and dazed he strained to hear what those voices were diagnosing in the distance but dozed off sooner than expected.

-We need to run some tests. We will bring him in as soon as possible.
The stretcher moved so quickly that he felt like a baby cradled in one of those high chairs with soft fabrics and sweet melodies. Tiredness and the hundreds of drugs in his vein delivered him directly into the arms of Morpheus, whom he embraced with willing desire. Whispering her name, like the mantra of a young man in love, he went to where she was waiting for him with lips full of passion.

"Why haven't they brought it yet?" Akim's father was getting up and sitting down again and again from the hard couch. He tried to calm himself but the waiting was proving to be insufferable. His young son had been in an induced coma for five days and his hopes were beginning to waver. When Nikola opened the door with two cups of hot tea, she thanked him from the bottom of her heart. Better to drink the brew than to release his fears and end up unhinged with worry.

-What's new? -asked a very distressed Nikola.

-None. He nodded his head and reached out to pick up the drink.

The young friend leaned his long body against the wall while cross-legged, he puffed on the cup to cool his tea.

-This is the biggest scare he's ever given us..... - Nikola muttered with a touch of annoyance and the father smiled warmly.

"He gave us? As if you were the father," he thought amused. Nervously he saw Akim's clothes folded on a chair and thoughts flashed through his mind. "Why does fate always tend to prey on the same ones? I could never stop any of those damned blows blackening his heart. It was only when he met the doctor that he thought the sun might be rising for him. "yet here we are, in a hospital."

-Thank you." He murmured sincerely as he looked at Nikola and saw her concern.

-Why? I couldn't be anywhere else. The young man answered so confidently that tears almost came to his eyes, and they would have if it had not been for the nurse who came in at that moment with his son's body on a stretcher.

Frightened to see Akim totally unconscious, he jumped off the couch, but was instantly reassured by the medical assistant.

-Calm down. He is asleep. Medications often cause such effects. He'll wake up in a few minutes. You don't have to worry. The danger has passed.

The father snorted loudly as if a thousand-pound slab had been lifted off his back and tried to take a sip of his tea, but the trembling of his hands made him spill much of the drink on the floor. The nurse left and Nikola sat down next to him by the stretcher. It was time to wait a little longer.

-Did you hear that? -Nikola said looking angrily at the dozing friend. He keeps calling her. Knocked out, asleep or stoned. It's always her," he grumbled between his teeth in annoyance.

His father would have liked to explain to him that true love is not forgotten on this plane or the next, but he did not feel strong enough to argue with Nikola's inexperience in love. Exhausted and nervous, he waited patiently as he had been doing for the previous four days. Akim had to wake up soon or he himself would have to be committed for temporary insanity. He loved his son and needed him in his life again. He may have looked like a young man molded by the hard knocks of life and some might even fear those wide tattooed arms but he knew the real Akim.

The young man opened his eyes but was unable to focus anywhere. Darkness was all around him. His head was splitting in two and his throat was sandpaper and of very poor quality, by the way, he thought confused by so many medicines.

-Fuck... -The words came out almost by themselves as I tried to move my left arm.

-You are awake.

-Dad? Is that you? -Are you there? -. His father's face paled at the sound. Nervously, he reached out to turn on the lamp on the bedside table next to him and nervously pointed the spotlight at him.

-Fuck! You've blinded me." He protested, opening and closing his eyes with force.

-Can you see me? -he asked, his voice strangled with fear.

-Of course I can see you. What the hell is wrong with you?

Akim replied in his typical bad mood and his father smiled in relief. His son was back.

-You're welcome.

-For nothing what?

-You're welcome.

Akim didn't bother to understand. His gaze focused on the now plastered arm and the father patiently explained.

-You're in the hospital. You had a stroke. Do you remember?
-Akim kept looking around. "Yes, we are alone. He answered knowing exactly who his son was looking for.

The saddened young man lay back as best he could but as he dragged his other hand through his hair he realized that half of his head was bandaged. Trying to spin some memories and he spoke in a most confused manner.

-I remember coming out of the store and something hit me in the back. I tried to turn around to defend myself but some guys grabbed me. I couldn't get free. He answered, narrowing his eyes as if he could remember something better.

-Did you see them? -Nikola entered the room at that moment.

-I thought you were going to rest. The father scolded him like a little boy and Nikola smiled mischievously.

-When you rest, I will. Now let your dear son tell us what the hell happened.

Akim frowned at his friend's irony. What was wrong with him? It was he who was in the hospital with a broken arm and a devilish turban on his head.

-What do you say? Have you seen them? Could you recognize them? -He asked again, interested.

-Philips." He whispered in embarrassment.

He didn't finish answering when he heard Nikola curse loudly and his father walk away from the bed.

-I'll fix it. Akim answered trying not to worry them but his father added to his friend's insults.

-Don't worry? Don't worry! You heard it Nikola. My son tells me not to worry.

The young friend's eyes widened without daring to answer. It was the first time in five days that he had seen Akim's father lose his composure. The man looked like a runaway locomotive and he wasn't about to stand in his way. His friend was an asshole, and if his father beat him out of bed, he deserved it.

-Don't let me worry! You know you've been in a coma for five days? In a coma! Damn it.

"No, the truth is that I didn't know. That's the thing about being in a coma.... You don't remember to count days." He thought with a touch of amusement that he preferred to hide. In all his years of life he had never seen his father so angry.

-At first I feared for your life, then for your blow to the head, but now that you have awakened, I see that you have not suffered any injury. You're still as dumb as before.

Akim glared angrily at a Nikola who unabashedly burst out laughing. He pressed his fingers to his temples trying to find some sanity in this crazy situation. He remembered Philips and some thugs, kicks, blows and darkness, but nothing else. Now he was in the hospital, according to his father, after being in a coma for four days. Four or five days, he had said? Anyway, with the mood he was in, it was better not to ask. And Brenda, why wasn't she there worrying about him?

-Did Brin...? -He couldn't finish the question. His father instantly turned to the window and his friend snorted angrily.

-Don't even think of bringing it up again. You almost scared us to death but you only think of her. You call her in your sleep and ask for forgiveness as if you were a fucking prisoner. We are sick and tired of your crazy love, not to say that.... You've got our balls all puffed up," Nikola grumbled, his fists clenched in fury.

-Dad! -. The door opened and the tender voice of a child echoed through the walls, silencing them all.

Lucien ran and was about to jump on his father's cast arm when Nikola lifted him up and gently pulled him close to kiss him on the cheek.

-You have to be careful, your father is hurt.

-Godfather, will he be cured? -The boy asked interested.

-Nikola answered with a sideways smile while Akim snorted in annoyance. The boy did not understand anything so he preferred to tell his father about his latest exploits.

-Nurse Carmen showed me the newborn babies and took me to the playroom. She is very kind, she gave me a ball and bought me an ice cream.

-Nurse Carmen? -Akim asked curiously.

-Yes, Uncle Nikola told her that he was my godfather and that we were alone in the world and she offered to take care of me until you woke up.

-Alone in the world? -. Akim asked smiling wickedly as Nikola gently rested the child on the ground.

-How about saying goodbye to your father. You have to go to school tomorrow. You have missed too many days. Grandfather spoke to the little boy in a commanding voice, but with a big smile on his face.

Akim looked down as he realized the discomfort he had caused. His family had really had a hard time and all the blame and worries originated from him. As usual.

-Nikola, could you take him with you?

-No." Grandfather looked at him in surprise, but the young man continued speaking as if nothing had happened. Grandfather looked at him somewhat surprised, but the young man continued speaking as if nothing had happened. You have not moved from this room for five days of hospitalization. You must rest. Grandfather was about to argue but Nikola didn't let him. I will spend the night here. If any problems arise I will call you.

Lucien held his grandfather's hand and the man saw that he was exhausted. Nikola was right, Akim was much better and out of danger. He should go home and try to get some rest.

-I will come first thing in the morning.

-I don't need anyone to take care of me. An angry look from his friend silenced him before he could utter any more words.

When the little boy and the grandfather found themselves outside, Nikola cursed loudly without sparing any insults and Akim stretched out on the mattress pondering whether it was really worth being awake.

-Your dinner. A very blonde nurse with a pleasant smile came into the room, holding a plastic bowl in her hands. The doctor will come later to check that you are all right. She said as she helped him to sit up on the backrest.

-Thank you. He replied, choking back the pain of crushed bones.

-We are here to help. The woman said smiling as she fluffed her pillow and glanced sideways at her friend.

Akim ducked his head to reach for the spoon. The soup looked awful but he wasn't in the mood to witness his friend's advances in front of his delicious nurse.

-Thank you so much Carmen, I will never be able to thank you for everything you have done for us....

Nikola continued talking as she walked through the door with her arm resting on the blonde's shoulders. Akim shook his head and looked at his cast right hand realizing that drinking the soup would be a titanic task for someone as dexterous as him. He was on the fifth spoonful and the thirteenth curse when Nikola entered the room again with a smile on his face.

-Goddess. He said looking at the ceiling.

-If you say so... -The friend answered as he abandoned the broth and tried to prick a pea that, shot by the pressure of the fork, left the plate and went directly to hit the TV screen.

-Come on, let me help you. Akim was about to refuse but he had too much appetite.

He finished the whole dinner. Not a single pea was left. His head barely ached and his body seemed to start responding to him.

-Nikola stammered as he pushed the now empty food tray away.

-It seems so.

They were both silent, and Akim didn't know how to bring up the subject without bringing up his colleague's fury. The last time he remembered her, she had left the nightclub with tears in her eyes.

-Nikola... -He said in a conciliatory voice.

-I haven't seen her. I wanted to let you know but I couldn't find you.

-You didn't find her? -he asked worriedly.

-No, not in the office, not at home, not on her cell phone. It's as if the earth swallowed her up.

-Son of a bitch. Akim spoke loudly and Nikola was instantly enraged.

-Forgive me for not spending more time on it, I was worried that my best friend was about to get it or become a bit more of a jerk than usual.

-The insult was not directed at you.

-Oh no? He mumbled, not quite believing it.

-I'm serious. The night I was attacked, Max was on the premises.

-How?" he asked with interest.

-Brenda didn't know she worked nights.

-Didn't you tell him?

-No, but apparently his ex did it for me.

-It's not so bad either," Nikola tried to play it down. She'll understand. She's an intelligent woman.

-Yes, well, there is also the little problem of the photos.

-Photos?

-Nikola's eyes widened in disbelief and Akim felt like a piece of garbage. It's not what you think. She caught me off guard. It was the only time and I broke it off instantly. In fact, I was even rude to reject her.

-And you say that Max has pictures? What a coincidence that it only happened once and he was there at that very moment, don't you think? -he said suspiciously.

-You too? I have never been unfaithful. Nikola looked at him with a face twisted in distrust and Akim smiled unwillingly. Not to her.

-Then more in my favor.

To tell the truth Akim had not had time to think. It had all happened too fast.

-That's not the worst of it...

-Mother of God, brother, problems come to you by the handful.

Akim nodded before continuing. -That idiot tried to buy me and I turned him down, but the jerk swears that not only was I unfaithful, but I cashed his stupid check.

-What figure are we talking about?

-One too high.

-A very good figure would make anyone think twice. He said with a nod of his head.

-You too? I didn't collect that money. Do you think I would do something like that to him?

-I would even change my last name for less. He replied amused.

Akim lay back on the bed. He felt exhausted and not because of the wounds. If his soulmate doubted, what could he expect from Brenda when Max told him. He should find her as soon as possible.

"Five days. It had been five days." He thought furiously. That bastard wouldn't have stopped at his lies, of that he was sure.

New moons

Tears no longer calmed her. The deep pain mixed with the shame of deception, plunged her into a sadness whose bars were too heavy to free herself. To put an end and write a new chapter where the liars no longer had a place would be the best option, but how to do it when your heart is still calling out to him? The warm water sailed over her numb figure while with her palms pressed against the wall and her face turned towards the cold floor, she begged for the blessed drops to wash away the hypocritical memories.

Oblivion, he was her only lifeline. In love and dreaming of a far-fetched reality, she behaved like a brainless ingenue, believing in strawberry fairies and love glitter. Falling in love with a younger man, for heaven's sake! How could she be so naive? Did she really believe in the unimportance of incipient wrinkles or in experience as a rising value? Stupid and a thousand times stupid. Tears streamed down her face mixing with the heat of the shower and she felt even worse than before. Remembering Akim gave her a sense of pain and helplessness that disarmed her as a woman. She offered her feelings to a con man of hearts and on a silver platter. She gave them away to an unscrupulous liar, one capable of pretending just to get a measly paycheck.

-No!" he shouted, slamming his fists against the wall as he remembered the damn money. "That's what my leap into the void for you meant?" he thought painfully. You took it all with your lies.

She turned off the faucet and stretched out her arm to wrap herself in a towel. Motionless, staring at her figure in the mist-covered mirror, she was grateful that the steam had fogged it. How many times would that ingrate and his explosive girlfriend have mocked her? How many times would she have stifled her beloved's mocking laughter between her large, perfect breasts? Brenda dropped the towel to the floor and couldn't resist the self-censure.

She was no longer a young girl. The rough skin on her feet, her hands scarred by the years, her buttocks struggling not to sag.... How could she not see the lies in his words? Pious hands covered her face to allow her to weep in solitude at her own shame.

He took a huge sip of his late macchiatto as he looked out the glass of the huge window of the cafeteria. People were strolling by, some smiling and others even looked happy. She took a second sip and as she looked up she spotted a little girl who, releasing her grip, picked up the cloth doll that had fallen into a small puddle. The little girl looked at her mother with a sad face but the mother did not hesitate to smile. The woman quickly reached into her purse for a tissue and dried the tiny pink dress while the girl waited anxiously. The mother, proud of the results obtained, extended the doll to the little girl who now, without crying, wrapped her little rag doll in her arms while she gave a huge smile of gratitude to her mother. They both walked happily hand in hand and Brenda thought deeply. The mother offered a solution to her daughter's terrible pain with a simple tissue. Surely the doll would remain wet for a while, but the girl was over it. Perhaps it was all about something as simple as a tissue, drying off and continuing the journey. Wrapped up in her thoughts she didn't realize that her wait was over. She lifted her face and joy hid her bad memories.

-Anne, you look beautiful! -She said excitedly as she looked at her high pregnancy status.

The woman smiled with a glow that lit up the cafeteria, and Brenda felt herself infected by her joy. The change in Anne Foster was astonishing. When she began her treatment with the doctor, Anne had looked weak and insecure, but now she was a radiant woman, shining with her own light, and Brenda was happy to have been part of such a change.

-Please sit down. When you called me I didn't think you would come with me. She said amused as she looked at her advanced state of pregnancy while she got up from the couch to give him an affectionate kiss on the cheek. I can imagine how proud Reed must be.

-Please don't talk to me. That man thinks I'm an invalid, he won't let me do anything. He won't let me lift a finger on my own.

-And you are delighted. The doctor answered with a confident diagnosis.

-Of course, but I'll never admit it. They both joined in an accomplice's laughter as they sat down on the comfortable sofas.

-A coffee?

-I can't," she replied sadly, "The doctor took me off caffeine but a Breakfast tea with a splash of milk is allowed," she said trying to get up from the couch but falling back on her buttocks due to the weight of her huge belly.

-I'll order them. How much longer do you need? -she asked curiously as she looked at the expanse of her belly.

-In a fortnight I'll be out of accounts. He replied, snorting with fatigue.

-Then I'd better hurry. Brenda replied with a smile as she hurried off to the Starbucks counter. The two talked tirelessly and Anne filled her in on all the details.

The doctor listened with amusement to all of Anne's crazy talk and smiled at Reed's excessive care. Having that relaxed conversation helped her to forget her own problems and start being herself. She appreciated the interest of her friends, but sometimes to rise from the ashes you need to stop being reminded that you are a pitiful woman, and the talk with Anne was one of the best things she had encountered in the last three days.

-And you, everything okay? -Anne asked curiously and Brenda shook her head.

-Yes, of course. Now tell me about that urgent thing that couldn't wait.

Anne stirred in her chair and Brenda narrowed her eyes trying to guess what would be such an urgent reason for a pregnant woman on the verge of explosion to escape from her prison of cotton balls. She seemed to be taking her time and Brenda couldn't contain that spark of curiosity that since she was a child she never knew how to contain.

-I'm waiting... -She said intrigued.

-I don't really know how to start...

-The beginning is usually the best way." He said with a small touch of amusement to cut the tension of the moment.

-If I only knew which one it was..." He answered with a seriousness that frightened Brenda. -He answered with a seriousness that frightened Brenda. You see, it's about Jane, my sister, do you remember her? I think I told you about her.

-I remember her.

-And do you remember I told you that I had run away with a man?

Anne's sister was locked in a relationship that she had not had the courage to end, and the arrival of that man made her understand the reality. Yes, today more than ever that story seemed clearer than ever to remember.

-You told me he was Reed's best friend, didn't you?

-Yes, Suraj. He's a lovely man, he's a very nice person. It was love at first sight. She was very confused but Suraj waited for her, he never gave up. Both of them are made for each other.

-You'd think you were trying to sell it to me," she smiled, but when she saw the woman's seriousness, the smile faded instantly. What exactly is going on with them? Anne, if they need a therapist, it's up to them to make the decision. No matter how much they worry you, the patients are the ones who should....

-It's not that... -She said, raising her hand nervously. It's not what you think, they're both fine. Or so I think.

-So?

-Suraj is in jail. The doctor opened her eyes and drank from her coffee cup, understanding much less now than before.

-Brenda, I need your help. You are the only one who can save them. He is not guilty, I assure you, I would put my hands in the fire for Suraj. He would never commit such a heinous act.

The woman's voice began to tremble and the doctor was afraid that so much tension would harm the baby.

-Anne, honey, I'm a psychologist, not a lawyer. I think you have the wrong person.

-Brenda, you don't understand. His life could be in danger and I don't know anyone better than you to help him. I swear to you, Suraj would never harm those women.

"Harm, women?" she said to herself intrigued.

Anne began to talk about some strange rapes and deaths that made her skin crawl and made her want to run straight to the exit. If this Suraj guy had committed those murders, he deserved to be locked up and the keys flushed down the toilet.

The woman spoke more and more nervously and Brenda felt sorry for her. It was clear that she firmly believed in the man's innocence, but she knew from her own experience what a man is capable of deceiving a woman in love.

-Honey, I'd really like to help you, but I still don't see what you need from me," she said with a friend's pity.

-Brenda, you are the only one who can help us.

The pregnant woman began to explain herself with such fervor that she did not have the courage to confess that people do not always show themselves as they are. She herself, supposedly a professional of the human mind, had fallen like a fool in front of a money-driven swindler. Anne talked and talked and the doctor began to feel the woman's doubts growing inside her as well. What if this Suraj was innocent? What if he was really involved in a story that did not belong to him? Not all men were such liars and swindlers as Akim.

-And those psychologists that you say analyzed him, have they presented their report? -she asked, curious and interrupting the story.

-No, they didn't even deign to visit him. It's as if they wanted to implicate him and avoid major problems.

Brenda began to see some anomalies in the case that ignited a spark of curiosity inside her. Most likely, this Suraj was just a psychopath, but she had nothing to lose by going to visit him.

-And in what prison do you say he is in?

Anne took a long sip of her tea and Brenda waited wondering what all the intrigue was about.

-Tangier... -He whispered with barely a sound.

-I'm sorry? I didn't hear you," said the doctor leaning over to hear her better.

-Tangier. He commented in a low voice.

-Is it a prison or a neighborhood? Where in London do you say it is located?

-In Morocco. She replied shyly as the doctor began to turn pale.

-Morocco, Africa? Do you want me to travel to Africa?

At that moment a tall, dark man with a somewhat strange gait approached Anne's ear to speak to her in a whisper in her ear.

The young woman ducked her head like a child caught with a stolen lollipop and the man with piercing eyes greeted her captivatingly.

-Dr. Klein. Reed spoke in a thick voice as he glared at his girl. I thought we agreed that I would take care of everything and you would stay home. He said as he sat down next to her and tenderly caressed his wife's bulging belly. Are you all right?

The man spoke with such affection that Brenda felt a deep sense of envy. Months ago she would have been delighted for them, but today, thanks to Akim's deception, her heart was transformed into a selfish one eager to obtain that which was once promised to her and which turned out to be the most dastardly of lies.

-I am perfectly fine, and now that Dr. Klein has said she will help Suraj, so much the better.

Brenda's eyes widened in astonishment at the news and she was about to answer that there was no way she was going to Africa when Reed asked enthusiastically.

-Is that true? Dr. Klein, your reputation is impressive, an analysis like yours could get my friend out of jail.

-Yes, well... -I was about to comment on the ridiculousness of the offer when Anne groaned a deep, deep groan.

-It is nothing. An isolated contraction. He replied as he let out another whimper and Reed instantly jumped to his feet.

She had never witnessed a birth before and had no interest in this time being the first, so she wanted to end the madness as soon as possible.

-Well, as I was trying to explain, your friend? -A new moan from the pregnant woman distracted her from her conversation. Reed nervously stroked the tightness of his wife's belly and asked curiously, ignoring the doctor's explanations.

-Every how many minutes? -He asked in a low, serious voice but received no answer from his girl. How often? -he grunted between his teeth.

-Maybe twenty or maybe ten, I'm not sure.

Brenda opened her eyes more than frightened and looking for some calm before screaming hysterically for an ambulance to be called urgently. However, Reed decided to act without waiting. He took his girl by the arm to guide her towards the exit.

-I'm fine!

-We are going to the hospital. Dr. Klein, I can't tell you how happy I am to know that we are counting on you. I will send you a message with all the information, but we are leaving now.

-Yes, well, the truth is that I... -Brenda wanted to say something but couldn't for a change. They were both walking out the door towards the car with extreme urgency.

Frozen in place, she watched them walk away unable to believe the mess she had just gotten herself into. It was not possible.

"But I don't want to go to Africa! What am I going to do there?" he thought, sweating all over.

Fearful for her future she sank onto the couch. She could still refuse. If only she could wait for the baby to be born and then she could explain herself....

-Another latte macchiato," he said to the waitress who was coming to clear the table.

She was a professional and it wasn't her habit to abandon those who needed her. After all didn't Akim say she was a specialist in getting into trouble? "For heaven's sake, am I really considering this madness?"

She accepted her third cup of coffee of the day when someone very familiar approached her with an exaggerated smile.

-How did you know I was here? -he replied with acrimony.

-Max replied as he sat down next to her.

-Now you're spying on me too. He said without much desire to speak.

-Don't be silly, you know I'm not. I just care about you. I wanted to know how you are feeling. We haven't seen each other for days.

-What exactly do you want? -. He said trying to get rid of her presence as soon as possible.

Max frowned angrily but didn't dare answer. He knew him too well to know that he hated the way he expressed himself but he didn't care. He no longer felt responsible for his bad moods or his mental frustrations. If he was angry then let him eat it with potatoes and some Ketchup, she thought with a wry smile.

-I thought we could have breakfast together. He replied hopefully.

-I'm leaving right now.

The man sighed loudly and spoke with a serenity that made her feel like the worst of women. He was demonstrating a calmness that she did not possess. She had had it before, and plenty of it, but not today.

-You can count on me. I will always be on your side.

Regretting her hostile manner of greeting him, she nodded her head. Max was not to blame for anything, indeed, if it weren't for him, Akim and his siliconed girlfriend would still be making fun of her stupidity. Their relationship was over, but an immense amount of blame rested on her. She no longer wished to hide in the walls of an unhappy marriage.

-I appreciate it, but I need to be alone.

-I'm not asking for much more than a cup of coffee and a slice of that cake we love so much. That's all. What flavor was it? -asked the scoundrel with amusement in his eyes.

-You don't play fair," she replied reluctantly.

Max smiled so tenderly that Brenda was confused. He still loved her and seemed to be willing to start from scratch. Could she be making a mistake? Max always proved to be a good partner. Akim, however... He taught her passion, that was true, but he also taught her the pain of deceit and conning.

Max went to get the cake and came back with a slice and two spoons. He talked as if nothing had happened between them and Brenda knew at that precise moment that she would travel to Morocco as soon as she bought the ticket. Distance would be the best option for both of them. They both had to go their separate ways. In other arms she enjoyed a passion that although fraudulent she could not ignore, if she did and went back to her ex, that would not make her a better person than Akim. With Max, her skin didn't bristle and her blood didn't boil needily. With him her heart didn't beat wildly nor did her eyes fill with tears asking, why did you cheat on me? No, maybe her path was lost and she would never again feel what that young man made her feel, but that mattered little. She had no desire for consolation prizes. When you know the whole, you are no longer satisfied with small portions.

Don't look for me

-What do you think you're doing? -Brenda asked tenderly as she watched Rachel place some of her hundreds of creams in a travel toiletry bag.

The woman looked at her as if she had asked the most foolish of questions and the doctor smiled tenderly.

-You are not going.
-Sweet, you don't believe that yourself. I'm coming.
-Rachel, I...
-I'm here.

Connor entered his living room using his own key, and Brenda thought she should take it back from him someday. Those two took that brotherhood thing literally.

-You too? -She said exhausted as she watched her friend dragging a small suitcase.

-What about me? -He answered as if it wasn't about him.

Brenda summoned all her composure and tried to explain herself. She didn't want to hurt them, but she wouldn't give in either.

-Neither of us will be traveling with me.
-Both Rachel and Connor looked at each other and smiled.
-I need to do this by myself. I want to be alone. It's important to me. She commented seeking understanding.
-No way. Connor said.
-No." Rachel affirmed.

Brenda scratched her forehead trying to find the right words without being rude. They were her friends, they loved her and didn't want to see her suffer and she understood that perfectly but it was time for them to understand her reasons. The last few days turned out to be the worst of her life. She was devastated. She was heartbroken and ashamed. This trip was not only about helping

Anne and Reed, it was also about distancing herself from everything that still made her suffer.

-You guys, you can't imagine how grateful I am but I can't take you. I need to put my broken pieces back together and this work concerns only me. I ask you to please understand me, without you I could not.... -I have been lied to, I have been deceived," she smiled as she heard Connor's grunt. I've been a fool and accepted lies from the wrong person. I can't forget that even though I was tricked by a phony, my answer was always sincere. He conned me but my heart still responds to him with sincerity. I want to hate him and I try to forget him but I am not able to. It is stored so deep inside me that I tremble to think that I can never banish it -. Her eyes filled with tears and she cursed herself for behaving so vulnerably.

Connor wanted to have a say but he wouldn't let himself. He was baring his deepest fears out loud and realized it was infinitely necessary for his mental health.

-I won't deny it. I can't. My body and my heart awoke with the kiss of a frog who never became a prince.... Everything I gave was sincere and even though my feelings were trampled on, I must rescue something good from all this or I think I will go mad with grief. I have to look for my cure and for that it is necessary to get some ground to stand on. Please understand and support me. I need you both, but here.

Rachel closed her eyes as if she was the first to understand her and nodded gratefully. With grief tearing at her voice, she asked sheepishly.

-Connor?

-I'll kill him for what he did to you," he replied between his teeth and with his fists clenched tightly.

Brenda approached him and knelt down in front of the chair to be at the same height. The friend moved his body forward to the edge and reached out his long fingers to stroke her hair.

-I hate it...

-I am so sorry. The doctor apologized from the bottom of her heart. In the last few months she had confronted her true friend and leaned on the con man. What a shoddy psychologist, she thought saddened.

-I have nothing to forgive. If I had found the evidence Max gave you before, I would have hanged him with my own hands.

-Can you ever forgive me? I was a fool. She said, resting her face on the man's broad knees.

-You don't deserve to suffer so much for him. He answered as he lowered his face to place a kiss on the crown of her head. That bastard will pay for what he has done to you sometime.

She did not answer. She merely accepted his caresses and absorbed the warmth of his strength.

-Shall we take the bags outside? - Rachel spoke with her voice cracking.

-Please...

Connor got up and walked through the door with the suitcase. Rachel took her place next to her friend.

-I'll be fine.

-I know that," he replied enthusiastically. Sweet, haven't you thought that maybe it was all the result of a mix-up? I say that because I saw him in Ibiza and I can't believe such cruelty. He seemed sincere to me, even in love?

Rachel wanted to continue but Brenda interrupted her with such confidence that she preferred to be silent instantly.

-Isn't that what con artists do? -He answered as he stood up and held out his hand. Once he got what he was looking for, he disappeared. He didn't even care to explain himself. When he was discovered by Max, he left with the money and his sweetheart. Don't give it any more thought. Let's go outside, my cab should be about to arrive.

Rachel accepted the answer. Brenda was right, that guy was a scoundrel who cheated them both.

-When I get settled, I will send you an email with all the details. Rachel, I'm asking you please. She said while pasting the address of the hotel on a corkboard, which the actress used to rehearse her scripts. It's for emergencies. I don't want anyone to find me. Only in cases of extreme urgency.

-No Max? -he asked as he straightened the note on the corkboard with a second thumbtack.

-He least of all. I need this time for myself.

-You haven't told him you're leaving.

-I wasn't able to. Rachel please...

-Don't worry. No one will know where to find you.

They both walked towards the exit and Brenda felt such great sorrow that she felt sorry for herself. She confessed to having been cheated on and said she accepted it but it was not true. For a brief period of time she felt she was the luckiest woman, the most adored. She recognized a love she never thought she would feel and today she was leaving with her soul torn and without hope.

He got into the cab and without feeling able to look at the friends he was leaving behind, he set off on a new course.

-The cell phone you are calling is switched off or out of coverage".

The little message was repeated over and over again and Akim trembled with helplessness. Since he woke up he called constantly but she didn't answer.

"Not a damn thing!" he thought in disgust. Even if he hated it, even if it was nothing more than to insult him, but why the hell won't he answer!

The cast on his arm had been replaced by a bandage and his head hurt a lot less. He tried to get out of bed and although at first the dizziness nearly knocked him down, he managed to stand unsteadily like a drunk. If he managed to reach the chair, the next objective would be to make direct steps to the closet and from there straight to the street.

-What are you doing?

His father spoke in distress as he entered the room and rushed over to hold him under his shoulders to keep him from falling flat on his face.

-I'm almost there. He replied hopefully as he looked at the half-open closet door.

-Come on, sit down and stop fooling around. She said as she helped him sit back down on the bed.

-You don't understand... -Akim spoke with despair.

-You haven't been able to talk to him. He affirmed when he saw his son's cell phone on the mattress. Maybe if you give him some time....

-I will go to your house. You'll have to listen to me. You may find it hard to believe the stupid picture with Lola, but the money thing is a complete lie. I'll prove that his bastard ex set me up. I will gather all the evidence. You will understand that he is the only one who is a fake. He would never betray her, not even for all the money in the world," he said, putting so much emphasis on his words that even he managed to encourage himself. You'll see, don't worry about me," he said, looking at his father's discomposed face. I'll make it. She'll forgive me and we'll go back to the way we were. I love her. She's my life, I'll prove it to her.

Akim rose from his seat with a slow but determined step. He approached the closet looking for his clothes as he watched his father deny again and again with concern.

-Dad?

-I cashed the check. He said without giving himself time to breathe.

The young man's heart stopped at that very moment as his hands let go of what they were holding. If it wasn't for the shoes hitting against the hard floor causing a loud sound, Akim would have sworn he was still in a coma and this was one of those horrible nightmares.

-What are you saying?

-I cashed the check. I'm sorry.

No, it wasn't true, it couldn't be. His father had sold him, for money? She wanted to scream at him, to hit him, to bellow, but she was barely able to babble.

-Why?

The man walked around the room, dragging his fingers through his graying hair.

-That man would attack you or the child. I had to do something.

The young man shook his head and covered his ears, refusing to listen as his father spoke, running over his words in an attempt to explain himself better.

-That same morning I cashed the check and sent for that Philips guy, but the bastard didn't show up. I was too late. That pig had left you in a coma," he said, wiping the sweat from his forehead, "I couldn't risk it, if he came back, if they were looking for Lucien... I couldn't....

The father was trying to demonstrate the reality of the situation, but Akim was not able to understand the reasons. He was squeezing his head trying to stop listening

-It's me he was looking for! You had no right," he said angrily. I lost her because of you," he growled through his teeth. You ruined my life.

-Life you wouldn't have if that man came back," he said. he shouted worriedly.

Akim didn't answer him, he just breathed furiously as he searched for his clothes in the closet.

-Son, I know exactly what you are going through. I understand you better than anyone, but I had no choice. Akim fidgeted nervously as he shook his head and despair filled his father's voice. She will understand. The truth is the only way you have to explain yourself. When she hears us, she will accept it.

-Will she accept it? -She'll accept that I used our relationship to get money from her husband? She'll accept that she's a fucking paycheck to me! Do you really think so?

Akim spoke with his heart torn with grief. At one time he thought he had a small sliver of hope but now... Now everything was very different. She would never accept the honesty of his feelings. Never. She would believe that he used her to pay off his debts. A number on a piece of paper...

-I will accompany you and explain that the decision was mine and mine alone.

Akim smiled half-heartedly as he wiped the moisture from his eyes. He couldn't remember crying since that day he had covered his mother's face with the aging gray blanket. His progenitor had not only stabbed him in the back but was now proposing to present himself to Brenda as a parent requesting guardianship for his wayward son. Now he was no longer just a con man, he was an idiot incapable of defending himself.

-You've done enough. He said with a torn voice.

-Akim...

-I don't want to see you again.

-You're angry and I understand that, but I won't leave. I know you and I know you're not sorry.

-Go away.

- Together we can...

-Go away! -He shouted angrily as he turned to look at him with fire in his eyes and pointed to the door that was opening at that moment.

-Akim! -Nikola shouted from the doorway as he closed the door so that no one in the hallway would hear the discussion he himself had been listening to as he walked towards the room. Nikola was ready to defend grandfather above all else but the poor man raised his hand to silence him.

-I'll leave. We'll talk later. Son, I remind you that I'm your father and I'm not afraid of your hellish eyes or your overfed muscles. I'm leaving now because among other things I have to pick up my grandson who gets out of school and needs to eat. He said as he left, closing the door with a loud bang.

Akim punched the wall with the fist of his bad arm and cursed loudly. Nikola smirked in amusement as he reached for the cold pack lying on the bedside table. He brought it over to him and the young man put it on his sore arm as he growled even more angrily than before.

-What the hell are you still doing here!

-Did you throw me out too? I thought the stupidity was only directed at your father.

Akim shook his eyes. He was not for his friend's imbecilic conclusions.

-Did he tell you? -Nikola nodded and Akim felt doubly betrayed.

-What do you plan to do? -He said as he walked over to the window and bit into Akim's breakfast apple.

The friend looked at him with a look clouded by fury. Was Nikola really such an imbecile as not to realize that he had lost the love of his life? He would have grabbed him by the neck and beaten him until he realized how miserable his life was if it weren't for the fact that his arm hurt like a thousand demons put together.

Nikola continued to eat the apple in complete silence until only the core was left, which he threw into the garbage can with a full basket, when he finally decided to look at his friend.

-What? -He asked, trying not to sound so hopeful but not quite succeeding.

Nikola raised one side of his lip in a smile and Akim opened his eyes in complete hope. He knew him perfectly well, that one in front of him was his best friend, his brother, and that look was of someone who hadn't exactly been doing very legal things. The young man waited anxiously to discover Nikola's malicious glare.

-You see, it turns out that my idiot friend woke up from an induced coma, and I thought that since he's stupid and would be hospitalized for a few days, I could make some inquiries for him. He commented while looking at the nails on his right hand.

-Speak. Akim's growl echoed off the white walls.

-This is not the way to talk to someone who cares so much about you. He replied with a smile.

-Speak before I break your mouth." He snarled with clenched fists.

-With a kiss? -he answered, raising his eyebrows in amusement.

-Fuck!

-It's okay, it's okay. I know they are not together. Akim took a deep breath of relief. Something was better than nothing.

-You were scared, weren't you? -Nikola smiled without impudence.

-Go on. Akim did not want to acknowledge his friend's one hundred percent correctness. One of his greatest fears is knowing that Max would have taken advantage of the situation to gain lost positions in his Brin's heart.

-She is on a trip.

-Where? -he asked, getting more and more nervous.

-I have no idea but she is alone. Max and his friends are in London. I checked it out myself.

-What about Rachel? -he asked, trying to come up with a plan.

-She's in London too. He answered enthusiastically. So what do you say? -Nikola asked, knowing the answer perfectly well.

-I change and we leave.

-You have a plan. He said with that mischievous smile of his.

-Akim answered as he pulled on his jeans, still a little dizzy.

The nurse came through the door with some papers in hand as she spoke in the voice of an angry mother but instantly transformed into a loving cat when she discovered Nikola in the room. Akim shook his head as he pulled on his shirt. It was amazing how women fell for that rascal's smile.

-Signing a voluntary discharge in his condition is foolish. He would need at least one more week to recover.

Akim looked at his friend and smiled elatedly. That asshole was in all of them. Nikola lifted his shoulders and replied with a superior air.

-I figured you'd want to get out of here as soon as possible.

The young man hugged him as he slapped his back with two strong slaps.

-I owe you one.

-You really owe me a lot. He said holding up the keys to the bike.

Akim smiled with complete joy as he accepted the pen from the nurse and urgently signed the papers.

-You drive. He said as he turned to watch in astonishment as Nikola planted a tremendous kiss on the nurse's mouth.

-Akim shook his head as he listened to him as he hurried his pace. He was dizzy but not because of the scarcity of health but because of the hopes that seemed to return to his life.

-Akim, your father? -Nikola said as she put on her helmet.

-I know, I know, we'll talk later. I have other emergencies now.

-You're crazy, man," he said as he started and revved the engine.

To tell the truth, he was. Completely and utterly mad with love, he thought as he held on tightly to keep from falling.

Truths

Rachel trembled at the image before her. It was impossible for him to be there and in front of her door. How long had it been since Brenda had left? Three days? No, a week! What was she looking for? Frightened, she tried to slam the door but couldn't, the man blocked her with his foot. She looked around trying to find something to hit him with and run away, because she was sure those two would kill her and then steal every last vase.

-Rachel, please. I'm not going to hurt you. I just want to talk.

Akim tried to speak softly but the gravity of his voice and that foreign accent made her tremble even more with fear.

-I have nothing of value. It's all in the bank. Here you will only find trinkets. Here no money dirty bricklayer.

Akim and Nikola looked at each other quizzically and Rachel took advantage of the distraction to flee into the living room. If she made it through alive, she could escape through the garden. Nikola closed the door hoping that no one would hear the screams of that madwoman while Akim caught up with her and lifted her into the air like a sack of potatoes.

-Stop it at once! -Akim threw her on the sofa while cursing for the blow that woman gave him on his bad arm.

-Okay, okay. They're behind Marilyn's painting, take them all but don't hurt me.

The young man frowned trying to figure out what the hell that crazy woman was talking about when she tried to run away again and this time he held her by the waist and shouted at her without any patience.

-I have no idea what you're talking about. I just want to know where she is.

Brenda stopped struggling and he let go. The woman fell face first again against the couch in a most undignified position and

Akim smiled as he saw her there with her hair curled and her face scrunched up against the couch. Rachel sat up as best she could as she tried to pull her clothes back together and pushed back her glossy mane.

-Bricklayer, aren't you going to rob me?

Akim clenched his fists at his sides. That woman was insulting him even when he didn't think about doing it.

-No, I'm not going to steal from you. I'm not a thief." He snarled through gritted teeth.

The woman made an incredulous face and the young man tried to search his brain for some reason that would justify not hanging that stiff.

-I am not here to hurt you.

-Oh no? Then why are you coming into my house with another bully just like you? Angrily he shot a glance at Nikola who was stretching smiling at being considered a muscular thug.

-Woman... I don't want anything from you. Not your jewelry or anything that belongs to you. I simply want to know where she is. Akim spoke with pain at the memory of her and Rachel frowned indignantly.

-Liar! You can't fool me. I am a prestigious actress and I know how to recognize a bad actor.

Akim was about to answer him with a series of insults when Nikola held him by the shoulder to interrupt him.

-Ma'am, we are neither thieves nor rapists. My friend needs me to tell him where the doctor is. When he speaks, we will leave through that door and you will never see us again. He said proud of his tremendously polite tone.

-No way, you dirty bricklayer! -He spat each letter in disgust and Nikola opened his eyes in bewilderment. As handsome and kind as he was....

-Max lied," Akim stammered wearily.

-You bastard! -Did you have to hurt her? I offered you money... -He answered in pain.

-I don't want your lousy money! I only want her." He shouted in exasperation at feeling misunderstood.

-You broke his heart!

Akim broke in two as he heard the woman's accusations. Brenda was heartbroken and it was his fault. Damn it, he needed to find her and explain to her that it had all been the result of hundreds of circumstances gathered against him. God, he would never hurt her. How could he do that when he loved her more than anything in the world?

-Rachel, please," he pleaded wearily, "you have to believe me. I never cheated on her. I swear I love her...

Akim walked shuffling his fingers through his black hair when a slate of notes caught his eye. It was Brenda's. He would recognize that handwriting anywhere. He moved closer but still distracted by Rachel's stiff upper lip, which kept getting in his way every few minutes. Out of the corner of her eye she tried to spot the letters written in pen on the paper, but was unable to. Not without attracting the attention of an actress who kept insulting him with phrases like "dirty bricklayer" or "beast with painted shoulders". He stealthily turned his gaze to Nikola, trying to make sure that so many years of friendship would be useful to be able to connect by telepathy. He thought and thought of different alternatives to get hold of the note, a quick option would be to throw Rachel aside and steal the card without further ado, but no, she would start screaming and the last thing he needed was to end up in jail as a delinquent. He had to get his hands on that card without a complaint.

He spoke almost without thinking trying to catch his friend's attention but nothing, Nikola continued to eat strawberries from that glass container.

-She loves me and I... I love her! -He shouted at the top of his lungs, finally getting Nikola to raise his head and stop searching for the ripest fruits.

Akim looked at him with fury in his eyes and he raised his eyebrows as a sign of "what the hell is wrong with you". If it wasn't because he was his best friend, he would have killed him on the spot. Akim pointed at the cork of notes with his eyes as if trying to tell him how important it was to get hold of the pinned information and he nodded closing his eyelids. "Just as well," he thought without stopping talking a string of nonsense to distract Rachel who seemed to show some confusion and he needed those seconds of distraction for Nikola to get hold of the loot. Determined, he continued talking, as he wrapped his arms around her preventing her from moving and seeing what was going on behind her back.

-Please, I need to find her. She has to know that I love her. You have to help me. You can. He said as he gently squeezed her shoulders pinning her in place and obstructing her vision.

The woman must have been frightened by the contact because she started screaming like a madwoman. He tried to explain himself and tell her that he would never hurt a woman when the door burst open and all three of them looked at the Scotsman covering the length and breadth of the entrance shaft. "Shit," he said to himself before taking the first punch in the face.

That bastard had fists like hammers, he thought as he tried to get up from the floor. His legs barely responded when, as he stood up, he received the second impact that slammed his bad arm against the wall.

-Shit... -he repeated as he felt his shoulder crunch against the cold floor.

He was still not recovered. Fuck, he had just gotten out of the hospital and that red demon kept attacking him. And why didn't that idiot Nikola stop him!

-Wait, wait... -He said, raising his hand. I didn't come here for this. He spoke while wiping the blood from his split lip.

-Go away!

The Scotsman's shout echoed throughout the room and Akim stood up with his muscles tensing. He may not have been in any condition to fight such a beast but if this one wanted war, he would have it. It was at that moment that Nikola approached and spoke calmly, stopping the giant.

-We are leaving. We didn't mean to scare you. He said with his hands raised.

Akim continued to glare angrily at the Scotsman and the Scotsman approached him without listening to a word from his loyal friend.

-You will go away. You will disappear from his life. He spoke with his teeth clenched in fury just inches from her face.

-I won't... -He whispered with a small grimace on his split lip and moved closer until their bodies almost collided.

Nikola shook his head and grabbed him by the shoulders to pull them apart as he talked nonstop.

-We will leave. There is nothing for us here. She said as she pushed him from behind towards the exit.

-If you come back, I'm going to break every bone in your body. Even your little friend won't be able to save you!

Akim was about to turn to face him when Nikola stopped him by the shoulders.

-They don't have anything here that we don't know about.

They both looked at each other. Nikola smiled with a wicked look as she showed him a corner of paper hidden in her pocket and Akim breathed gratefully.

With the scent of a woman

Brenda argued in front of the mirror trying not to be late for her appointment with Jane but again that troublesome hijab decided not to cooperate. At first she refused to wear it but then realized it would be best not to draw attention to herself. With strong tugging she continued to struggle with her long hair to cover it with the silky fabric but it looked worse and worse. Annoyed with the result she ran downstairs to meet her new friend and devise a slightly more daring plan. In the week they had been together in that country, they had barely made any progress. It was time to make strategic changes or Suraj would have no chance of getting a fair trial. She had tried everything but the bureaucracy wouldn't let her get close and she was tired of wasting so much time. "No risk, no gain," she told herself with conviction.

Anne's sister, appearing on the hotel landing, was sorry for her. The young woman was exhausted but even that failed to dull that wonderful gleam of optimism in her transparent gaze. "I wish I could feel the same way," she thought hopelessly. The hours were running out and if she failed to make progress and develop her report on the incarcerated man, the man would most likely rot in a cell moldy with age and poor maintenance.

-The cab is waiting for us. He said as the young woman responded with the greatest enthusiasm.

-Jane commented sheepishly as she remembered the last eight times the drivers had tried to swindle them out of every last coin in their pockets.

-Relax, this time the cab was ordered by the guy at the front desk. He said smiling as they walked out the door.

-If you say so... -Jane stammered uncertainly and she smiled at his serious expression as she looked around rather nervously.

Not that she considered herself a coward, but those men used to watch them like real eaters and she was pretty tired of it. No matter where they went or how many times they refused them, more would always show up. It was as if because they were foreign women their refusal meant nothing. Those guys deserved a lecture from Rachel in the Amazon group, she thought amused, they would teach those macho guys how to behave with respect.

They both got into the car parked outside the door and drove to their destination.

-Where are we going? I thought we were going to use the visitor's permit? -Jane asked as she pointed to the envelope she was protecting in her purse.

-It's still a few hours away, and I don't think cell custody will allow us to get in any sooner. We have time." Brenda answered hurriedly.

Despite reiterating his confidence to a very worried Jane, he kept looking at the map on his cell phone screen. This time she would not pay triple this time.

-I don't think it's this way. He said confidently, pointing to the screen.

-It's this way. He answered coarsely and Brenda began to get angry.

These men had been treating her like a piece of furniture for a week and she was fed up. Ready to engage in a dialectical battle, the chauffeur stepped forward and answered in a better mood.

-The main street is usually jammed at this hour. We'll get there sooner this way.

Brenda narrowed her eyes and focused her gaze on the center of the driver's rearview mirror to show him that she would be watching him. The man, instead of feeling threatened, smiled in amusement. He looked like he was old enough to be able to retire but that didn't make her trust him. She had been defending her position as a woman for days and that old man would not win her over with a loving grandfatherly look.

-Have you been in town long? -he asked politely.

Jane was about to respond but the doctor put her hand over hers to silence her. That woman was too sweet and that would make them pay double for the ride.

-Enough. He replied, his eyes narrowing again.

Jane watched her curiously but she cleared her throat trying to make it clear that she shouldn't worry. She was there to defend them both.

-A woman to be reckoned with. She replied smiling.

Brenda was about to answer when the driver stopped. Both women looked at each other in bewilderment as they saw the narrowness and darkness of the street.

-What... what are we doing here? -Jane asked in fright.

The man stretched out his arm in the passenger seat and turned his body back to look them straight in the eye.

-This is their destiny," he replied, reassuring them.

Brenda looked at the place and shivered. It looked like an abandoned place. The sidewalks were broken and the street was unpaved. The sunlight could barely reach it due to the narrowness of the road and the car could barely fit on that tiny road.

-Are you sure? -The doctor asked, swallowing her breath and wondering why she always got into such trouble.

-Yes, number 33. It's right over there. The yellow portal.

That thousand-year-old piece of wood was a door, and he would never learn, he said to himself, stroking his forehead, which was beginning to sweat.

-Are they coming down or not? -The driver asked as he pointed out that the meter was still running.

-No." Jane replied confidently.

-Yes. Brenda figured the hotel guy knew where they were going and he wouldn't risk taking them to a place where they would be robbed, raped and cut to pieces and lose their jobs, would he? -They're waiting for us. We don't have to worry. She replied uncertainly.

-Jane answered flatly, and Brenda would have liked to laugh at her fear, except that she was just as frightened as she was.

-It's all right. I think it's better. You stay in the car and keep the engine running." She said trying to make a joke but sounded too terrified.

-Ladies, am I going to get paid or not? I have another trip.

-But aren't you going to wait for us? -Jane asked, clutching her purse.

-I was hired to bring them, not to wait for them. I have another trip to make. If you'll do me the favor of paying me and getting out of the car... both of you. He said as he watched Jane cling to the seat with her fingernails.

But what was wrong with that heartless man who couldn't take pity on two poor, helpless tourists? Men, he said to himself angrily. They are never there when you need them.

-Come on, Jane. She pulled her friend down by her elbow, leaning on each other.

Not that she needed the physical contact so she wouldn't start crying, no. She was a prestigious and brave doctor. She was a prestigious and brave doctor, but she was doing it for poor Jane, she thought as she rang the doorbell trembling and glancing to the side. A creaking sound from the hinges and the old wooden door swung open. Brenda swallowed dryly. They had no escape, they should go in, she told herself as she reached into her pocket for her cell phone. If they didn't steal it, the police might someday find their bodies in some lost puddle, she thought, choking on her own fear.

-We're looking for Mr.... -Brenda took out the paper that she was holding tightly in her hands because of her nerves. Mohamed.

-Which of the four? -. He asked, analyzing them from top to bottom, or rather, from waist to toe. The five-foot woman had a hump on her back the size of a watermelon. The woman grumbled in a strange dialect and Brenda looked intrigued at a Jane who lifted her shoulders just as intrigued.

-Which of my four children? -she said, annoyed.

-Mohamed. Brenda repeated. Maybe the poor old woman was deaf in addition to being a hunchback.

-Which one? Stubborn woman - He repeated reluctantly.

Did all four have the same name? No, that would not be possible, Brenda was about to answer again when a man of elegant bearing approached the doorway.

-I'll take care of it. The black-robed old woman left, saying something that Brenda thought she recognized as a long list of insults.

-Why are you looking for me? -he asked without moving from his spot.

"So much for hospitality," she thought somewhat annoyed.

-Are you the guide? -The man nodded while he kept analyzing them.

-We want to hire you.

-Why?

-I beg your pardon?

Brenda didn't believe his question. What did he care about the reasons? He was a simple guide and they were willing to pay him. That was all he should be interested in.

-Why? -The man asked again without waiting and this time stopping his gaze on Jane's angelic face.

-Ahem. The doctor coughed trying to get his attention but he did not look her in the eyes until he considered it appropriate. We need a city guide and your name was recommended to me. He answered sharply.

-I am without men

Brenda's eyes widened uncomprehendingly. -I, uh, we... we're not looking for men. She answered confused and very angry.

What did the guy think he was doing? They might be foreigners but they were not willing to be treated like whores. She was about to defend herself at the top of her lungs when that man raised his long, thin arm to silence her.

-You must be the doctor's chatterbox.

-Oh. Brenda squeezed her chest, offended and ready to kill him with her dialectic when the man blinked and shook his head. My nephew called me and told me they were coming. I can't guard them. I have no free men.

-You see, he misunderstood us. We were just looking for a guide. We know how to take care of ourselves.

The man reached out and brushed Jane's chin.

-Believe me honey, you need it. She replied smiling and with a hint of mischief.

Brenda felt offended. Did these guys think that because they were two women they couldn't take care of themselves? Morons. They were just looking for a guide so they wouldn't keep wasting time looking for places on outdated maps. That's all. She was about to leave when Jane spoke with a confidence she didn't usually display.

-Why do you say we need help?

The custodian smiled at the sweet voice and Brenda shook her head in disgust. Men, their pants were falling down over an angelic face and sweet little green eyes.

-You are not tourists. You are here for the English.

-How do you know? -. The doctor asked, narrowing her eyes suspiciously.

-Honey, everyone knows it. You need protection and I have no free men.

-But you can help us? -Jane spoke in a honeyed voice and Brenda wondered what exactly she was up to.

-I'm not a custodian, not anymore," he said, dragging his hand through his incipient gray hair.

-Be our guide. Please...

Jane stared at him and if it wasn't for the fact that she was sure she adored Suraj she would have thought she was trying to seduce him. Mohamed snorted but she smiled at him again until the man replied in a low, somewhat raspy voice.

-All right. Wait for me at the corner. My car is a black Mitsubishi Montero. He said turning around without another word.

-And what car is that? -Jane asked curiously.

-How should I know? The doctor commented as they opened the door to leave. Why did you do it?

-The sweet look? -She said amused. I didn't want him to turn us down.

-We don't need it. She replied offended in her pride as a woman and an active Amazon.

-We need it and you know it.

Brenda remembered the time they were wasting by always being lost around the city and Suraj's need for time... and yes, maybe Jane wasn't so wrong after all.

-You were very clever. And that little look was most effective.

-Men... -She answered as if that were enough and they both burst out laughing as they walked out the door.

-Who are those guys?" Jane spoke as she realized that, as soon as they stepped through the door, they found themselves semi-circled by three men. Brenda felt the trembling in Jane's hands as she clung to her arm as if she knew how they would get out of it.

-Please. She said as she tried to make room to pass. Maybe these men didn't want anything to do with them after all.

The men made room for her and the doctor smiled in relief, until one of the men spoke to them in a deep voice.

-These foreigners are pretty....

The men burst out laughing but Brenda was not distracted. She tried to walk to the corner. They weren't that far away. One of them stood in her way while the other two followed right behind. They were so close it was possible to feel the heat of their bodies. Jane looked at her frightened but she pressed her hand between his to instill confidence.

-Gentlemen, please... We are not looking for trouble.

-Cute and polite. He continued amused.

-I'll take the blonde." A voice was heard from behind.

-I like this one. Said the one in front of her as she reached out to drag the doctor's hijab and drop it on the floor.

The men behind her nodded with laughter and Brenda felt her heart pounding. She had to think. Maybe if she kicked the one in the balls in front of her they could run around the corner and race to Mohamed's car. He was thinking how to explain his plan to Jane when the voices behind his back continued to speak viciously.

-I'm not sure Asim, I like it too.

The men laughed fiercely and Brenda knew she couldn't waste any more time. She hoped Jane would run quickly because she intended to fly. With no margin for error she lifted her foot with all the strength she could muster and kicked the assailant in the balls in front of her so hard that he arched in pain.

-Run! - Brenda screamed at the top of her lungs and Jane needed no further incentive to run like lightning.

The doctor tried to dodge the body of the man lying on the floor when a hand grabbed her arm. She pushed hard trying to get away from the assailant and thought it would be impossible when the man just let her go. Without looking back she ran and crashed head-on into the van that was waiting for them with its doors open. They both jumped into the car and the guide accelerated powerfully. The two hugged each other nervously. They had just saved their necks by pure miracle.

-I thought they had caught you....

-I'm fine, I was lucky," she said to herself without wondering why that man had just let her go, "Good luck....

From a distance and knocking out the third of the assailants, who fell next to the other two, the stranger smiled under his cobalt blue turban as he saw them headfirst into the van.

A matter of luck

Brenda smiled when she saw the jailer's angry face as he read the visitation permit for the umpteenth time. The man could not refuse. The seal of the Ministry of the Interior was absolutely authentic. This time he would not be able to forbid them to enter.

-It's all right. But only you. The jailer pointed his finger at the doctor.

-The permission is for both of us. She will enter with me as stipulated in the document," she said confidently, "because otherwise she would be obliged to talk to her superior and we wouldn't like that, don't you think so, sergeant? -she commented, elongating the last vowel.

The chubby man stretched the collar of his uniform and extended the letter directly to her face. The doctor, far from being intimidated, smiled in relief as the soldier opened the doors and let them pass. They both walked through narrow corridors until they reached what appeared to be a group of cells.

Cold, damp and hopelessness covered the desolate walls. Both walked in complete silence, each one thinking about their own stories. Jane was probably anxious to abandon herself to the embrace of her beloved, but her case was very different. She would meet an innocent or a serial killer for the first time. Freedom or sentencing depended on the right questions and analysis of her experience.

-It's here.

Brenda walked behind a Jane who rushed toward the barred door. Opening the cell, the young woman threw herself into the arms of a man with an incipient beard who held her tightly as he rested his face on her hair. The two embraced and kissed, thirsty with need, and she blushed and lowered her face, allowing them some intimacy.

-Are you all right? -He whispered carelessly and she nodded without speaking and with tears in her eyes. -Are you sure you're not lying to me? -He said as he wrapped his broad hands around her delicate face and wiped her cheek with his thumb.

Jane nodded again and again as she rubbed her face in his strong hands. He watched her spellbound and the doctor studied every gesture, every behavior. Her analysis was beginning at that very moment. The man looked up at her for the first time, focusing a penetrating gaze that made her shiver.

-I am Dr. Brenda Klein. She answered straightening her body like a complete professional. Suraj watched her with interest and she hurried to inform him. Reed Blackman sent me.

The man relaxed his shoulders when he heard Blackman's name and Brenda tried to sit down on the old wooden bench to the side and open the briefcase with a folder full of papers.

-The doctor is here to help you," Jane spoke in a rush of words. She will get you out of here. The man kissed the woman's forehead with a sad smile and Brenda decided to speak clearly. Her duty was to be completely honest and not to create false hopes. She was there to help, that was true, but what she would never do would be to let a murderer loose.

Suraj must have noticed the doctor's frown because with an affection that made Brenda's heart tingle, he spoke to his girl with the utmost gentleness as he tucked a lock of her hair under her hijab.

-Honey, the water here is vomitous. Would you buy me a bottle?

Without thinking twice, the woman ran out to get the bottle of water when her man grabbed her waist and gave her a tremendous soap opera kiss before allowing her to leave. The young woman smiled at him with a blissful face and Brenda looked down at the papers. Once his girl had left, the man changed his voice. The tender being transformed into the tough London inspector she had been told about and Brenda doubted her initial impression. Could he be faking a romantic relationship to actually hide a deep case of split personality? The worldwide case known as Dr. Jekill and Mr. Hyde.

Something curious but not at all out of the question, she thought as she wrote in her notes.

-I asked. He said earnestly as he sat down on what would at some point turn out to be a cot but whose glory days were long forgotten.

The man looked into her eyes and Brenda shivered. His gaze was deep, capable of disarming her and her years of experience if she was not careful. The dark complexion clearly indicated his Indian ancestry, perhaps from the group of men who had come to England from the colonies, she thought curiously. The blue of his eyes and the long dark lashes indicated to her the mixture of races. His confidence and bearing were that of an expert, cultured man with an exquisite vocabulary, but there was something about him that Brenda could not discover and that warned her to be careful.

-Well, I would like to introduce myself, I am a doctor in psychology in cases of...

-I know it," he said in a deep voice. It's the one with the bomber. Brenda looked at him intrigued and Suraj answered naturally. I am a police inspector for the City of London, I would be a fool if I didn't know her. Half of London knows your reputation.

-Only half? -He replied, trying to break the ice and get her to open up.

-The other half is an imbecile. He replied with a fake smile and Brenda smiled along with him.

-I don't think I can argue with that.

-Discuss you.

-I beg your pardon?

-I think in the position we are in," he said, looking at the dark prison and the closed bars in front of them, "you can talk to me about you.

Brenda smiled a second time and replied affably.

-It sounds perfect to me. Okay Suraj, I want you to start telling me everything you remember. I want to know what exactly happened. I need all the details, your impressions, the conclusions you have drawn. It is essential that you don't hold anything back and that you trust me or I won't be able to help you, am I clear?

-Perfectly." Suraj nodded as he tilted his head to one side to begin his explanation.

-Jane and I have been traveling for months. One day we woke up determined that Morocco would be as interesting a place to visit as any other.

-Whose idea was it exactly? -He asked with a touch of unimportance, as he always used to do when he questioned.

-If you are wondering, I didn't do it, I didn't kill them. Jane is the only important thing in my life and simply because of how much I love her, I would never put her through such suffering. I didn't touch those women. He confessed, holding his head in both hands.

Brenda regretted her clumsiness. The man was an expert in criminology and understood her intentions before she even voiced her questions. She should take a more direct stance if she wanted to know the truth of the facts.

-You say you're innocent and that you didn't know these women. So what exactly were you doing at Lunas de Oriente? I understand you don't exactly go there for coffee.

-That's not important. He answered gruffly.

-Well, I think so. Those women frequented the place and some even swear that at least once they saw you leaving the same room as them.

Suraj did not answer and Brenda continued to demonstrate that she was sufficiently informed.

-Those two young women had their throats slit in an alley outside the store after being with you. You were the last person to see them alive.

-That does not represent any proof. He replied with a hardened face.

-No, it is not, but it is clear that you are not telling me the whole truth, so I repeat, if you say you are so in love with Jane, then why were you cheating on her with those girls? How long were you with them?

-I haven't cheated on her, I never have." His voice showed that he was beginning to get angry.

Brenda saw him clench his fists and looked around the cell, realizing that this place was neither her country nor did it have the security of her clinic. She should be careful or she could become the third woman to have her throat slit, after all those cops at the entrance were no guarantee of security.

-Well, then let's not call it cheating, but you'll have to admit to me that you knew them.

-I don't even remember their faces.... -he commented in sorrow.

-Are you sure? Maybe one of them interested you more than you thought. Maybe, without realizing it, one of them started to win your heart and you felt anger for what was starting to happen to you. Jealousy for not having her?

Brenda asked leaning her back against the back of the bench, interested in the man's movements more than his words. Many times gestures showed much more truth than hundreds of unfinished sentences.

-I love Jane. He said again like a mantra.

-But you admit to cheating on her." The instant she mentioned the word, Brenda cursed herself again for her clumsiness.

-No!" The man exploded but didn't seem to want to attack her. He decided he would tighten the noose a little more. Jane was his weak point and apparently key to the story.

-But she wasn't with you. She was waiting for you at the hotel while you were hanging out with other women. What exactly happened to ignite your anger? Jealousy, rage, out of control? What did they do to you? Were you afraid Jane would find out? Were you afraid she'd think you didn't love her and that your feelings weren't true?

Brenda was about to continue to strafe with questions and look for an uncontrolled reaction from her patient when he screamed out loud and jumped off the cot.

-Not her! Lock me up if you want, but don't let Jane have anything to do with all this.

Brenda trembled at the sincerity of his words. His feelings seemed true but that did not mean innocence.

-You say you love her but you hide the truth from her. She said expecting a confession from the incarcerated man but the female voice at the entrance froze her in place.

-Jane entered with a bottle of water in her hand, which she handed to her boyfriend, while he shook his head. The young woman waited for the policeman to lock them back in the cell and leave before continuing to talk. I was with Suraj in that room.

-No, I will not accept it," he said, holding her by the shoulders.

-Accept what? -The doctor asked curiously and Jane sighed heavily.

-He wants to protect me. Suraj believes that if I accept to the authorities that I was in the Lunas de Oriente, they will have no pity on me. Here the laws are harsher for us than for them.

-They'll lock you up and throw the key into the sea! I won't allow it.

Suraj moved angrily around the cell and Jane waited for him to calm down before hugging him and resting her face on his torso. The doctor for her part waited for them both to calm down so she could get some information that would clarify what the hell they were talking about. According to Jane, she had been with Suraj in the room, but he denied it, why? Both said a few words to each other softly that she was not able to understand, then Jane gave him a delicate kiss on the chin and looked at the doctor with decision.

-You need the truth.

-Please. He replied with a deep headache.

-Suraj and I... from time to time we visit places different from the common couple. Brenda bent her neck trying to understand and Jane wanted to clarify her words, although the woman seemed to have trouble finding the right phrases. We have shared sex," she said almost breathlessly.

-¿Y? -she asked curiously. Not that she was the most liberal of women, but she didn't live outside the real world either.

This time it was Suraj, who, resting his strong hand on his girl's shoulder, took her place in the story.

-In the Lunas de Oriente, in some clandestine rooms, certain couples with this type of taste meet.

-I understand." Brenda thought she didn't really understand anything but wanted to reassure them so they could explain themselves.

-If I had imagined it, I would never have done it.

-Never, what? -Brenda waited, but this time it was Jane who continued speaking.

-It was not your idea but mine. You should not blame yourself. He said looking straight at the doctor. I was the one who proposed to go to the room. We met those girls but we hardly said hello. Our room was another one. We didn't... I mean that...

-Jane was the only woman in our room," Suraj answered seriously. Well, doctor, do you believe me now? I had nothing to do with those young girls. Maybe someone saw us in the same hallway, maybe someone even introduced us, and to tell you the truth, if so, I don't even remember it. Jane is and has been the only one, games or no games, I have not been with another woman.

Brenda thought and thought as the couple hugged and comforted each other. If Jane had always been with her boyfriend, and as hard as it had been for them to confess, she believed them, then who wanted to involve him in such a cruel crime? These women had been mercilessly slaughtered.

-Do you have people who want to see you in jail?

Suraj smiled while still holding his girl in his arms and replied in amusement.

-Everybody.

-Reed Blackman asked me to get you out of here. -. He replied, breaking the tension.

-Everyone but him. He rectified dryly.

-Maybe if I confess.... -Jane spoke to the ex-cop, but he refused outright.

-You would only make things worse. A woman would be judged more harshly for prostitution, no, not a chance.

Jane turned red at the accusation and Brenda instantly felt sorry for the young woman. What they did in their room was their business alone and no one should judge them.

-Suraj is right. Certain activities are not allowed here and if we add to that the fact that they are not married, we would only make things worse. Someone wants to involve them and the first thing is to find out who and why.

Brenda wrote in her report some conclusions. Now that he was able to see the situation clearly and understand the obscurities in Suraj's statement, he believed her version. He came across as caring, protective, maybe even overly so, and that led him to think more of Jane than of himself. No, he would never play with her freedom, so who and why did he want to see him behind bars?

-Tonight I will prepare a report to be delivered to the Minister of the Interior. With that and a few phone calls I hope you will be free.

Suraj and Jane watched her as if she were an alien and the doctor smiled self-sufficiently.

-One, which has one or two contacts. It would be a temporary freedom but it's something. All three smiled but it was Jane who seemed the most elated. It was obvious that the woman was suffering from her silence.

When they both left, night was beginning to fall and Mohamed was still waiting. He opened the car and the two got in silently until Brenda remembered a question she had preferred not to ask in prison so as not to worry Suraj.

-Jane, when you went to get the water bottle, did anything happen?

-Why do you say that?

-Your hair was disheveled and your hijab was misplaced. You were as red as a tomato, I don't know, you looked agitated?

Jane nodded as she removed her headscarf.

-It was nothing serious. When I was on my way to the warehouse some guys decided to be affectionate.

-Did you have to run? -she asked worriedly.

-No, no. A man in a blue robe chased them away. I was lucky.

Brenda nodded in appreciation that at least one of them understood a woman's rights.

The car pulled away towards the hotel as they both stood in silence. Night was lighting up the city and they were both exhausted. The emotions of the day had proved too strong. Getting lost in the city, convincing a grumpy guide, punching a jerk in his parts, interrogating a suspected murderer. Too many emotions for one day.

The van sped away as a man in a deep blue suriyah covered his head and the entirety of his face leaving just a thin line of his intense gaze free. Attentively, he watched them climb into the car and smiled as he saw them depart safely.

Passions of Africa

Hundreds of visits, writing everywhere, some very worn soles and at last the long awaited answer. Somewhat more relaxed, she waited, watching the people strolling by the window while Jane walked from one side to the other, carving grooves in the floor of the old wood.

The sergeant was not very eager to comply with the orders of the Minister of the Interior but waiting calmly was much better than raising another complaint. Freedom was just a door away and discussions were no longer worthwhile. It was freedom with charges and an inability to leave the country but for the moment that was much better than that dark, dank cell. With Suraj free they could investigate who the hell was behind that nonsense, because two poor girls may have met an unpleasant death but the inspector was not responsible. He didn't fit the profile of a serial killer, let alone a dismemberer of innocents. Someone was trying to implicate him and it remained to be seen why.

She looked out the window again and let her thoughts fly. So busy in her reports, she had not had time to remember whom she should not, however now, seeing Suraj's love for Jane, she remembered the moments with Akim, his way of talking to her, the sweet words when making love, the caresses given in the dark of the night and the hundreds of foolish things she believed to be true.... There could not be a more idiotic woman and a more deceitful man.

Jane's gasp made her look into the room. Suraj appeared walking slowly and the young woman threw herself into his arms as seemed to be the usual for them. "At least sincere love exists..." The man lifted his face above his girl's head and Brenda found that he thanked her with a twitch of his lips. She smiled at him accepting his thanks as she spoke with a lump in her throat.

-I think we should leave.

The couple did not separate even to walk to the car and Brenda feared for her physical integrity, because those two would hit the ground at any moment. Amused, she climbed into the car in the passenger seat, leaving Mohamed perplexed.

-To give them a little privacy. He explained to the chauffeur, who kept watching the two of them cuddling in the rearview mirror.

-Cheeky Europeans. He replied angrily as he watched them merge in a passionate kiss.

The vehicle stopped in one of the many traffic jams in the city and Brenda opened the folder with the reports of the ex-incarcerated man. She began to read and study them carefully. She had at least an hour ahead of her until she reached the hotel, rested for a few minutes and set off in search of the definitive clues. Suraj was innocent, she was sure of it, and she would leave no stone unturned and no person unanalyzed until she could prove it, after all she was Brenda, Brenda Klein, protector of lost souls, she told herself amused while she made notes on the side of a sheet of paper.

After a two-hour traffic jam, a hasty shower and tea drunk on her feet, she hurriedly got dressed. Mohamed was probably already in the doorway waiting for her. A little nervous about what she was going to do, she decided to put on her head scarf and leave as soon as possible. The sooner she left, the sooner she would return safe and sound, or at least she hoped so. Cautious not to be discovered by Jane or Suraj, who were just in the next room, she walked almost on tiptoe down the hallway. She didn't get two steps when she remembered that the couple hadn't been alone for a month and the last thing they would be thinking about that night was her and her follies. Smiling at her conclusions, she walked briskly and collided head-on with the body of a man who, leaning on the stairs, interrupted her passage.

-Excuse me. She said trying to dodge him. The man covered from head to toe, including his face, with long blue cotton clothes, did not respond, nor did he move, so she decided to jump over his legs. The man grunted loudly and she smiled in satisfaction as she went down the stairs to the hotel reception at full speed. You should have moved," she said cheekily. You would have thought the man held back a laugh but without paying any attention to her she walked briskly towards the exit.

Mohamed was with the van on and waited to see her get in to ask her destination.

-The Moon of the East. She said like a complete detective but the driver replied angrily.

-No way!

-How?

-I said I will not take her to that den of sin for all the gold in the world. Allah would not forgive me.

Brenda took a breath trying to calm down. The man didn't understand that she was the one who decided where to go and where not to go.

-Mohamed, I'm going to the Orient Moon, with or without your help.

-You devil woman! We are not in your country. If you go in there, you won't come out alive. They will seize her as soon as she goes through the door.

-And why would they do such a thing? -she asked intrigued.

-For prostitution. He replied angrily. Here you have a prison sentence.

-What a stupid thing to say," he said cheerfully, "I'm not a prostitute. Come on, take me to the happy room and wait for me at the door.

-Stubborn woman. He mumbled as he accelerated the car. -I hope she left the will in writing.

Brenda shook her head. Mohamed was exaggerating. He would just order a drink, ask a couple of questions, get some information and get out of there as soon as possible. "Prostitute? Her?" she remembered how she had to confess to Max her feelings for Akim for not being able to lie. "Prostitute," she muttered with a restrained laugh on her lips.

The blue-clad man watched as the car sped off and cursed loudly. With alacrity he raised his hand and a cab stopped instantly. With a raised finger he signaled the cab driver to follow the van in front and he did so without question.

Hidden glances

The scent of incense and jasmine clouded the senses as we passed through a room clouded by bongs and the crackling of candelabras. Hundreds of brightly colored candles danced to the sensual percussion of the lute and tar while couples conversed intimately on large, brightly patterned cushions.

Dazzled by the baroque décor, she walked slowly, taking in every detail of the place. A central stage, now empty, occupied the heart of the room while a bar at the side was dispatched by waiters who drove her senses crazy. Distracted by their splendorous bodies, she walked, forgetting her red dress of vaporous translucent silk, which she had chosen for the occasion. A man or two focused their gaze on her figure and to tell the truth, she felt a little uncomfortable with the intrusion, but playing the role of an uninhibited woman was her best option. With a somewhat exaggerated smile she approached the waiter out of the most erotic of fairy tales and ordered a Martini.

-I beg your pardon?

"Phew, bad start. You're not supposed to drink alcohol in this country," he thought, wrinkling his forehead at his clumsiness.

-Pour her a glass of Arak. A man with a thick voice, eyelashes like the night and a look like the deepest of deserts, spoke while he undressed her with his eyes.

-Thank you." Her sultry voice brought an instant sinful smile to the man's face.

He didn't introduce himself, he simply waited for his drink to be served, but kept his eyes on her. Brenda began to feel like a young girl at a prom. She moved one foot in time to the soft music as she absentmindedly scanned the room. Maybe this way that guy would go away and leave her alone because he was starting to intimidate her. After all, she was a recent divorcee and a prude by birth, she told herself, drumming her fingers on her glass.

-My name is Mohamed. He said after five long minutes.

"Are they all named the same?" She wondered with eyes wide as saucers.

The man seemed to discover her thoughts because he smiled, showing his perfect, gleaming teeth.

-It's a fairly common name.

-It seems so. She replied with a silly smile, "I'm Brenda.

-Hello Brenda.

The man demonstrated in every word, an air of superiority that he hated and that in London he would not have tolerated, but he was in Morocco, he said to himself while biting his tongue to avoid sending this arrogant man to the back of the room with a kick. The more she talked to him, the more she wanted to hang him.

-European, then?

-From London and you? -He spoke with a stupid grin as he sipped his drink.

-From here.

-He was about to say shit, disgust, crap when he saw the amused look of that macho bag of bones and did not want to indulge him - ...strong. It's a bit of a strong drink.

-You women are so delicate. He replied as he finished his glass in one gulp.

"So delicate, I'd kick what you're delicate with." She decided to ignore his stupid comment and proceed with her plans.

-And do you come here often? -Brenda asked while she thought about drinking a second glass of that lye.

-Whenever I can. - "Interesting."

-So you'll meet a lot of people?

-Enough, and you?

-No, I'm alone. He answered barely wetting his tongue and leaving the wet sheen of the drink on his lips.

She may not have been a sex bomb and in psychology school they did not teach seduction techniques, but she was no prude and she had read many novels. The man who did not stop devouring her with his eyes, came closer, decreasing the distance between them, their bodies almost rubbed and the sensation was most unpleasant, but if that arrogant man had information, she would get it out of him.

-I'm alone too. What do you say we keep each other company?

Brenda smiled that fake, goofy, vase-woman smile.

-The night is young. He replied mischievously. Besides, I'm waiting for someone.

-I thought you were alone? -he replied with mock disappointment.

Brenda adjusted her neckline and smiled again.

-Now I do, but I met a man on the trip and I'd like to go back and... talk to him again. You know what I mean... -The man cleared his throat when he saw the woman's decision. It was clear that he also wanted to "talk" with her. You might know him. I have a picture of him on my cell phone, you know, the kind you take without thinking?

The man looked at the screen so interested that she could have sworn she wanted to see something with less clothes on. The man raised his head in utter disappointment at the image of Suraj in solitary.

-I've seen him a couple of times.

"Yes!"

-Have you seen him? -You don't know if he was accompanied? I just wouldn't want to... you know...

Brenda asked without showing too much interest even though inside she would have strung him up by the neck until he sang La Traviata. She waited patiently for that lout to speak, but the idiot was slower than a wheelbarrow pulled by a donkey. Snorting inwardly, he discovered that in the distance, a young woman with thick black hair, did not stop watching them for a moment. "Poor naïve, in love and horned", she thought saddened.

-Why don't we talk somewhere more private and I'll tell you everything I know? -He stretched his torso until their bodies were almost touching, whispering in her ear.

Brenda instantly tensed up, what could she answer? This was no place to be alone with anyone, but on the other hand, if she could get something out of him it could mean Suraj's freedom. She thought and thought about anything foolish that would free her from having to accompany the jerk, when she heard him curse out loud.

The arrogant man turned around to face the man next to him, who had apparently pushed his elbow, causing him to tip over his glass. Intrigued, she raised her head to see who was responsible for such a brazen attitude and found another tall, strong man, but covered entirely with a kind of deep blue frock coat. The fabrics of the same color completed a turban that hid his forehead, nose and the whole of his face. Barely a narrow opening to leave a gaze as cold as the night and as blue as the most transparent sapphire. Her heart pounded at the sight of that man. To tell the truth, she could see nothing but cloth, but something made her shudder. It was curious, but she had only felt something like that once and that was when... she shook her head, it was not the time to remember it.

-You had to be a Tuareg to behave like an idiot," the man, whose eyes barely showed a thin line, didn't answer but didn't move away either. Brenda tried to observe him a little better but the room illuminated by the small flames of the candles did not help much. The idiot turned to her again but this time with anger in his eyes. You could tell he was annoyed by the interruption. The doctor instantly became alert. If a careless push had made him like that, what could happen when she refused to accompany him? She smiled like a fool and invented the stupid but so useful resource that all women always keep up their sleeves.

-I have to go to the toilet.

She was about to leave and decide to look for a less furious prey when he grabbed her by the arm with a force that made her shriek in pain.

-He said, leaving far behind the apparent kindness he had shown so far. Brenda was startled but also irritated enough to jerk her arm free of his grip.

-I go where I want and with whom I want. I don't need permission.

She walked away to another room when Mohamed reached out to grab her by the neck but barely brushed her hair. She heard him swear again before that guy in the wide blue cloths grabbed him by the neck. Without waiting and thanking him for the gesture, she walked with a quick step, leaving those two behind. Looking for an escape route, the girl who was watching her before, shook her head and pointed to a door at the back on the left. Thank you, she mumbled through her lips as she ran over. She quickly entered the new room.

The man with an icy gaze and a body covered by blue cloths, watched her leave while with one foot he continued to squeeze Mohamed's back, who cursed loudly.

Run while you can

She entered another room, which was no less attractive for being smaller. The young woman guided her to a small wooden table and pointed to a very wide and apparently very comfortable pouf; she nodded gratefully and sat down waiting to know the reason for such a laudable rescue. She did not ask. Not aloud. She just sat and waited. The girl approached a waitress who instantly brought them a teapot and two small crystal glasses on a finely wrought copper platter.

-Mint tea. He said holding the teapot up as if waiting for consent.

-Please. The doctor spoke kindly.

The woman poured the steaming drink into both glasses and Brenda waited solicitously for her to begin speaking. Patience was not one of her virtues but in these distant lands she had been cultivating it for a week.

-My name is Lina.

-I'm Klein, Brenda Klein. She discovered with amusement that she loved to simulate 007 in action.

-I know. He replied, sipping his drink.

-Do we know each other?

-I've seen her at the hotel and walking around the city.

Brenda would have liked to say like any other tourist, but she preferred to keep quiet. That girl had focused her attention on her and she needed to know why.

-I also saw her in jail. He spoke with a hint of fear.

-Were you following me? -She didn't answer and Brenda started to get uncomfortable. Well, if you wanted to talk to me, here I am.

-I didn't want to talk to you.

-Oh no? -Brenda sipped her delicious tea, trying to calm her nerves. Either she was going crazy or she was surrounded by crazy people.

-May I know why you brought me all the way down here and bought me tea?

-I saw her ask Mohamed. He doesn't know anything.

-But you do.

-Yes, you want information about the Indian. The one who was imprisoned.

-How do you know so much about me and I know nothing about you?

The young woman raised her shoulders in a sign of caring little about her deductions and the doctor shifted uncomfortably on the pouf.

-Lina, either you tell me what I'm doing here or I'm leaving," he said, using an old-fashioned but effective lantern. She wasn't going to move from there, not even as a joke. If that little girl knew something, she wanted to know it too.

-You must promise to help me with Mohamed," he said, hiding his face, which was as red as a tomato.

-Which one?

-Moha, the man in the other room. She replied confused.

Brenda smiled and answered instantly to release her from her fears.

-I'm not interested in him. I'm sorry you thought your boyfriend and I had a thing.

-He is not my boyfriend.

-Okay. She replied reluctantly, hoping to end that crazy conversation and focus on her personal interest.

-I want you to help me. The young woman spoke, biting her lip nervously.

Brenda frowned, thinking seriously that this conversation had neither head nor tail, so she decided to get up and continue her research in other directions. She had no time for such absurdities.

-Lina, was that your name? -The girl nodded and Brenda spoke, pushing the tea cup away and trying to get up to indicate that the conversation had come to an end.

-I have no idea who Mohamed is but you should not focus on him. You are a beautiful young lady and you can have as many Mohamed as you want. Now if you'll excuse me, I must go. He got up and was about to leave when Lina spoke in a rush of words.

-I know who the girls left with that night. Your friend was not with the men who took them.

Brenda instantly stopped in her tracks, perplexed by his confession. Damn it, if the authorities had that information Suraj would be in the clear.

-How do you know? -His heart was beating impatiently.

-Help me. He said with the stubbornness of youth.

-Lina, if you tell me who those girls left with, you could free an innocent man. My friend is accused of a double murder he didn't commit.

-Help me and I will help you.

-Help you what! -He shouted, his nerves shaken by the girl's stubbornness. What could he expect from her more important than saving an innocent man from jail?

-With Mohamed.

-And again with the same little song. I can't help you. I don't know him. Today is the first time I've seen him in my whole life.

The doctor began to explain herself in a desperate manner. She did not know what the hell she was referring to when she kept repeating the request for help. She wanted to explain the seriousness of withholding such information when the screams in the next room put them on alert. Lina got up as if triggered by a spring and ran to the other end of the room.

-It's the police. Run. This way.

Brenda wanted to say out loud that she wasn't doing anything illegal when she realized that she was in a Muslim country, surrounded by illegal alcoholic beverages, and dressed somewhat provocatively.

Let's run! She said to herself as she tried to run away, but she bumped into some people and others who, like her, were seeking refuge wherever they could. People were moving like dizzy ducks and she cursed when she bumped into a woman who, instead of running away, was in the way. Damn heels, if she had known she would have to run with such urgency she wouldn't have worn them. Lina was looking at her worriedly insisting that she hurry up and she was trying, but what a way to run into people! She was about to start hitting everyone in front of her with her purse like a soccer quarterback, when some arms lifted her up and carried her quickly towards Lina. The little girl opened several doors and Brenda bit her lips in rage. She was being carried like a sack of potatoes in a very undignified position, but what could she say? with such high heels she would be the first one they would have behind bars. She leaned her face on the man who was holding her up while she looked at the view they were leaving behind. "By the skin of her teeth," she thought clinging to her savior's strong shoulder. "They sure are strong," she squeezed them for a second time as the man grunted in annoyance. "And well, what did you expect me to do. I'm hanging and jiggling back and forth, I'll have to have some fun with something," she said to herself as she smiled to keep from crying.

Lina opened a huge metal door, pointed the way to the alley and disappeared. The man began to release her slowly, causing a most pleasurable shudder to run through her from her nose to the smallest toe. Could it be that in all these years she had missed so much? Who knows, maybe maturity was giving her new pleasures. Whatever it was, he liked those arms from the first touch. For heaven's sake, so much saffron, candles and Arabian dancing were turning her into a shameless libertine. It was either that or feeling like a free and divorced woman suited her to perfection.

-The Tuareg," he murmured as he recognized the blue robes.

-Get in that car! -Her chauffeur's shouts brought her back to reality.

-But... -She said ashamed when she noticed that her Blue Knight released her from his embrace -Get in right now! Samir will take you to the hotel.

-Samir? But who is he? And you? And him? -She asked in distress, but the driver wouldn't let her. He practically dragged her the twenty meters down the alley and shoved her into the car. Brenda moved to the side waiting for the two men to get in next to her but Mohamed slammed the door and banged on the roof, signaling for the new driver to leave immediately.

Puzzled by what had just happened, she turned to watch through the rear window as the figure of the two men dwarfed in the distance. She took a deep breath fearing for them. Mohamed could have run away with her and she didn't understand why he hadn't. And her Blue Knight? No, he didn't need her, he was a savior, surely he would have his own means of escape, perhaps one of those cars with huge wheels and capable of flying over the desert sands or maybe a motorcycle to flee in the middle of the city or a camel for a romantic ride through... "My mother, I've gone from being a demure woman to becoming a harem casquivana". She thought shaking her head, better to stop fooling around and try to get some rest. First thing in the morning she would talk to Suraj and confess to him the little nocturnal mischief and her latest discoveries.

-That woman is made for getting into trouble. She doesn't know where we are and the danger she's in. Mohamed took a close look at the man next to him and asked him curiously. Did you help her?

-Yes. He replied in a very deep voice as he watched the vehicle drive away.

Mohamed continued to analyze him from top to bottom. He could see that under the long djellaba down to his feet there was a strong and well-shaped body.

-Are you Tuareg? -He said, pointing to his clothes. Would you like to work for me? That woman needs permanent custody and I'm not in the mood for that. Mohamed sensed that the man was thinking about it and continued with his offer. It's a bit insufferable but I'll pay you well. Those foreigners either pay well or they don't leave the country, you know what I mean.

Mohamed mistook the gentleman's angry look for one of disgust at having to deal with that insufferable doctor, so he continued with his plea to convince him.

-Blessed women," he said at length, "they are insufferable. I don't understand why those Europeans give them so much free rein. If it were up to me they wouldn't leave the house. Taking care of children is what they were born to do.

The blue knight grunted and Mohamed tapped him twice on the shoulder.

-That's right, my friend, because we need them, otherwise.... So what do you say? Good and fast money.

-I will protect her.

Mohamed didn't know what exactly that meant but everyone knew that these Tuareg were most sparing with words.

-Well, let's have an arak to celebrate. I know where they put them at a good price, by the way, what's your name?

The gentleman didn't answer and Mohamed decided he didn't need to. If he could just get that blissful chatterbox off his back, that was enough.

Bargaining

Brenda tried to forget that sea of past sensations but the memories took on a life of their own. That warmth so protective, those arms so safe, that jolt of feeling him skin against skin, became an accumulation of feelings burning in her veins. Meeting the gentleman in blue robes led her once again down a path she had to forget. She could not fall back into the arms of desire. Not so soon... With melancholy she gathered her hair in a high ponytail as if with that simple act she managed to put her innermost thoughts in order. Discarding the hijab, she decided to recover part of her essence and go out into the street with her hair in the wind. Totally distracted, she walked down the stairs thinking about those arms that shook her without intending to.

Better not to imagine. He had more important matters to attend to. He would head straight to the central market. A busy tourist site where he remembered perfectly well having seen the same logo that the young woman wore embroidered on her T-shirt. This Lina admitted to knowing things but she ran away before she could convince her to testify and she had to find her. In a hurry she wanted to go through the hotel door but the shout of Suraj, who was in the armchairs of the reception, stopped her in her tracks.

-Where are you supposed to go?

-Good morning, how was your first night off with Jane? The man opened his eyes smiling and the doctor felt herself start to turn red with embarrassment. She should think before she spoke, she scolded herself.

-I didn't want to, well I did but it wasn't....

-I heard you went out last night. He commented, changing the subject.

-How do you know?

-Mohamed.

-And why should I tell you anything? -What a gossip," she thought in disgust. He doesn't care where I come or go. I'm on my own.

-As the man closest to you he felt he should know your antics.

-What a stupid thing to say!

-Doctor, I don't make the rules here. Don't kill the messenger," he replied amused, "Brenda, why did you go to that place? It's no place for a woman like you, much less alone. Don't do it again.

The doctor was about to respond when the inspector grabbed her by the shoulder and spoke tenderly.

-Jane told me everything you did to set me free and I don't think I can ever thank you for it, but from now on I'm on my own. I couldn't bear to see either of you hurt.

-Don't worry about me, I can defend myself. I'm used to getting around in complicated places. You should have known me in better times.

-This is not England," he replied with a frown. You must go home. You have done more here than I can ever thank you for.

-You don't have to worry about anything. I plan to do some sightseeing, that's all. He lied brazenly.

-Good.

-What about you? What are you planning to do this morning? -She asked with great interest and as if she was not hiding her daring plans.

-I spoke to a friend of mine last night. He's a member of the defense department. They may be able to help me.

-That's great! -She replied with excessive enthusiasm. "Too over the top, I'll have to take lessons with Rachel," she said to herself in amusement.

-Yes, we'll see." His thick voice sounded too hopeless but Brenda was not daunted. She would help him.

-Well, I'm off before they sell everything and I run out of gifts. Brenda walked slowly away trying to fool the perceptive inspector when he shouted from his seat.
-Won't you call Mohamed for a ride?
-It is not necessary. Downtown is close by. It's a beautiful day for a stroll -. "And I'll be damned if I'm going to call that tattletale a tattletale." Traitorous male chauvinist.
With map in hand he left.

After an hour of searching and too many turns in circles, she knew that she could not find that place without help. She was totally disoriented. Those stalls were all the same. Furious with her lack of orientation she approached one of the hundreds of spice stalls.
-Sir, if you could help me. The man looked at her as if she had horns on her head, but the doctor continued speaking. You see, my good man, I am looking for a hairdresser's, "I think", it is one of those places that do henna tattoos, or so I thought. I'm sure it was around here but I'm not able to find my way around.
The man furrowed his eyebrows that joined into just one. He didn't like tourists very much.
-Are you going to buy or not?
-No, but if you could help me....
-Do I look like a tourist agency?
-No, no, I just wanted to know if you know of any henna tattoo stores for girls. One like this. He said trying to show the picture he had on his cell phone and that he had gotten thanks to St. Google.
-Do I look like a girl?
-No, no, I didn't say that, but maybe you know where it is and could help me? -he finished speaking almost in a whisper. The clothes horse turned to a couple of Germans ready to buy and turned his back in his face.

At first, she wanted to shoot him with her eyes, but immediately she realized her mistake. Of course, since she was so stupid, that man was there to earn his children's bread, how thoughtless she was. Maybe that store was the only sustenance, his own and that of the five children waiting for him at home... and the dog, surely they had a dog? Smiling with her deduction and sure not to make the same mistake again, she headed for a most interesting stall. Yes, she would ask there. She would buy a nice silk scarf and then politely ask. "How pretty is that blue," she thought amused as she realized how much she liked that color lately. A very fine line in his eyes was the only thing she had been able to distinguish from that man, but she was unable to forget him...

"Blond or brunette?" she wondered when the clothesline startled her with its scream.

-Are you going to buy something! Or will you keep pawing through the merchandise?

-Oh, yes, sorry, I want this one. She said excitedly, wrapping her fingers around the silky garment.

She caressed it ecstatically. It was perfect. It was supposed to be used for belly dancing but she would buy it on a whim, she would never use it for anyone. Disappointment led her again to remember Akim and the daring she would have indulged in to win his love.

-What about that one? - she asked, pointing to another one in purple tones. He picked one up in each hand and asked interestedly, "How much is this one?

-Which one?

She looked at the outstretched hand with the blue handkerchief feeling she was being quite clear but the man looked at her as if she was not from this planet.

-This one. He answered showing the garment on his right hand.

-That twenty euros.

-Euros? But your currency is the dirham.

-We adapt to tourism," he said with a yellowish, stale smile.

"So much for that," she thought deciding it was far better to play dumb than to have another argument.

-I imagine this one will also be twenty euros? -. He commented out loud when he realized that the only difference was the color.

-Which one?

Brenda narrowed her eyes but didn't get to notice if he was really playing her for a fool or not.

-This one," he said, raising his other hand. The left one.

-Ah, that one. Yes, twenty euros.

Brenda shook her head but did not open her mouth.

-I'll keep them. Forty in total. He said as he took the money out of his pockets. Distracted and as if the matter did not concern her, she wanted to show him the screen of her cell phone.

-I wonder if you know of a store that does tattoos like this? I'm looking for a friend of mine...

-There are sixty of them. He answered in a deep voice.

-I beg your pardon?

-The handkerchiefs are sixty euros.

-But he said twenty. She commented somewhat puzzled.

-Each one twenty, together sixty. If you want another one, I'll let you have all three for seventy.

-But doesn't that make sense? -He commented, mentally adding up to know where exactly he was going wrong.

-Four and I'll give you a purse,

-I don't want any purse. Okay, fine, I'll give you sixty. He said rummaging for more money in his pocket to finish the transaction. Here you go, now I would like to ask you if....

-Don't you want the other one?

-No thanks, with these two I have enough. As I was trying to ask him ....

-And why doesn't he want it? I give him the purse, a pair of slippers for a hundred euros.

-No, thank you. I was asking if...

-Well, eighty.

-I'm not interested. He answered, gritting his teeth.

-I see she's tough. Sixty euros and she takes three handkerchiefs and a leather purse.

-Sixty? No thanks. I'm just interested to know if you know a woman with a...

-Forty, and two handkerchiefs and a one hundred percent leather purse. The shopkeeper interrupted again and Brenda's eyes widened.

-Forty? But if he charged me sixty for only two handkerchiefs?

-Ugh, woman, you really know. All right, fifty euros and purse plus purse.

The doctor forgot why she was there. Her blood was boiling in her veins. Was this man making fun of her or was he just naturally like that?

-I wanted a handkerchief, you tried to cheat me out of two, and now you're selling me a purse and a wallet? Are you out of your mind?

-By Allah, woman. She's going to ruin my business. All right, two handkerchiefs, a purse and a wallet for one hundred and ten euros.

-Five seconds ago, it was a hundred.... - He said, sobbing.

-But now I give him a leather headband.

-I don't want any tape!

Half an hour later and carrying five handkerchiefs, two purses, a purse, a travel backpack and three hair ribbons, she realized that she would not get much from those salesmen. She was about to leave for the hotel when a loud noise distracted her. She walked a couple of

meters away, leaving her purchases on the table of the last booth, and looked interestedly at the couple arguing loudly.
 -But he said thirty! Why the hell is he asking me for fifty now.
 -Why do you have two pots now! They are hand-painted.
 -But I only want one... just one..." The poor Italian whimpered faintly and Brenda was most amused. -The poor Italian whimpered faintly and Brenda was distracted in the most amusing way.

-He will approach the lady and answer all your questions. A thick-voiced man whispered in the merchant's ear.
 The clotheshorse tried to turn to tell him who the hell he thought he was when he found himself almost six feet tall. The djellaba covered him down to his feet and the tunic showed only a delicate line of gaze, as blue as his robes and as cold as the iciest of ice.
 -I am not an information center. He said trying not to choke when he discovered her fiery gaze.
 -I don't give a shit what you are. I heard you talking to that asshole saying that you knew perfectly well which store she was looking for. He said pointing to his shopmate who was still in shock when he saw those huge hands holding his friend by the neck-. You are going to look for the lady, you will give her the information she asked for and you will offer her your respect, did you understand everything?
 The blue-robed gentleman's gaze seemed to smile wickedly and the clotheshorse, although he wanted to send him to hell itself, realized that his six feet six inches could do little with that specimen of a man.
 -I don't have to do anything like that and you're not a Tuareg, I'm sure you're just as stinky an Englishman as she is. He spat with what little courage he still had left.

The blue knight grunted and squeezed his already tight neck even tighter causing his sandals to come completely off the cobblestone.

-You don't care who I am or where I come from. You will do what I tell you if you want to continue to have a business, do you understand me? -. He commented as he turned his furious gaze toward the store.

The companion was quick to squeeze the bags between his arms protectively and the man nodded as he coughed trying to get some oxygen into his lungs. The blue knight released him and held out the doctor's shopping bag, which he had forgotten in his tent, as he crossed his arms expectantly. The clothesline trembled just ten steps to collide directly with Brenda's body who was still focused and amused by the Italian's discussion. The poor tourist was trying to explain that he didn't want the skin of any dead animal, that he was vegan, but there was no way, that salesman didn't understand.

-Madam, you forgot this in my post.

-Oh, thank you. I was just about to go get it. He commented, picking up his purchases.

The clothesline seemed not to hear her because he spoke without pausing as if in a hurry to leave.

-That store you are looking for. I'm not sure if it's the one you want to find, but two blocks away, straight down the first exit, you'll come across a wooden crafts stand. It's very large, you can't miss it. There you will turn left and bump straight into the women's room. I don't quite know what they do but in the doorway they have a logo like the one you showed me on your cell phone screen.

The doctor tried to close her mouth but could not. She had been looking for that information for two hours and when she thought all was lost, there it was.

-If she asks for Hana, I'm sure she can help her. He clarified running over the words.

-Thank you. He commented in disbelief.

The man was walking away saying something about Allah and hellish demons when, without reason or logic, he turned to clarify.

-Thank you very much for your purchase.

Brenda could have sworn she said it with a certain tone of disgust but she was too delighted with what she had achieved to be bitter.

The bags hanging from the stall just behind her moved aside to make room for a smiling man who watched her hurry away. With satisfaction she pulled her blue linen back up over her nose and like a shadow of the night he followed her.

Caramel and beauty

"How can it take so long. A few simple questions and that's it," she said to herself as she walked up and down the sidewalk trying not to think about how much trouble she used to attract like trash to flies.

What if there was a back door and someone had taken her? What if she was in danger? What if someone had beaten her up and put her in a van and wanted to dump her body in a field somewhere? His nerves began to show him hundreds of ways of torture that made him even more frantic. Without thinking very well what he was doing and dominated by a thousand horrendous nightmares that made him fear for his safety, he crossed the street and went inside. He didn't care if he didn't understand what was going on there or what that business was about, he wouldn't breathe again until he saw her completely safe. Ready for anything, he entered the store like an elephant in a pottery store, when the women there began to scream like crazy schizophrenics.

-But... but... but... But what?

He looked from one side to the other. Some were trying to cover their breasts but had their arms up numb from something sticky. Others, with their bodies lying on stretchers and their legs in the air, were trying to cover their caramel-colored skin? He tried to think quickly but was distracted by the slap from behind of a woman with her purse.

-Ouch, ma'am, I was looking for... Auch.

-Pervert. Badly educated. Shameless.

The man would have liked to explain to himself that he had little interest in their beauty sessions or whatever those torture tools were attached to their bodies, but it was at that moment when a woman with a long, broad mustache like a Chinaman from China began to beat him with a small stick that was just as sticky.

-No, ma'am. Ouch!

He wanted to dodge the old woman but his stature caused him to collide with a rather low bookshelf that hit him squarely in the forehead.

-Shit." He cursed loudly when, dizzy from the blow, he rested his hand on a jar of a burning and mellow liquid - "Fuck, what the hell? -He wanted to wipe it off but realized that when he touched his turban it got stuck between his fingers leaving his face uncovered.

The women screamed even louder and he wanted to flee but could not. The old woman, who was a tough cookie, took advantage of her hands, rendered useless by the sticky fabrics, to hit him with the stick on the little hair that had been left uncovered. The wood was left hanging from his forehead like a lady's hair roller one morning at the hairdresser's, and his first reaction was to remove it, but he lost his balance due to the strong pull. Disoriented and in pain, he collided with a door that opened instantly, leaving in full view a woman completely sprawled out, with her legs spread wide, and a large mixture of that coppery gunk where she should never have looked. The man tried to say he didn't mean to but was pummeled by another woman, who with spatula in hand hit him in the free arm leaving another contraption now attached to his body.

Cursing again, with two sticks attached to his body and one hand stuck to his turban, he fled in terror, praying never to witness anything like it again.

-Fuck, fuck, fuck," he said to himself as he peeled the cloth sticking out of his hands. As he saw Brenda turn a corner running after a woman he cursed and began to chase her. If she went down the street to the right, I'll intercept them first, he said to himself as he ran at full speed with a thin wooden stick dangling from his black hair.

Minutes before...

Brenda entered the store smiling and expecting to bump into Lina, but it was not so. The woman she was looking for was not there, or at least not in sight, she thought optimistically since she had been lucky for a few days and seemed to be accompanying her like a guardian angel that never abandons you.

-It may not be your turn yet. If I make some time... -He thought as he watched the women ask for their turn to be waxed.

-Excuse me, what did you say? -commented the pretty young lady at the front desk.

-I was wondering if I could get one of those henna tattoos. He smiled.

-Do you have an appointment?

-Ugh, no," he said in a sad tone. You see, I've only been here a short time.

-I'm sorry, but there's nothing I can do.

-Are you sure, please, I would love to have one. The young woman seemed to be thinking about it and the doctor counterattacked. It's so important to my... my mother. She always read me those books about Arabian princesses and I imagined I was one... and of course... now that she is no longer with us..." She commented appealing to the old man. -He commented, appealing to the old resource of grief.

-If you can wait a few minutes, I have a cancellation, but it will have to wait. She replied sympathetically.

-Yes, yes, of course. Of course.

Brenda made her way to the tattoo waiting room, guided by the receptionist and with a broad smile on her face. Lina's tattoo was exactly the one on the sign on the door and she hoped she was one of their employees. She had a slight intuition and although it wasn't much, that was better than nothing. Sitting obediently, she waited her turn reading a magazine.

-Mrs. Klein, come this way.

A sturdy woman with a smiling look guided her to a booth while showing her a catalog of beautiful designs awaiting her decision.

-I like this one.

-An invocation to the dead? -she asked intrigued.

"Ugh no, not that," she said to herself without understanding anything of what those tattoos depicted.

-This one?

-Do you want to have children? -she asked intrigued.

-What about this one? -She spoke in despair.

The woman seemed to realize her incomprehension so she decided to intervene.

-You don't know which one to choose? -she commented amused.

-No idea. He answered just as smiling.

-Well, I explain, these tattoos symbolize mainly desires, for example this is the sign of fertility, this is the happiness of a better life, this is the discovery of love.

-The truth is that love and I have not been on a very good run lately. He said trying not to give much importance to the last drawing.

-Well, then we'll tattoo this one. It is the bud of a flower and it means a new beginning. Leaving the past behind to give your life a new lease of life, what do you think?

-Perfect. That's mine.

Brenda offered her right hand and waited. The two talked for a long time while the woman worked on her arm. When the tattoo was finished the doctor asked for young Lina.

-I can't help you. There are many Linas here. It's a pretty common name. She said as she finished her artwork and angrily closed her painting case.

-Maybe if not now, at some other time you might remember her and be able to give me her address or some way to contact her," she commented hopefully.

-I'm sorry, I don't know anyone like that. I'm going to look for the cashier. Without giving her a chance to reply and leaving behind a small door that did not close behind her, the woman left.

Brenda, curious and tireless as always, followed her walking on her toes so as not to get caught. She leaned her ear against the wood and listened to her talking on the other side of the door.

-What kind of trouble have you gotten yourself into?
-None, Mom, I swear.
-Then why is that Englishwoman asking about you?
-English? Is she here? And what does she want?
-I have no idea, but if you get into another one of your messes I swear....

Brenda decided it was time to intervene. The girl had done nothing wrong. She stepped through the door determined to prove to both of them that she posed no threat when the women froze at the sight of her.

-Run! -The mother ordered her daughter before Brenda could say a word and the young girl, faithful to her mother's order, ran out of a small back door.

The doctor decided that if she ran after her and managed to catch up with her it would be better than giving a thousand explanations that would never be understood. The alley was narrow and there were two alleys on both sides.

-Right or left? Left." He said to himself, thinking he had lost it.

Brenda turned without any optimism when she almost collided with the young woman who was facing her as if she was waiting for her.

-Lina, I'm not going to hurt you," she said hastily.
-I know, he told me.
-Him? I don't know who you're talking about.
-The man with the stick on his head.

Brenda looked at her intrigued but preferred not to ask. Luck was on her side again and she wouldn't waste time on young girl nonsense. The little girl would be raving from the heat. It was logical.

-What do you say we have lunch together. I'm starving and need an iced tea before I die of dehydration.

The girl smiled in satisfaction and the doctor breathed a sigh of relief. If she could get Lina to tell her what she knew, Suraj might be free much sooner than she thought. The two walked together as Brenda stopped in place.

-Wait, I forgot my purchases at your mother's store.

-Shopping? -she asked interested.

-Yes, the truth is that I was just looking for a scarf," he replied with a smile, "but I've been sold half a yard sale.

-Don't you know how to haggle?

-It doesn't look like it.

They both laughed out loud as they turned back toward the store.

Hiding behind a thick, tall palm tree, the blue knight, or what was left of him, was pulling the stick out of his hair as he cursed again and again at the sight of the huge tuft of black hair stuck to the wood. The turban was totally sticky and unusable. He walked the opposite way to the women, ready to buy a new turban and in search of a place that would offer him a beer. How could women suffer such martyrdom? He thought, stroking his arm now with a bald spot the size of an orange.

Alliances

The intense African sun was felt in every corner like a judge ready to sentence anyone who passed under its yoke. Brenda wiped her forehead and looked for a lovely little table under a group of leafy palm trees that offered them the right atmosphere for a long afternoon of confessions. They ate quietly talking about various banalities. The important thing was to gain the young woman's trust. Lina should feel safe by his side, she had no intention of harming her in the least, but she needed to know the truth.

The girl kept talking about Moha as if he were an unreachable god and Brenda was tempted more than once to laugh at her naivety. She was barely in her twenties but she kept saying that she would die without his love. Blessed innocent youth that makes you believe that your heart stops for a look that never comes or a caress that was never real. Tears may have made you feel like you were drowning in a sea of pain, and your heart would break into a thousand pieces just remembering her name, but she as an expert adult knew perfectly well that none of that was true. Your legs keep walking, your lungs keep breathing, the broken heart keeps beating and the sorrow for love ends up being a silent companion that walks by your side.

-And that's why I need you to help me.... -He commented once more.

The doctor sighed and tried to express with the utmost tenderness an open secret. After all, she had experienced it herself, and not so long ago.

-You can't force anyone to love you. I am a doctor, yes, that's true, and yes, it's also true that I know a lot about human psychology, but that doesn't give me the power to create what doesn't exist.

-But he cares about me. I want him to see me as a woman... one of those women who go to the club and he stares at me like a fool.

Brenda smiled at the man's matter-of-fact, decaffeinated description.

-Honey, I'm afraid everyone gets a little "goofy" around women like that. I saw them dancing too, and I think I'm on Mohamed's side this time. She replied cheerfully as she sipped her cold tea.

-But I want him to look at me.....

-Maybe competing with them is not a good idea. Maybe if you could show them your qualities without having to become who you are not, it would be a better solution.

Lina sipped her refreshing mint tea while Brenda took advantage of the fact that they were no longer talking about Mohamed to get into the real reason for their lunch together. She didn't want to come across as unpleasant, she really liked the girl, but an innocent man's freedom was at stake so she decided to be very clear when talking about the really important issues.

-Lina, last night you told me something about those young girls and I need you to tell me everything you know.

-I don't know much. I shouldn't have said anything... -The young woman suddenly turned pale and Brenda felt the need to stretch her body across the table to bring her hand close to hers.

-Yes, it is necessary. Thanks to your collaboration we can save an innocent man from being tried for a murder he did not commit.

-But I don't know much," she commented sadly.

-It doesn't matter.

-You are a very good person.

-Not as much as I would like. Now tell me everything you know. The doctor wrapped her fingers around the young woman's hand so that she could feel the warmth of her confidence. You are not alone, you have nothing to fear.

She tried to instill confidence in her and her soft and tender words seemed to get the desired results because Lina began to speak softly so that only she would be able to hear her. The doctor moved the chair closer to the young woman's side and tried to record every detail of the conversation in her memory.

The girl spoke without pausing and Brenda did not breathe so as not to interrupt her.

-... and that's all I know," she said as if telling it for the first time would free her from a weight of immense dimensions.

-What I don't understand is why these women were so interested in Suraj. Were they infatuated with him? Love at first sight?

-No, no," he said with an elongated smile. Those two knew little about love. They didn't do anything without payment," she commented as she drank casually.

-But you say they had been trying to have something with Suraj for days and he turned them down. I don't understand. I understand that prostitution is forbidden but, according to what you say, they were doing it all for money, but whose money? I find it hard to think that Suraj would pay for sex and then decide that he didn't want anything to do with them.

The young girl started to turn red with embarrassment but answered so confidently that Brenda felt proud of her courage.

-No, he always refused. He seems to be enraptured with his wife.... -Brenda didn't add any comment because it was totally true, Suraj was totally in love with his girl. Those two proposed to play with him but he refused. Always... -he choked, "his wife is the only one in the room. He replied with a downcast look.

Brenda knew perfectly well what Lina was talking about. Suraj had confessed to her that they had shared sex, what she did not know was that only one woman, Jane, was involved, but honestly it was a subject that did not surprise her, they were adults and free to make of their sexual encounters the experiences that best suited them. For Brenda, mutual respect were the only rules. Lina's redness showed her youth and incomprehension, so she preferred to ignore that issue and focus on the real heart of the problem.

-So you mean that someone would be interested in bringing you closer to these women intentionally?

-I don't know, but whoever it was, he would pay in euros and those two were overjoyed.

Brenda thought about her new friend's last words. She repeated them over and over as she pressed her lips together with her hands as she thought of a couple of somewhat far-fetched but possible ideas.

-So will you help me? Will you tell me how to be as interesting a woman as you are? -The little girl spoke with such confidence that she instantly distracted Brenda from her musings.

-Like me?

-Yes, you're so smart and you walk so confidently," she said, shaking her shoulders as she sat back in her seat, causing the doctor to laugh out loud at her new friend's assertions.

-I don't think I'm the right person to help you, but I'll help you, of course I will. The young woman clapped her hands happily and Brenda commented just as enthusiastically. But you will have to help me too.

-I've already told you everything I know. Those women were... whores..." he whispered softly. -he whispered under his breath. They worked for Kazim.

-And according to what you said, that Kazim goes every Wednesday to the premises.

-Yes, to look for the proceeds, or at least that's what they say. She commented doubtfully.

-Well...

Brenda thought about her idea but noticed something strange in Lina's face that made her hesitate.

-What's wrong? What are you afraid of?

The girl with her shoulders bent looked down at the ground and Brenda asked again. She had to know all the ins and outs or the next neck cut in a dark alley would be hers.

-Lina...

-Mohamed is a good boy. You have to promise me they won't do anything to him.

-What exactly do you mean? -She asked, feeling her knees trembling. Was the young lover involved in the murder?

-Kazim and Mohamed are friends. Well, not good friends, Kazim is bad. Bad for Mohamed, but life is not easy here. You have to promise! Moha can't go to jail. Kazim is the bad man -. she shouted in distress.

Brenda took a deep breath. Maybe Lina was right and life was not easy for a man of limited resources in a country with so many social differences, but that did not make him any less guilty. If he had anything to do with the murder of the girls she would help put him in jail herself.

-I will find the guilty and help the innocent," he said, speaking without promising what he could never promise. If Mohamed was guilty of such a horrendous murder, justice would be the only one to pronounce itself.

-Come with me until I get a cab while I tell you an idea that might help you.

The young woman was hopeful about her new friend and Brenda preferred to omit Mohamed's name for a while. She did not wish to feed him false hopes.

Learning to fly

Two days, I had been following her like her shadow for two days, but nothing. Brenda seemed reformed. The little girl would arrive at his hotel and the two of them would lock themselves in for hours on end. Once in a while he was tempted to listen behind the door being very careful not to be discovered but nothing. Sometimes he heard music and sometimes loud laughter but nothing out of the ordinary. Maybe in other circumstances that would be a good sign, but she was Brenda, Brenda Klein, a woman who attracted trouble like bees to honey. No, normal was not for her.

The blue knight took off his turban and djellaba, breathing as he felt the coolness of the night entering his room. In that country even the night was hot, he thought as he opened the window and leaned out half his body to look at the night lights of a city that refused to sleep. He was tired. The weight of remorse was weighing him down. He did not feel good about himself. He was not sure of anything.

He sighed thinking he would go to sleep early and rest all night when a petite woman's figure with her hair pulled up high made him curse. And there was his blissful Dr. Klein trying to get out in the middle of the night, alone and who knows where. The man put on his djellaba, held the fabrics of the blue turban with his left hand while with his right he opened the door to run after her.

-This has to end or you will end me," he said as he ran to keep track of him once again.

Brenda entered the restaurant ready to eat the world. She had been cooped up with Lina all day and needed to recover her energy. That and to get some air. If she heard that blissful belly dance again, her head would implode. A very kind man guided her to a table and she obliged politely.

Over-decorated and with obvious Arab touches everywhere, the doctor doubted that Italian food was served there, but she couldn't take it anymore. She needed pasta urgently. She didn't want more rice or more curry. She needed a pizza with tomato, pepperoni and lots of mozzarella. Yes, the kind that sticks to the plate and no matter how hard you pull up the cheese stretches and stretches but never quite comes off. She opened the menu hopefully and pointed gratefully. Yes, pizza, here you are! The young waiter walked away with her order as he offered her a drink. Brenda opted for agua fresca with two ice cubes and the bigger the better.

The blue knight entered silently and sat down in a corner. From there he could watch her perfectly from a distance. The huge column in front of him offered him the perfect cover to hide behind. Carefully he slid the turban that covered his nose and rested it on his chin. His face was thus exposed, but he was not afraid. It was impossible for her to discover it from that spot. He watched her and smiled as the little chocolate eyes sparkled with excitement at the sight of dinner.

The gentleman paid his bill as he sipped his coffee without taking his eyes off her. She may not have been one of those magazine cover models but there was something about her that made him wish he was a real man. Seeing her walking through an unknown country and trying to free a man, who she thought was innocent, made him think about how many things Brenda would do for a real love.

With his eyes fixed on her face, he drank from his small cup and thought about the ridiculousness of the situation. He had followed her, admired her and was enraptured by her courage. He was in love again and with the same woman. "Idiot," he said to himself finishing his coffee in one sip. Enjoying the view he waited for the moment to leave when jealousy gnawed at him unable to contain itself. There was that guy again. It was the fourth time he had approached his table, hadn't it become clear to him that he wanted nothing to do with him? Trembling with fury he drummed his foot against the floor. She couldn't intervene. It was foolish. This guy posed no threat. Simply a man attracted to a woman, but hell.... "Don't touch his arm! He said no." He was about to intervene when he noticed that she with a broad smile brushed off his unwanted presence and left for the exit. He promptly arranged the cloths over his face leaving barely a thin line across his eyes and waited a few seconds when he saw the Don Juan also rise from his seat. "What's he trying to bump into at the door and buy her a nightcap? Not a chance," she thought as she stretched her leg out more than was cautiously correct and caused the man to fall face first onto the cold floor. Smiling she jumped over him and headed for the door.

He looked for her, trying to follow her as he had been doing all week, but nothing. He turned his head this way and that, but there was no sign of her. Fear began to take hold of him. His foolish decision to stop the flirtatious dandy distracted him from his real duty, to take care of her. He cursed himself over and over again sweating from nerves as he managed to see her pacing back and forth near the corner.

-What was he doing? I was arguing, but with whom?

-I have no handkerchief to cover myself, but you can't stop taking me for that nonsense.

-I am not as liberal as you Europeans and I do not sell myself for a few coins. Either she covers her hair or I don't take her," said the chauffeur with a very bad temper.

Damn the time she left the damn handkerchief at the hotel. An archaic old man all over the country and it was right up her alley. Better to walk and find a cab stand. She walked briskly toward the main street when at once the idea occurred to her to return to the restaurant. They would surely find her a ride. She turned sharply to change course when she couldn't believe who she found walking behind her.

-Hello!" she shouted, raising her hand. "I hope it's him, or this piece of paper won't be erased from my record," she thought in amusement. She walked quickly towards him. She had barely seen him a couple of times but she was almost sure it was him. That same penetrating gaze and that leg-shaking sensation she felt every time she saw him. There was something about that man that made him exciting. Maybe that air of mystery, that hidden face, that magnificent body she was sure he would hide under layers of soft blue linen or that touch of Omar Shariff in Lawrence of Arabia or maybe a little bit of everything....

-What's the coincidence? Do you live around here?

The man didn't speak and Brenda remembered that he was mute. What a fool she had become. How could she not remember that silent touch that made him even more intriguing. God, if Rachel could hear me she'd say that after all that happened I've become a libertine, she thought amused, and maybe she was right. Why not, what did she have to lose? Twice she had tried to go down the path of respectful love and both times she had been wrong, why not experience a little of that never-tested sass. A complete and refreshing adventure.

-Can you help me get a cab? I need to go somewhere and with your help I'm sure I can. By the way, do you remember me? Because I do remember you... -He said with total clarity and double intentionality.

The man did not answer, of course, he is mute, she said to herself, thinking again how silly she was becoming in front of that Arab soap opera actor. Brenda took a breath and breathed in courage before grabbing him by the arm and clinging to his body.

The man could not believe what he was seeing. She was guiding him and kept talking as if she had a parrot stuck in her throat. She was smiling for no reason and every two minutes she was batting her eyelashes like a teenage girl at her rock idol. "Is she hitting on me?" he thought in a daze.

Brenda let out an eyelash-fluttering laugh as they got into the cab and it made him furious. Yes, damn it, she was hitting on him. Rage began to well up in his skin. She couldn't be doing that. She couldn't be interested in him, well yes, in him yes but not in a stranger. Damn it, she was jealous of him herself.

"Fuck," she thought as she felt the warmth of his fingers stroking her arm. She was looking for something and it was very clear to her what it was but how to give it to him when she was dying because of her own jealousy. The car stopped and she looked behind the window to see where they were. Damn his luck. What was missing, the Lunas de Oriente.

They got out of the cab and he cursed himself over and over again. She was sure he was a mute and that would hide his identity for the moment, but for how long, how long would it take Brenda to discover his deception and how long would it take him to prove to her that he wasn't a fucking stalker? He let himself be guided to the front door of the premises like an inexperienced youngster and praying to God, Allah and every being up there to help him because hell would be unleashed on his head very soon.

"Since when did my Brin become such a sensual and charming woman? It's as if the distance has served her to grow while I..." He was at a loss, devastated, committing one stupidity after another looking for a solution he didn't know how to find. He was about to run his hand over his head to drag his fingers through his hair when he noticed the unbearable turban that kept his face anonymous. She talked and talked while he thought and thought.

It wasn't good to lie to him, but he hadn't had much choice either. Brenda thought him a pig, a liar, self-serving and unfaithful, and that made him have very little chance of a friendly conversation. No, this was the only way to bide her time, besides proving with her own eyes that she and Max were not together. He hated to think it but the doubts were too intense to ignore. At first she thought that the cretin had managed to deceive her and advance positions, but now, seeing her so alone.... he didn't know how he could contain himself. Always so confident, so determined... so Brin.

-I guess I'm boring you, but of course, you're a mute and I'm a chatterbox, doesn't seem like a good combination, does it?

And there was that little look. It was clear that she was attracted to her unknown man and he smiled under the cloths. What would she think if you knew his true identity?

With relaxation he leaned his body against the wall allowing her to do. She displayed her feminine weapons of conquest and he felt delighted to be the center of her attentions. Maybe it wasn't such a bad idea. If he could win her over one more time, maybe this way, she would accept the truth of his feelings and the strength of their union. No matter what position or continent they were on, he was born to belong to her.

-... And that's how I got here. You see, lonely woman without commitment or destiny," she said in a bitter voice, sipping from her glass and looking down at the floor, "First I accepted a destiny without asking life for anything in return, and then when I thought it was time, I was laughed at.

His heart broke just listening to her. He wanted to scream, to explain, to tell her that none of it was true, but he was only able to raise his hand and caress her face with the tip of his index finger.

-Oh no, don't worry, I'm fine now. I have accepted my fate.

The man looked at her interestedly as he shook his head sideways and she seemed to understand the silent question.

-Yes, you see, it's very clear to me now, I must face my own challenges. I must decide for myself without thinking about anyone else. No, don't think I'm selfish, but I think that if I manage to do the things I like and live my own experiences, maybe in the simplest way, maybe one day I will meet someone who loves me and values me as I am. Someone who won't try to change me or ask me to be the girl I'm not. Yes, I know you don't understand anything but you see, it turns out that the man who lied to me, besides being a swindler, turned out to be much younger than me and of course, in my stupidity I thought he might be really interested in me... you know... as a woman.

Listening to her talk about their differences and their infamy made him feel like a complete wretch. He wanted to press her shoulders and shake her until he made her understand that the only differences that existed between them were the imposed ones and that he had been tearing them down for a long time, but he couldn't talk.

He was sick of social impositions, she had loved him and would love him again and for others to rot in their own envy. Slowly he moved closer until he almost pressed his chest next to hers. It was a risky move but he cared very little, he needed her, they had been too long apart pretending to be who they were not. She was not that calculating woman with cold feelings and he was no Tuareg nomad. He reached out his arms to wrap her in a tender embrace. He could not speak, not without being discovered, but what he could do was to give her the warmth of his body. To prove with his caresses that she was worth more than any of them, that he didn't give a damn about their devilish differences and that he was as much hers as the first day he saw her. He pressed her small body to his, at first trying to be delicate and not be carried away by that scent of jasmine, vanilla and smoothness of woman that only she possessed, but after a few seconds and almost without thinking about it, he pressed her more and more until he felt her totally glued to his hard chest. As if transported back in time, he rested his cheek on the softness of her hair and inhaled her scent, traveling back to those few days when their love was a reality. Those mornings when he woke up in her arms with a smile of a beloved woman. He took a deep breath and decided that the charade had to end. It mattered little if the time was right, she should listen to him and accept the truth. He would beg, he would plead, he would shout, he would do whatever it took, but she had to know that his love was as real as life without her was a living hell.

He was about to speak but his throat instantly went dry. No, it was not because of the heat of the desert or anything like that, but it was the result of a fear that gripped his insides. The fear of not being understood. He breathed and tried again to take courage but she brought her tender hand close to his chest to press him back and break the contact.

-I thank you for your understanding, but I feel fine, you don't have to feel sorry for me. The sorrows of the past are just that, sorrows that can't come back. He said sadly as he stretched his body on tiptoe to give her a sweet kiss on the cheek on the soft linen.

-Finally I find you! I thought you'd never get here," she said smiling, "Are you ready?

The young girl from the waxing store appeared as quickly as he took her by the hand while he felt his heart beating a thousand per hour and his blood rushing like a wild river. He would have gone out after her, asked her where she was going, begged her to forgive him, asked her to stay by his side and never leave him but, of course, for that he would have to be able to talk and move and not feel like a liar. He stroked his chin and closed his eyes thinking about how much he needed her and how much he wanted to feel her skin against skin again, when she turned to speak to him with a smile that lifted him to the fifth heaven.

-I have to leave for a few moments, will you wait for me my Blue Knight?

"Of course, I've always waited for you and I always will. What else can a man as much in love as I am do." Too many words for a mute, he thought as he simply nodded his head.

Hidden feelings

He sat at a table waiting for what he thought was an eternity. Not having her around upset him. Separations, short or long, forced him to think of moments of loneliness that became unbearable without her by his side. If she did not return soon, he would go room by room destroying everything in front of him until she was returned to him. Nervous, he took a drink of his third Arak and set out to begin the search. Thirty minutes represented about half a dozen problems in Dr. Klein's universe. Determined, he stood up and arranged the linen over his face as he watched the few lights that were on go out and be replaced by others in very intense shades of maroon. A sort of futuristic smoke began to billow from the large central platform and belly dance music enveloped them with its notes. Five young ladies, dressed in pastel colored gauze and coins around their waists, entered, slamming their hips to the sound of the tar. Their faces were covered trying to hide their features but the fine gauze let their smiles show as they moved their legs and arms to the music. They were all very attractive, but there was one, with a deep gaze as dark as the thickest chocolate, that left him with his jaw unhinged.

-No... no... -he whispered, unable to believe his eyes. She was there. Brin, his Brin... swaying her hips like the most sensual of courtesans.

At first he thought of tearing the turban off his face and taking her away from there as soon as possible and having the men present drool over others but he could not. Again he was frozen in place. She was smiling and waving her arms like a Saracen sinner, and one too sinful for a poor man who was dying to feel her skin again. Saliva choked halfway down his throat and blood flowed through his veins like uncontrolled cataracts. Too long apart, too much torment, too much loneliness.

Wrapped in a cloud of incense, and with her hips shaking to the sound of Arabian tambourines, it was much more than her poor heart could bear. He looked down trying to bring a glass of alcohol to his mouth but collided with the devilish cloth that he could not move without being discovered. Burning with desire, he clenched his fists trying to stifle a hunger that devoured him from the core.

The women began to move around the room in opposite directions but their eyes of fire always followed the same one that chained him to her figure. Their gazes met and an invisible thread of steel bound them together, never to separate them again. There was no one else but her. She and only she concentrated all his attentions. His Brin moved delicately and parsimoniously closer and closer to him and he had to restrain himself from stretching out his arms and loving her in front of everyone. He cared little for modesty, he wanted to feel her, he needed her, she represented his future, his reason, his destiny, his only meaning.

The delicate bare feet barely brushed the linen of her long, bluish djellaba and the current that coursed through him was the same as that of a hundred power plants put together. His skin bristled and his eyes sparkled with desire. He needed her and she wanted him. Well, maybe not exactly him, but right now nothing else mattered but feeling her skin against skin and experiencing the brush of her heaving breath sighing in satisfaction.

She smiled as her rough fingers approached his delicate face without brushing it. Wrapped in her enthusiasm, arms stretched with a life of their own and broad hands encircled her waist in intimate possession. Both bare skins, hands and waist, brushed against each other feeling his touch and the moan escaped his lips desiring to devour each other. His doctor was teasing him with full intensity and he didn't plan to resist, not anymore. He pressed his fingers into her delicate hips demonstrating that this was no game, and she smiled in such a libertine way that he wished he could drag her into any dark corner and rip that amusement away from her for a somewhat more pleasurable kind of satisfaction.

"You're going to kill me..." He thought bringing his face close to hers whose body kept moving under his hands, teasing him like the most irresistible of temptations.

The broad, unrestrained fingers traced her silhouette up the smooth skin, brushed the side of her delicate breasts and reached the delicious face which she wrapped like the most delicate of treasures. His broad, rough fingers wrapped around her cheeks and he smiled beneath the turban. He was a selfish bastard who would never think of giving up his love. Brenda was there, in front of him and trying to conquer a stranger and he would prove to her that no matter the distance, no matter the thousand and one disguises he wore, destiny would always bring them together. Whether as an Englishman, an immigrant, a Tuareg or a simple bricklayer, he had been born by and for his love.

-Don't go... -She whispered close to his ear moistening the fabric of her turban before separating and walking away towards a group of men.

Her hands, desolate at the loss of their contact, clenched tightly and her knuckles turned white from clenching as she approached those two guys who seemed to be eating her with their eyes. She couldn't say she didn't understand them, the whiteness of her skin stood out above anyone else. The men spoke to him and she smiled with mischief in her eyes and jealousy gnawed at him as doubts assailed him as always. Could it be that his fervor for her made him see what wasn't there? Could he be looking for simple flings? To imagine just for an instant that she no longer loved him, even if it was with her face covered, was too painful to admit. Blinded by jealousy he moved closer trying to discover what they were talking about but the music covered their voices. Her lips were moving and she was answering more and more smiling and in front of every funny gesture of those men the rage was gnawing at his insides. It was he who was there for her, it was he who gave up everything to be by her side, it was he who would die if he was not by her side, it was he who wanted her above all and not them, he thought choleric and frustrated.

The music stopped playing and the girls left but not her. She was still there smiling at those two strangers. Wait a minute, wasn't that the guy he threw to the ground that night? Why was she talking to him again, did she like dark-haired guys with the look of a jerk, she thought more and more disgusted. The second jerk reached out to grab her by the elbow and knew that was as far as his patience had gone. He reached over with the intent to intervene when Brenda released her grip and with a slightly exaggerated smile, accepted the card the jerk offered her. She was acting, but why? "What a mess you're going to get us into again." He thought now smiling as he remembered how boring his existence was before he met her. "And to think I emigrated to run away from danger..."

Brenda greeted the men, returned to her side and happiness settled back into her being.

"Wasn't he planning to get dressed? For heaven's sake, he was no saint," he said to himself with sweat running down his body. The barely covered hips moved in a transgressive and very sinful way, he thought without being able to take his hungry gaze off that body that kept him tense with need. He would have her, by God he would have her, he said to himself as he held her by the hand and pressed her to a body that awaited her painfully exalted. She moaned a little quizzically but he smiled wickedly. "No honey. You've played with fire and you're going to get burned. I promise you that."

He practically carried her to one of the doors that he knew exactly where it led. He didn't know the place but he was no innocent. Couples didn't go there to talk. With a jerk he pulled her into the room barely lit by a couple of candles and bolted the door shut. He thought he saw her hesitate and felt selfishly happy. His doctor was still there, she might be trying to hide it but he knew her and he knew his Brin was dreaming of more than a liberal romp.

He tried to move slowly so as not to frighten her but the need was too strong to hold back another minute. Two of his fingers blew out the candles and he moved closer with restrained impatience. Checking the complete darkness of the place, he held her tightly as he pulled the uncomfortable cloth to expose her face. Everything would be perfect as long as she didn't speak, he thought as he threw himself over her half-open lips and filled his lungs with the breath of her sweet breath. Oxygen was barely enough for him, desire stronger than survival itself. He would die if he did not possess her. He had to feel her one more time. She had taught him the power of sexual love and he wanted it back. To live again with something that wasn't just passion. His doctor had shown him a path where sex and heart came together in a heady mixture that he needed to savor again to feel complete.

With lips quivering with need he kissed each small portion of her neck as she stretched backwards giving him greater access to her breasts which hardened expectantly. Grateful for her fervent response he mixed kisses with small nibbles that made her moan in arousal. With full intent he lifted one hand to strip the soft silks that covered her breasts until he let them fall to her waist. Famished he imprisoned them between his lips with complete brazenness while with his hand he opened the scarves that served as skirts gaining access to the center of her womanhood. His long fingers ran along the dampened lace of her undergarment and he understood that tearing it would be the quickest solution. He had no time for foreplay. He needed her with extreme urgency. His body was dying to possess her and his crotch was clamoring to return to its lost home.

Feminine hands intertwined behind his neck, tugging at his hair, and a delicate leg was raised over his hip to offer him better access. Howling in silent pleasure, he traced intense kisses over the sweet skin, which, bristling and burning, received him with fervent pleasure.

Impatient to reach inside her being, he grabbed her under her buttocks and lifted her off the floor to carry her straight to the nearest wall. She raised both legs, crossing them behind her waist, and he was grateful that he didn't need to speak to demonstrate his need.

With the force of two of his fingers he tore the lace of the delicate garment and struck the center of her womanhood with the power of his hardened erection to the point of torture. He had both hands under her buttocks and she would not be able to free herself from the damnable garment without his help. She let out a light chuckle that sounded like heavenly music to him as with those gentle hands she lifted his garment releasing an erection that twitched gratefully. Naughtily she stroked him up and down hard and had to bite her tongue to keep from moaning in pure satisfaction. How much he had missed her. If he could speak without being discovered he would have howled like a wolf at the most delicious delicacy.

With uncontrolled madness he attacked her lips as he pressed his grip hard to lift her up and leave her in the exact coupling position. Embroiled by the desperate need he thrust hard entering fully into that wet channel that took him straight to paradise. The moan of satisfaction almost escaped from his chest but he stifled it against her mouth kissing her fiercely.

Pinned against the wall and the sturdiness of her body, surrounding him completely, he rammed into her more and more powerfully than the previous time. His taut muscles wrapped possessively around her and his head sheltered in that small hollow between her neck and ear as his body took her without restraint. Brenda moaned excitedly tearing at his back with her nails but he didn't care. Her reactions were exquisite balm of sweetness. Agitated he tried to have some control and wait for her to find the peak of pleasure but the desire was too intense to restrain himself. With feigned self-control he began to slow down his thrusts and thus give her more pleasure but thank heavens she refused. Annoyed with his attitude, Brin nervously raised her hips nervously urging him to regain his previous rhythm, and he grinned wickedly. He moved once, twice, three times forcefully pushing her against the wall and lifting her to the heights as her tight channel squeezed him tightly between her wet walls. "Yes...," he said to himself as he realized that she had reached the peak of desire. Without fear of leaving her unsatisfied he let himself go four more times until he felt her taut body release in endless spurts of satisfaction.

She was breathing heavily and he... he was barely breathing. His forehead rested on the wall and his body with muscles like flans was barely able to move. Her body joined to his, still burning with desire, she rubbed against him and it was not long before she was lying on the floor and begging for more.

With a force of will that he himself was unable to recognize, he fumbled on the floor with his blue robe and other fabrics, and covered himself before she was able to react. With extreme speed he covered her face and tattoos. God, she looked delicious, with her eyes closed, her lips red from kissing and her skin rosy from the roughness of his beard, it was his dream come true.

Brenda did not move. She was still standing by the wall in the same position with her eyes downcast as if she were embarrassed? "For heaven's sake! It's Brenda, the polite doctor, the proper wife," how had she not realized it before. She would never have done anything like that, let alone with a stranger. Proud to know he was the provocateur of her recklessness, he approached her tenderly. He thought twice and even three times until he accepted that although the time had come to confess his identity, he would not do it at that moment. She kept her taste on her lips and did not intend to spoil it. Not yet. Tenderly he embraced her and she cuddled into his chest.

With devoted love he breathed in her sweet scent of vanilla and jasmine before holding her hand tightly and pulling her out of that dark place. She tugged at him to stop him. In the pitch blackness of the room she was barely able to see what he picked up from the floor. They both went back out to the living room and he waited for her to get her clothes and change. They traveled to the hotel in complete silence. Well, he may never talk, but she used to do it for both of them. Would she be sorry for what just happened? "Please don't do this to me, not now, I still want you..." he said to himself frustrated at the thought of the hotel bed.

The cab stopped and he waited hesitantly until she held his hand inviting him to get out. "Yes!" his soul cried out loudly though she was unable to hear him.

They went upstairs to his room. This time it was she who closed the door while he was in charge of closing the curtains and turning off the lights. Tonight would be his and may the morning light catch him confessed because tonight darkness and desire would be his only allies.

Brenda looked at him strangely as he darkened the room but he came closer kissing her passionately and making her completely forget about her doubts. Bravely she tugged at his clothes and he dropped onto the bed with his arms at his sides. She wanted him and he would be the fulfillment of her most intense desires.

Determined she straddled his body now stretched out on the bed and reached for him with her hands. He had darkened the room so that she could barely make out his outline but she didn't find herself with too much sense in her brain to ask him for an explanation. This man was upsetting her and she was determined to devour him in bites.

In the past she would never have thrown herself into the arms of a stranger, but new times were coming in her right life. She would regain the freshness she had lost one day and act with the carefree attitude of passionate women who only think about living. Amused by her own reflections, she tugged her djellaba down, enjoying the warmth of a body, now half-naked, offering her the best of welcomes.

He got harder and tighter and Brenda wanted to scream euphorically, she felt so womanly, so desired, that she didn't plan to stop all night. This was her night. She would release her chains and let herself be driven by desires she should never have held back. The correctness of a formal life led her down paths of coldness that she wished to leave in oblivion.

An intense heat swept through her and with desperate desire she groped his figure with her hands until she found his hard torso and caressed the soft hair that tapered into a delicate line below his navel. Bold as ever, she leaned back against him and rested the roundness of her breasts on his burning skin, rubbing herself like a cuddly cat. He groaned through his teeth and she smiled as she felt the control of his masculine passion. Empowered by his reaction, she enveloped him with slow kisses that she scattered across his neck and trailed in a steady, direct path past his waist. Owning unsuspected courage, she caressed the hardness of his torso and savored her way down to his hips to lose herself in the perfume of his musky masculine scent.

"What's happening to me?" she said to herself as she felt her head spinning. Her fingertips traveled slowly down the hard figure and wrapped around the rest of his bluish clothes to tug at them tossing them to an undefined spot in the room. Gently she caressed his manhood, which now free, rose fiercely. The blood coursed through his veins unbridled and the wetness concentrated in the center of a feminine essence that desperately demanded to be satiated. With fervor he lowered his lips to the smooth skin of her manhood, which he began to kiss tenderly, but which in a few seconds became absolute necessity. The smooth tongue, eager to delight, enveloped him with her grip and tasted him from beginning to end making him moan under her touch. Strong hands gripped and tugged at his hair but she didn't care. She felt even more powerful. The pleasure he felt became food for her own pleasure. Her Amazon woman's body wanted to conquer him, to possess him with raw passion, she needed to feel satisfied in the deepest of her needs and she would do it there with this stranger.

Quickly she tasted him again and again until she felt the tension in her muscles and the sweetness of his essence peek through the peak of her desire, causing her to smile a valkyrie smile that she was sure lit up the darkened room. One last taste and with studied movements he straddled her legs as he quickly tore off his own clothes.

He let himself be done at all times as if he understood the need for her liberation and Brenda smiled gratefully as she felt the barriers begin to fall before her eyes. After a captive love and a ruthless betrayal, she was on a new path where she and only she was the driver, and she felt wonderful. Grateful to the man who allowed her to explore her new paths, she claimed possession of his mouth, drinking from a breath of life that painted better horizons.

-I need you... -she whispered as if with those words she was able to explain the need she felt to take him in that way.

The man's lips smiled caressing hers and made her feel a most fortunate woman. It was incredible how, without knowing her, he was able to understand each of her doubts and desires. Gently he kissed her face and chin until he lost himself again in that sinful mouth that incited her to more.

Knowing perfectly well what he was looking for, she settled on his erection and guided him with a sure hand inside her body. She wanted to enjoy every touch. She was neither with the right husband nor with authentic love, between them there was only an urgent passion to be satiated and she would take advantage of it. The prison bars of propriety or society would fall like a house of cards and she would enjoy the magnificent sensation of freedom.

He exhaled deeply as she mastered each entry and exit with total mastery. He was beginning to savor his feminine conquest. With each rhythmic movement, Brenda took possession of her own life and her own decisions. No longer would she accept lies as truth or conformity as daily nourishment.

Determined to enjoy her prom queen moment, she gently caressed the flat stomach that bristled under her touch. The man moaned lifting his hips to reach deeper as he squeezed her buttocks pushing her down firmly and making her smile with desperation. It felt so good to be a woman....

With his mind occupied only by desire, he let himself fall into the abyss of passion. Galloping the male body with the sole aim of achieving her own pleasure she let herself fall into the magic of passion. She may have been completely selfish but it was truly what she needed to feel the breaking of her own chains. The moans echoed in the darkness of the room and her compas lifted her into a heaven where she let herself be swept away. With each spasm that welled up from deep within her moistened body, something new was born inside her. One entry and another and another until the hardened man made her convulse and discover hundreds of colorful stars that burst inside her being to lift her up and then collapse her into unprecedented satiation.

Her limbs were still trembling as the man gripped her fiercely in his arms, and without leaving her interior, he turned her around placing her under his body, taking control of a session that seemed unfinished.

Still exhausted by the previous experience, she let herself be loved, when without being able to believe it, a new wave of intense heat began to surge under the hard and determined advances of a man who no longer accepted her domination. Burning with the new passion that was beginning to grow in her being, she clung tightly to shoulders that she scratched but from which she heard no complaint. He did not lose concentration, with one of his hands he held the weight of her body on the mattress but with the other he caressed her brazenly. With force and firm decision he entered her body more than four and more than ten times until she felt him tense. Enveloped with the empowerment of her freedom, she crossed her legs tightly behind her back showing him that she was eagerly awaiting him. The man advanced like a conqueror and, for the second time, she imprisoned him between her wet walls trying to hold him there forever.

-I can't... it's too much. ..... -She muttered without planning to. The spasms of her body engulfed him as she writhed under the muscles arms and legs that pinned her to the mattress.

A deep moan cut through the air before she felt the weight of a burly body falling against hers. Satisfied and happy with her own discoveries of freedom she waited for the man to move to lie down next to her and fall fast asleep, a smile on her lips.

Reality dawns

The morning was beginning to dawn and he looked out the window at the light of a city that was still sleeping. Like her, he said he was in love when he saw her sleeping so relaxed. The soft body barely covered by the white cotton sheets, took his breath away. A glimmer of melancholy seized him as he saw the empty place beside her. He should be there kissing her and drinking in her morning passion, yet he found himself nervously waiting for a moment he didn't want to come to take away his only chance at happiness.

The time had come to discover her identity. This was not how she had imagined it, she thought, dragging her fingers through her dense hair. In her head the plan had always been very different. He would explain to her the deception he had been exposed to and she as a sensible woman would understand, he told himself nervously as he puffed on his cigarette smoke by the open window. In his plans she would willingly accept that he never forgot her and that he was always there to protect her. "And about last night, will she understand with the same reasoning? No, maybe not... " he said to himself nervously and taking another long puff on his cigarette.

Brenda started babbling awake and he didn't turn around. He hated having to face her. His future, both of their futures, lay in the rightness of her words and he doubted very much that he would be able to find them.

-Why...? -Those simple words, torn with pain and coming from her sweet lips, pierced his heart and broke it in two.

Brenda opened her eyes sleepily as she stroked the sheets and felt the chill of loneliness. She leaned back in bed and saw the figure of a broad-shouldered man in his underwear looking out the window.

She smiled happily to discover that her blue knight had not left, but when she looked at him closely, with the morning light brightening the room, she discovered some tattoos on his broad shoulders that made her cover her mouth so as not to scream in outrage. She was confused, it couldn't be. "God yes..." she said to herself, clutching her lips with her hands. That body, those arms, that silence, that darkness, how was she not able to notice it. She was so eager to feel alive again that she let herself be killed.

-Why...? -She asked with tears in her eyes and Akim turned around with his heart in his fist.

-Brin please, I need you to calm down and allow me to explain.

-Why? -She asked again with wrenching pain and he rushed to her side. He tried to hold her hand but she raised it quickly as if his touch would soil it. Isn't all the damage you've done to me enough? Are you looking for more money?

-What? -Akim stood up nervously and answered quickly. You have to believe me, I have never cheated on you.

-Oh no? -She answered, looking at her blue clothes on the floor.

Angrily she tugged at the sheet trying to cover her naked body and soul as she searched for some clothes. The nudity made her feel even more vulnerable and she hated to find herself in such a situation. How could she be such an idiot? "It was always him," she thought hurrying to put on a long t-shirt that would cover her bodily nudity, because the sentimental one, that was another matter.

-I'm here because of you.... -He spoke with something that sounded like pity, but she was not fooled.

-I can imagine, Max's check wasn't enough and you've come for more?

-Stop it! Stop talking nonsense! -He shouted angrily and she watched the distance that kept her away from the exit. She had never thought of him as an aggressor, but at this point nothing surprised her. You know perfectly well that it's not the money I'm after," he commented, tormented and somewhat calmer.

-Nonsense? But who the hell do you think you are to talk to me like that! You make fun of me, you use me and now you come to insult me? Do you want to keep on laughing at me with your little friends? -The fury welled up in his gut.

-Brenda, please... there's no little friend... He made it all up. None of what he said is true. She commented with a pleading voice that made her hesitate for a moment, but then she reacted as if her life depended on it.

She faced him fearlessly even though he was twice her size. If he was looking for money or fun let him find some other sucker because she was cured of fright.

-Liar. I saw you!

-Have you seen me? What are you talking about? -He froze in place, narrowing his eyebrows as if he didn't understand what I was saying.

-Max showed me the evidence," she said, spitting out each word with the bitterness of the deceived. I'm not stupid!

-Then don't act like one. He replied just as furious and answered her with the same fire in his eyes.

-But who the hell do you think you are to come here and insult me? Go away and don't come back. He said with weariness in his voice as he frowned hard.

-I'm not going anywhere and you're going to listen to me. I'll explain everything you want to know, I'll tell you everything that happened and you'll decide, but you have to let me talk. I'll tell you everything that happened and you'll decide, but you have to let me talk. Do we have a deal?

The nervous smile settled on her face and she, after hesitating and being unconvinced, nodded her head in agreement. If he wanted to talk, then let him talk, then he would leave and she would be alone enough to cry over her stupid mistakes. With exhaustion she turned to the window and bent her face to the ground waiting to hear what was supposedly so important to him.

-Brin, you are too intelligent a woman to accept any lie disguised as truth. Listen to me and evaluate for yourself. He commented patiently behind the delicate body that refused to meet his gaze.

-And what is your truth? -he said with a bitter smile.

-It is not my truth, it is the only truth. Between Lola and me there has been nothing.... -he said as he tried to hold her by the shoulders. She snorted and felt the need to correct herself instantly. Well, not since I've been with you, I swear.

Brenda took a deep breath as if to allow him to speak and he felt the words choking fast in his throat. Precisely to him, who just a short time ago could barely express his feelings, was now dying to confess. Blessed woman and blessed the day I became a fool in love, he thought without a hint of amusement.

-The photo Max showed you is nothing more than a montage. She held me by the shoulders, it was a moment, there was never anything between us. I let go instantly but he got the picture, I imagine they were waiting for me, I can assure you they weren't.....

-The money... - Brenda spoke, cutting off his explanation, and a part of him was relieved to think that the subject of Lola didn't matter to him, at least not too much.

Akim nodded and continued talking behind her back. She tensed and moved her shoulder to shake off his grip and he didn't insist. Knowing he was offering her a chance to explain herself was too much good luck to miss.

-Max came to my house, that's true. He offered me money in exchange for never seeing you again.

-That's not possible. She turned around with a surprised and accusing look on her face. He would never do something like that. It's not his style.

Brenda defended him and jealousy burned her insides like a cauldron of boiling oil. He bit his tongue until it bled so as not to argue. He would not raise his voice, he would not give that wretch the satisfaction of winning her so easily.

-It seems that he has decided to change his style because he came to my house and offered me, in front of my father, a most succulent check.

-And you accepted. She answered with tears in her eyes. He hurried to wipe them away with his fingers and thank heaven she didn't reject him.

-How can you even think about it. Haven't I shown you how I feel about you?

Akim's voice rang with such a soft, smitten tone that even he was surprised at the sincerity that flowed from his lips. He gently wrapped the small face in his strong hands and wished he was able to say in words what his heart was desperately crying out.

-Never, do you understand me? No one will ever be able to buy my love for you. What figure could I put on the only meaning of my life?

-But he showed me the income. She said confused and Akim ducked his head as he let go of her face and walked around looking for the right words.

-When he came to see me, as I said, my father was at home. I didn't react very well to his proposal and we had an argument, then I left. The check was left on the table and my father thought that if he cashed it he could save me....

-Saving you from what? You're blaming your father for collecting that money? That's your fancy explanation? -Brenda moved nervously towards the bed and he stayed in place trying to contain his nerves and not scream like a caged wolf.

He was not used to receiving accusations and even less used to openly and frankly admitting to himself. A part of him told her to think what she wanted, that he could not stand it anymore, but the other part of him knew that life without her would not be life anymore. At her side the days took on a special meaning, he needed to get her back or die trying.

-I don't blame him. If it weren't for my father I wouldn't be alive now.

Brenda turned instantly with curious eyes and he felt a small measure of hope, perhaps all was not lost. Her hands were tense and she awaited his explanation with an anxiety impossible to hide and he took advantage of her excess of interest.

-The club where you saw me at night," he commented with a hint of embarrassment. I was there for work. I took it because I had debts to pay.

She walked as if every explanation from him was a cold water running through her body. She was beginning to doubt, she saw it in his gaze.

-Why didn't you tell me? I could...

-But I didn't want to," he said without allowing her to finish speaking, "damn it Brenda, I did it because I needed to be part of your world," he spoke with his lungs tightening in his chest. I asked a loan shark for money because I wanted to show you that I could make you happy. I tried to give you everything he gave you that you had lost because of me.

-Are you telling me you asked for money to spend on me? Did you really think I cared about that?

-It didn't seem important to you when we were going out night after night," he mumbled without thinking.

-I didn't know! I didn't think! -She answered annoyed and embarrassed.

She spoke guiltily and Akim felt he could no longer bear the shame. He should leave, go far away and forget her forever. Everyone was right, he was in too high a sphere for someone like him. He wanted to walk to the door and leave but his legs did not respond. He was static. He was barely able to breathe, his arms did not move and his heart, who knows, maybe if he had a stroke of luck, it would stop at that very moment and he would stop feeling the humiliation running through his whole being.

-Why did your father collect the money? -she asked interested. Akim, why?

Her small hands rested on his back and his whole body trembled with the light touch of her fingers. It had been so long since he had heard her name escape his lips that he was on the verge of begging her to end the torture of not having her and stab him right there. Any wound would be a thousand times more bearable than feeling like he was losing her.

-That night... I saw you at the store," he said, his eyes watering as he remembered her look of disappointment. I came out after you. I ran, I tried to call you, but Philips's men.... Philips is the pawnbroker," he said, clearing his voice against the knot that choked his words. They were waiting for me. I was in an induced coma for a few days," Brenda covered her mouth with her hands and he hurried to explain so as not to cause her any more discomfort. If anyone made one mistake after another, it was him. But I'm fine now, it took me a few days to wake up and when I finally managed to escape from the hospital, you were gone.

-Escape?

-Well, yes, the truth is that I hadn't been discharged yet. He commented with a somewhat feigned smile.

Brenda squeezed her forehead and felt the world fall apart. She had been hating him for weeks, believing in his scam and now everything she believed to be true was collapsing like a house of cards. She tried to organize the ideas in her head.

No, it couldn't be true, if what Akim was saying was true, then that meant that Max had conspired to separate them and that wasn't possible. He refused to believe him but on the other hand the pieces Akim was presenting to him were too logical.

-Your father used the money to pay off the debt. That's why he cashed the check. He tried to avoid the attack..." He said softly.

-Yes, but I swear I didn't know, if I had known I would have preferred to be beaten to death before you thought I was at your side for money.

Akim from the beginning felt how economic differences were a stumbling block in their relationship and although it was hard for her to admit it, she was largely to blame. How could she have been so foolish as not to realize that in each of their outings he was spending far beyond his means? So blind had she been living in her world of affluent society that she was unable to see the simplest thing in life. Sincere love.

-It was my fault... -he said, dropping onto the mattress with the full weight of remorse. I should have seen it. You were forced to... it was my fault.

-No, no, this has nothing to do with you. He knelt down in front of her to be at the same height. Their gazes met and the guilt hit her even harder.

-You were almost killed because of me," she whispered piteously, and he enclosed her face in his broad hands with all the love he could muster.

-The only thing you're to blame for is that you've filled my life with meaning. I had the idiocy with me before. The smile enveloped her face and she threw herself into his arms, not believing how blind she had been and how much she had suffered without his affection.

The man's mouth caressed the height of her head and continued down her face seeking her lips in an almost desperate way. What began as a tender kiss began to turn into a desperate breath of unfulfilled union. Teeth clashed and tongues danced with each other trying to win a battle of life and death.

Akim grabbed her by the waist and pushed his hard body onto hers forcing her to lie down on the soft mattress. With speed he positioned himself over her body and she closed her eyes wishing he possessed her that way. Raw, strong, needy. She wanted to erase any vestige of pain. He whispered words of love and she stretched her neck waiting for more. Wanting it all.

-Does this mean I'm forgiven? -He whispered as he bit her ear and positioned himself between her legs.

-It depends on how hard you try.... -. He replied happily.

-I will try my best, I promise," she said as the palm of her strong and determined hand ran across her belly, making it vibrate wherever it went.

-We'll see if you're up to it. She answered, raising the last sentence in a sort of moan as she felt his caresses between her legs.

Akim stopped caressing her and propped himself up on his elbows so that he was level with her face and smiled perversely at her.

-And are those heights too high? -One of his hands slipped under her shirt and began to caress her indecently.

-Oh yes, I have met a gentleman with blue clothes and eyes as hot as fire, very hard to beat. She replied, blinking excessively.

-Against a man like that I don't think I can compete. He pretended to get up but she threw her arms towards his head to entangle them behind his neck and drag him back to her lips.

Smiling, they kissed each other and let themselves be carried away by the force of the reunion. Akim positioned himself on her body and was beginning to tug her shirt upwards when the door opened wide.

-I, I'm sorry... I listened and...

They both raised their heads toward the door and Brenda wanted to die of embarrassment.

-Suraj, I...

-No, no, I heard sounds and called but no one answered and then I got worried, but I see you are fine.

Akim smiled without the slightest hint of embarrassment and Brenda began to push him off her body. When he did, she looked at him with a hint of annoyance, and he just lifted his shoulders as if he didn't care in the slightest that he had been caught in the middle of it. Caught red-handed, she stood up, trying to stretch the shirt that barely covered her as much as possible.

-Suraj, meet Akim.

He extended his hand in greeting and Brenda saw him laugh with amusement. What scoundrels those two were.

-I think I owe you an apology, but I overheard an argument and when you didn't answer I came in. I didn't think of such a quick reconciliation.

Brenda sighed indignantly but preferred not to comment, after all she didn't have many arguments with which to get away unscathed. She was caught in bed half-dressed and with a man in his underwear on top of her, few explanations would offer her a fair trial.

-I imagine that you are.... -he said when he saw the blue clothes on the floor.

-Her boyfriend." He answered so confidently that Brenda felt the colors begin to rise in her face.

It was the first time she had heard him call her that and the effects on her body were not all good. They were reconciling, yes, that was true. She had forgiven him and understood, but that didn't mean that everything had been cleared up. He still had to know the reasons that would have led Max to lie the way he had. Not that she doubted Akim, but Max? Was it possible that she really knew him so little? They had been together for half their lives, there had to be some explanation for all that madness.

Jane walked through the door and Brenda thought it was beginning to look like the Marx Brothers' cabin because one and all were coming in like a stranger. She sighed and sat down on the bed while the woman talked breathlessly.

-He called. He finally called. He told me that if you meet with them they can give you a name," she said excitedly to Suraj. You need to leave right away. With the final sentence Jane's enthusiasm sank and Brenda asked curiously.

-Who are you talking about?

-You see, one of the reasons I came and interrupted you," Suraj answered for her with a touch of amusement in his voice, "was because I have been given the name of a gang that may be behind the women's deaths.

-The informant just called and I took the message. Jane spoke enthusiastically but at the same time with some fear. You can't go alone, we don't know anything about them. It could be a trap.

-It's not. Those rats are just looking for some money. Don't worry about it.

-She is right, it can be dangerous. Akim will go with you," she said confidently. The young man opened his eyes asking why with a huge smile on his face.

-I was wrong... You would offer to help him because it is part of your essence," he shook his head as he spoke. Now I see it clearly. You would have offered to help him without being asked. He lowered his face to the ground as he felt the blindfold finally fall from his eyes.

I believe you. In everything. You are not a swindler," she whispered more to herself than to him.

She hadn't finished the last word when he came up to her and gave her a loud and possessive kiss, leaving Jane stunned and uncomprehending. The robustness of his embrace made her sway but her passionate lover broke away as quickly as he came. He released her smilingly and walked towards the door.

-My room is upstairs. I change and we leave.

-Upstairs? -Brenda asked between intrigued and somewhat annoyed by the deception, but Akim raised his shoulders without answering.

-I'll wait for you at the front desk," Suraj said as he walked him out the door.

When they were alone Jane looked at her expectantly.

-Not that I consider myself very curious or anything like that, but can you tell who he is?

For heaven's sake, even politeness was forgotten when Akim was beside her.

-I'm sorry, I forgot to introduce you. It's Akim.

-Akim," he parroted. Akim? The Akim, the pig, liar, liar, phony and swindler?

-Yes. He said in a muffled voice as he recalled the hundreds of appellatives he had poured out uncontrollably.

-Aaaah. He answered, stretching out the letters and not understanding a word.

-He explained everything to me," he commented, trying to justify his guilt.

-I can see that," she said, trying to hold back a laugh but unable to. Her eyes filled with jocular tears as they ran down her figure barely covered by a tight T-shirt. It looks like it was most convincing," she finished laughing her head off.

-Quite a lot. Brenda accepted the joke and burst out laughing along with Jane. It would be stupid to deny the undeniable.

-I'd better get dressed and wait at the reception. It's the only thing we can do. Brenda commented ruefully. Waiting around was not one of her strong points.

Ghosts of the past

He was on his fifth cigarette, third mint tea, and was ready to get up from his seat when he remembered her and sat down again on the terrace of the pretty coffee shop. He would not let her down. He tried not to get impatient. They had been in the same position for a little over two hours and still hadn't contacted the informants, but who could say for sure if it was worth the wait, maybe they would get something that would help Brenda's friend. Every strange character, every beard longer than usual, every look too intense or too distracted, every detail deserved to be analyzed, but nothing at all.

He drank the last sip from his cup, letting his restless thoughts travel along more pleasant paths and comforting the long wait. He relived her tender caresses of the night before and enjoyed a reconciliation that he intended to extend over time. One night was not enough for the agony he felt at believing her lost. "Wait a minute, that night of passion was not mine but the blue knight's," he thought with mischief blooming through his intense gaze, "he still owes me mine." The smile settled on her face like a small child's next to a candy store. He was happy. She forgave him, life was beautiful and the birds were singing, he told himself watching the people go by under a beautiful sunny day. His heart pounded, as it always did when he thought of her and he regretted not being cooped up in the hotel with her delicious figure lying under his body.

"What the hell am I doing here," he thought knowing full well the reason. Brin, his Brin. She asked for the sky and he stretched out his arms to hold it, she claimed the moon and he tried to catch it, she asked for life and he offered her his heart on a silver platter. A young lover's sigh escaped his throat and he was amused at his own foolishness. Who would have told him a year ago that he would become a love-struck softie. The cell phone rang and he answered knowing who it was. His new friend stood no more than thirty meters away, like a tourist statue awaiting the arrival of those who apparently didn't wear a watch.

-You've seen them.

-Yes. Suraj answered, observing two men who were moving a bit nervously but without leaving the place. They were acting as if they were waiting for the right moment. -I think it's them," he said seriously.

-Do you recognize any of them?

-No." He answered sharply. Wait... I think that's... Yes, that's the guy from the Lunas de Oriente.

-Yeah, I recognized him too." How could he forget the idiot he'd kicked in the ass for trying to go too far with his girl. He also remembered that Brenda had danced and smiled at him while he kept his card. Remind me when we get back to the hotel to kill her....

-What are you talking about?

-Nothing. Be careful, they are coming.

-Okay, here we go. I'll leave the mic open... By the way Akim, thanks for being here.

-He replied, giving the limelight and responsibility to his girl. Without her, life would be much calmer, safer and more boring, he thought amused. Most boring, he confirmed with some regret.

The two men, now joined by a third, approached Suraj and he kept his wits about him planning how he could win a two-on-three, because those guys looked anything but underfed. He listened to the conversation through the phone mike but with his eyes fixed on Suraj.

-Where is my money?

-First what I'm looking for.

Suraj's voice sounded behind the mic with such ferocity that Akim was grateful to be on his side. The nice man had turned into a scary and very unpleasant cop. "What a change," he thought with a raised eyebrow in bewilderment.

-You have no idea who you're up against. One of the henchmen growled under his breath.

-Neither are you. Suraj smiled with the devil in his eyes and the big man wanted to answer him with a strong blow when his boss stopped him with a finger on his chest.

-You've got balls, Indian.

-I guess we're not here to demonstrate my attributes.

-Do you have my money?

-Suraj replied calmly as he leaned against the wall.

"He sure has them square." Akim thought, sitting up in the seat. He was tall and with three strides he would shorten the distance and catch up with the first of the guys, the other two would be the cop's problem, he told himself worried about the situation.

-First the money.

-I thought we were here on business, but you're nothing but a nerd.

One of the bouncers grabbed Suraj by the neck but Suraj landed a right that left him dry on the ground. Akim stood up and was about to run to his side when he saw Suraj stomp the guy with a foot to the head as he calmly spoke to his leader. "Fuck the cop."

-Now that we have everything clear," he said with a touch of amusement as he squeezed his foot and made the gorilla's nose bleed as it grunted in pain, "let's cut the crap and tell me who killed them.

The boss smiled as he looked at Suraj with some pride in his eyes.

-Indian, join me. I need guys like you.

-I asked who killed them," he barked, showing that he was beginning to lose patience.

-I think the German, I'm not sure," the thug replied indifferently. Those women were whores. They tried to keep the proceeds, maybe he killed them to make it clear who's in charge in the area.

-I thought you were her pimp.
-No, that's German territory.
-And what are you looking for from me?
-Nothing.

Suraj kicked the man on the ground who was trying to get up in the kidneys and pushed him away as he grunted in annoyance.

-I'm getting tired and I guarantee you won't want to see me angry.

Akim approached them with parsimony so as not to be discovered. The men had their backs turned, but he imagined the look on their faces as they discovered the weapon that Suraj discreetly displayed when he opened his jacket.

-You are not the only one who is armed. The boss replied with amusement.

-Maybe not, but you will be the first to accompany me to hell.

The second thug wanted to respond but his boss interrupted him with a hand on his shoulder.

-I don't have much to give you, I just know they want you out. They paid a good sum and they'll do better if you disappear forever.

-Who? -he grunted through his teeth.

-Indian, I like you, I need men with balls like you, are you sure you don't want to work for me? I take care of my own.

-I'll think about it, now tell me, who wants me out.

-I don't know his name, but he speaks the tightest English.

-Is it English? -he asked with interest.

-One hundred percent. Of the dead white guys with very blond hair," I answered confidently. Maybe he's a racist or something because he was just talking about getting rid of the Indian who stole something very important from him.

Suraj looked at Akim with unfocused eyes. The cop tossed a wad of bills in the air as he asked inordinately nervous.

-Were you asked to be late for our meeting?

The man nodded and Suraj turned pale as he ran without waiting for Akim.

-What's going on? -He asked without understanding anything at all.

-Jane's ex-husband. He's paid them off. He's going after her!

Akim's eyes widened and he ran even faster than his new friend. Brenda was with Jane and if that madman dared to threaten her he would rip her eyes out of their sockets. Akim got to the car first and pushed Mohamed the driver, to take control.

-I've had enough of you! Why don't you just walk around town like everybody else! -The man shrieked loudly.

-Go away! -Suraj pushed the man out of the passenger seat and he fell to the ground under the momentum of the vehicle that accelerated without waiting for him.

-Europeans, because they pay in euros, or else.... -he said, getting up and rearranging his clothes. "And now how the hell do I get back to the hotel?" he said to himself cursing tourism in general.

Chained and released

-Please, you're not going to get anywhere. You'd better let her go.

Brenda felt herself trembling inside even though she tried to hide her fears. "Not again...," she said to herself as she remembered the death of Murray's wife.

The man was pressing a razor hard on Jane's neck. He had been like this for too long and he looked nervous. His forehead was dripping and his eyes were clouded with rage. Jane's every word made him a little angrier, so Brenda took up the defense and tried to convince the madman, but to little avail.

-No! I will never leave her. She is mine. She abandoned me, left me lying there like a stinking dog.

The man was almost foaming at the mouth and although I didn't know his identity it was easy to guess. Jane's ex-husband was there, in her room, ready to avenge his outraged love.

-I think I know what you're feeling.... Have you told me your name? -Brenda tried to empathize with his pain and gain his trust.

The man looked at her perplexed and somewhat confused. Nerves dominated his hand and although he tried to tighten his grip on the dagger, he kept moving in desperate danger to Jane's integrity. Brenda sat on the edge of the bed trying to instill some calm in him. If she could gain her confidence she could use any absent-mindedness to help her escape.

-Jane talks about you a lot," he lied as the man shifted nervously and dragged Jane's body, who, exhausted by so much pressure, looked at her in terror.

The doctor tried to tell her with her eyes to calm down, that together they would get out of this, but Jane was only able to cry and beg for her life. The man in some moments of poor sanity, seemed to sympathize with the woman and tried to tell her that he loved her and that they could still be happy, but she was not fooled, the husband was totally blinded by rage.

-Jane has always told me what a good man you are and how much she loves you. Brenda spoke confidently as she looked around for some object with which to defend herself against the aggressor. She knew very well that kind of behavior and she was buying some time before the end would explode at any moment. Jane, why don't you explain to him how much you have missed him? -She said distracted in her desperate search.

The young woman wanted to respond but fear silenced her. The man met her gaze and begged for an answer.

-Why? -I loved you more than anything else in the world? You were everything to me. What does that bastard bastard give you more than me? What's the matter, that Indian son of a bitch put you on all fours like the bitch you are? Is that it? You like being his whore and sleeping with all those men? That's it Jane! -He shouted foaming at the mouth. You think I wasn't going to find out Jane? You fucking bitch. He barked angrily as he pressed the knife harder against her delicate neck. Jane shrieked in fright and Brenda answered quickly trying to save her.

-No! Wait... It's not what you think. He made her do all those aberrations. The Indian made her. She didn't want to, we're both here because of him.

The man looked at her with confusion clouding his judgment and Brenda shifted nervously on the spot making up as many lies as possible. She had to distract him and get Jane released as soon as possible. The man's fury told her that time was beginning to run out.

-Yes, we were both deceived. We are here because of you. You must help us escape. Brenda's voice trembled.

-I... -The unhinged man was sweating like a fool. His forehead was dripping and his clothes were completely soaked, his breathing was agitated and he was out of control. He moved nervously as if trying to hold on to Brenda's statements. The doctor tried to use all her tools of conviction. She just needed to break that wall in front of her a little bit and they could both be safe. Just a small breach with which to attack and get Jane free.

-Yes. That man is a monster. We are both his prisoners, he threatened us. Thank heaven you're here to rescue us. Jane always trusted you to save her.

-How?" the husband asked without releasing her from his grip.

Brenda tried to approach calmly but he tensed up by squeezing the knife even tighter.

-You can put that knife down. We're glad you're here. Put it down and we'll tell you all about it...

-Is that true, my love? Did he force you? I knew it. My sweet Jane, you would never have left.

The man held her even tighter but just when Brenda thought he would finally release her, the door to the room burst open with a loud bang.

-Let her go, you son of a bitch! -Suraj pointed a gun at the man, but he covered his body with Jane's.

-You bitch! You lied to me! -The ex-husband moved quickly, ready to slit the young woman's throat, and Brenda was barely able to think. She was the only one who was closer. Without a second thought she lunged at the man's head clawing at his face. He ripped Jane's neck and threw her like discarded merchandise as he angrily lunged at Brenda ready to hang her.

-No!" Akim screamed like a demon on fire and threw himself on the man's body, not caring about the sound of the gunshot that echoed throughout the room.

Brenda was kicking her legs trying to free herself and get some air into her lungs when something crashed into her back and threw her straight to the floor. Lying face down on the cold tiles, she raised her head still dazed from the blow and looked back to see Akim knocking her husband down with one blow, who, dizzy, fell flat on his face against the desk. "Thank heavens," she said to herself as she saw the unconscious deranged man on the floor. Nearly crawling, she moved toward Jane and tried to cover the cut as she screamed madly.

-A doctor! A doctor, please! -She begged in fear as she saw the red blood seeping from between her fingers.

Suraj dropped the gun and dropped to the ground to hold his girl's head. The man felt for a pulse with his fingers trembling with fear but instantly took a deep breath as he looked at Brenda with eyes clouded with tears.

-She's alive. It's all right. It's just a graze.

Suraj tried to show her that the wound was barely bleeding but Brenda was unable to understand his words. She continued to scream for a doctor.

-You have to leave! They can't find you here.

Stunned she looked at the red blood running down her hands and, although she tried to respond, she was unable to. She just looked at the blood while Akim finished tying the hands of her fainting husband.

-Akim! -Suraj shouted uncontrollably. Get her out of here as soon as possible! If she gets connected, she'll be lost.

She didn't finish explaining herself when Akim moved quickly to take her away from there as fast as possible. Brenda screamed and twitched in disgust at having to abandon her friend but Akim didn't hear her. He held her tightly below the knees and lifted her up and fled up the service stairs to the upper floor. The doctor was twitching and shrieking madly but he didn't stop. He slammed open the door to her room and slammed it shut with a powerful kick. Without answering her insults he sat on the bed with her on his legs as he hugged her taking the air out of her.

-One day you're going to kill me..." He said, squeezing her to his chest.

Brenda stopped struggling and allowed him to shelter her in his warmth. Her tense body collapsed in his grip like a flan. Akim's arms clasped her in his warmth and still with fear in her body she leaned her forehead against the hard torso, trying to quell the cold that froze her blood. He smiled and she felt safe.

-Couldn't you just stand still like I asked you to? -Akim looked upset, but the glint in his eye showed that he was joking.

-He gave a loud laugh and she followed him with amusement on her face.

Akim held her chin with his calloused fingers, until he bumped his forehead against hers. Gently he brought his lips close together and drank from her mouth all the sweetness she was capable of offering. Each brush of their mouths loving each other freely represented a thank you to life. A thank you for being with her again, a thank you for rescuing her, a thank you for trusting her feelings, a thank you for loving her in spite of everything, a thank you for not giving up, a thank you for having found her.... "How could I have been so blind," she said to herself as she clasped her hands behind the back of her man's neck to hold him even tighter against her body.

-You'd better take a shower. Akim spoke with passion clouding his eyes. I'll lend you some clothes.

-Why can't I go to my room? -he asked a little more calmly.

-We're not in London. Two women alone fighting one man? First they'd blame you and then they'd judge you. Here things are very different.

-But Jane...

-She's going to be all right. The neck was no longer bleeding and Suraj was at her side. I'm sure she's woken up by now. Surely the shock was so great that she just fainted.

Brenda nodded accepting that reasoning, she herself had been on the verge of losing consciousness due to the terrifying fear caused by that man.

-Don't think about him anymore. Shall I prepare the shower for you?

Sweetness mingled with mischief in her beautiful fiery gaze and like a woman in love she couldn't resist holding him tightly by the neck to pull him to her lips for a loud, hungry kiss. Akim let himself be enveloped by her wetness and gave her complete control of the situation. Brenda was surrendering and possessing him like a private property owner and he was thrilled with the sensation of feeling completely his.

-Either you get in that shower or I throw you on that bed. It's your choice. He said, his voice hoarse with passion.

-Shower. She replied in annoyance at the sight of the dried blood on her clothes and part of her body.

Without looking back, she took off her clothes like a striptease dancer and entered the bathroom, closing the door with a mischievous look in her eyes. She knew what she was doing. She was provoking him but she was in those moments when a woman accepts who she is, what she wants and for those who don't agree, let them rot or keep their opinions where they see fit.

He had suffered her absence, he was on the verge of losing a woman he already considered a friend and he was not in the mood for more nonsense. As the wise say, life gives lemons and she would make lemonade, and if someone doesn't like it, let them burst, she thought amused. She would live with Akim for as many years, days or months as fate would give her, and the rest... she didn't give a damn about the rest.

He turned on the faucet and decided that a warm bath was much better than a shower and in company even better, he thought as he immersed himself and felt the relaxation of his numb muscles under the steamy water.

-Akim... -he said in a ringing tone as the door opened wide.

-I thought you wouldn't call me. He replied amused as he undressed and slipped into the tub behind his back.

Brenda smiled in amusement as she let him drag her body to rest it on his now moistened torso.

-Were you behind the door? -she asked, amused at the speed with which he had come.

-I recognize that if you hadn't called me in the next three seconds, I would have come in begging, but I think you saved me an intense moment of pathetic humiliation. He said smiling as he bit his ear.

-It seems so. He answered stretching his body to feel their skin-on-skin contact.

Akim pulled her body to cling to his torso as he kissed her neck with soft nibbles eager to feast on her body. With a life of his own, his hands caressed her moistened breasts that turgid and taut eagerly awaited his attentions.

He gently pushed her hair aside as he kissed the base of her neck and she felt herself fly. To be in his arms was to feel alive. To accept that life had meaning beyond mere responsibility. She dragged her body back letting herself be loved and Akim possessed her with his tender caresses. The sideways face tempted him and he accepted the challenge by possessing her lips with desperate need. The two melted into a kiss that left them breathless.

Moved by an urgency that he found most amusing, Akim held her hips tightly and pulled her body until he lifted her up and positioned her over his manhood that impatiently awaited her in rapture.

-Come, love...

He whispered in her ear as he urged her down on his body to possess him in her wet heat.

-Yes, yes..." He whispered, his voice hoarser than ever.

At that moment she felt like the queen and mistress of that man. With total slowness she went down, slowly but steadily. Feeling that she had the power to provoke his passion and uncontrollability lifted her to seventh heaven.

-You're going to kill me... -Akim murmured with his lips pressed to her moistened back as she wrapped him only a few millimeters, then moved up a few centimeters and left him again with the feeling of abandonment in his body.

Her muscular body tensed under his and strong fingers pressed against his hips urging her to take him completely but she refused. She loved the feeling of power Akim allowed her. Determined she played with him once, twice and even more than ten times until his hands closed on her hips to pull her forcefully into his body and leave her fully impaled. They both moaned from the sensation of feeling each other inside and Brenda discovered that their game had reached its end. With deep desire, her body moved up and down again and again seeking to possess him deeper and deeper.

Their uncontrolled bodies moved urgently regardless of the water that began to splash on the glistening floor. Possessed by need, Akim urged her on by raising his hips to wait for her while she, nervous with the need to be possessed, clung to the edges of the tub and let her head fall back, enjoying the uncontained moans of a man who never ceased to enjoy himself.

-Brin... I don't think I can... Oh, God. He stammered as she moved, possessed by an electricity that ran through her blood with a fury. Love, I'm almost there.

-And me. He answered with his eyes clouded by passion.

-Then come to my darling... come... I wait for you...

Akim's soft words gushed in a voice more than thick from his throat as she, transported by a sea of inexplicable sensations, pressed her hips down begging to possess him with more intensity.

Concentrated in a sensation of sexual freedom, Brenda let herself be swept away by passion to enjoy an awareness that was born inside her. With her body tense, she let herself be guided, once, twice, until her being exploded from her womb, and strong spasms energetically seized the masculine splendor that she appropriated deep inside her.

He cursed loudly before madly raising his hips and pressing hard on her hips pinning her down and penetrating her beyond explanation.

-Akim, please! -She begged when she felt that the spasms did not end, but the young man did not obey.

Possessed by a perverse spirit, he moved again and again until he made her explode a second time and exhausted her on his wet body. Exhausted and completely satisfied, she let herself be enveloped in a tender embrace. Lethargically, she released him from inside her but continued to be sheltered between his hard legs that covered her possessively.

Akim spread a few drops of shampoo on the long hair and began to massage it gently as the warmth enveloped her in a lovely rest.

-Close your eyes. Enjoy. I'll hold you.

-Let's go to bed. A tender voice whispered in her ear.

Sedated by his attentions she did not resist as he wrapped her in a large towel and laid her on the cool sheets. Akim laid her down with the utmost care and she felt so loved and wanted that she was afraid. Afraid to think it was all a dream, afraid of a reality in which Akim did not exist and afraid of a life filled with lukewarm, decaffeinated coffees. Gently he moved to her side and covered them with the white linen sheet while she lay on his torso caressing his heartbeat.

-I don't remember how many times you have saved me.

-Brin...

-No, let me speak. I don't deserve it, I don't deserve what we feel for each other. I realize that now. Since I've known you I've tried every way I could to sabotage the feelings that dominated me as if they needed my permission. I have put all the obstacles to what we have and I have believed all the lies of my incredulous brain but you have been stronger than my own distrust -she said analyzing each of her sentences-. I am tired of fighting against the truth. I can't anymore.

Akim tensed under her body and she lifted her face to behold his sky-like gaze.

-Does what I say bother you? -she asked shyly.

-What do you feel? -He asked without answering with some trepidation.

-With you my life took on a different meaning. What was important was no longer important and what was normal was no longer right.

Akim did not speak and she continued as if at that moment he was the therapist and she was the patient.

-I knew my life was missing things but it wasn't until I met you that reality hit me in the face. I guess a part of me needed time but then you came along and everything sped up. My heart was always searching for you despite my hundreds of refusals.....

The young man lifted her chin with one of his strong fingers forcing her to face her fears.

-What do you feel now?

-You know perfectly well. She said trying to hide her face but he wouldn't let her.

-I need to hear it and not guess it. I have told you and expressed in a thousand different ways how much I love you but I can't wait anymore. I want you to decide for me. I need to know that I am your choice.

Brenda took a deep breath and, taking a breath of courage, spoke for the first time with clarity, saying what he so desperately needed to hear.

-I love you more than I ever thought I could. My world without you is upside down. When you're not by my side I'm an unfinished puzzle.

She began to shyly stir at his confession, and was even about to pull out of his embrace when he clutched her possessively to his body.

-I still have a little more to go. He babbled excitedly.

-More? What else? -She answered distrustful and somewhat disappointed, but he did not allow her to run away.

-I want you to promise that you will allow yourself to love me. I want you to accept our age difference and reject anyone who tries to interfere between us. I love you and you love me, that's all that matters between us. If you promise to love me half as much as I love you, my heart will be overflowing with love. He said pointing his finger at himself. You will always be here. I will be your captive for eternity.

Brenda choked with emotion. No one had ever spoken to her with such love or at least no one that made her tremble to the last cell of her being.

-Eternity is a long time," he said, his voice trembling with emotion.

-It's the least I have to offer you. He replied with a delicate kiss on her forehead.

Both bodies caressed each other excitedly until the passion was reborn again, maddening the yoke of a love that never thought of surrendering.

Of jealousy and truth

Akim's voice sounded far, far away but it still managed to wake her up. She stretched out like a rested and very pampered kitten under the softness of a cozy bed. She tried to open her eyes but all she was able to do was to reach out and caress the naked torso next to her and lean against his chest, wrapping her leg around his to hold him to her side and try to continue sleeping. The man let out a small chuckle that made him shift under her body but she didn't even bother to scold him, she was too comfortable and satisfied to vary her endearing posture. She wrapped her arm around his waist and relaxed as she listened half asleep and half awake to his cell phone conversation.

When he cut off the call, strong hands lifted her up to place her fully on his body while lips tenderly traced her neck.

-Aren't you going to tell me what Suraj said? -From what little she had managed to understand, Jane was perfectly fine and that was the most important thing, she thought as he just kept biting her shoulder and she rubbed herself on him eager to feel his lips.

-Mmmm

-Akim, let's go... -She said unconvinced but lifting her torso to move away from the temptation.

The young man smiled at the sight of her bare breasts and reached out to caress them tenderly. -Is this your idea of making me talk?

Brenda laughed and looked at him in amusement.

-Don't be silly, tell me what happened to Jane, is everything all right? And Suraj? And that man? Did they catch him?

-One question at a time, I'm a man and you know what they say about us. Akim stretched under his body in amusement.

She wanted to move to the side to let him free to begin to spill everything he knew but he held her by the waist tightly so that she remained sitting astride his legs. She grumbled trying to look like a serious and somewhat offended woman but the truth is that her interpretation was not very convincing, after all she felt in heaven and in the presence of a fallen angel just for her. Careful not to hurt him she rested her elbows on his torso and waited for the news.

-Jane is fine, it was just a scratch. They'll be here in a couple of hours.

-And Suraj is free, won't he have problems?

-One at a time... I'm a man and I can't do any more.

-Dumb.

-Now I don't count anything. He said stretching his arms up and crossing them under his head.

-Let's go!

Brenda gave him a small punch in the chest to make him talk but he instantly wrapped his body around her and threw her backwards onto the mattress to stay on top with her hands holding his.

-He begged. He commented with a wicked look.

-Never. She said laughing her head off.

He seemed to think about it for a second and then nodded defeatedly.

-It's okay, you always get what you want from me.

-They're both fine. Jane's ex-husband confessed to being the one behind Suraj's accusation.

-Really?

-It seems so.

Akim began to kiss her breasts with dedication and Brenda did not want the passion to cloud her judgment.

-But that's it? That's it? So he's no longer charged with the murder of those girls?

Akim lifted his face above his neck to answer.

-Basically. She said, ducking her head again and making one of her nipples go wild, which became erect at the touch of his lips.

-But... but... but... -He answered, trying to focus his words logically. So it's all settled then. Just like that? There's no more? Is that possible?

Akim smiled over her body and replied as he turned his burning lips to the other eagerly awaiting breast.

-I'm a man of few words, but yes, it seems so. I imagine that when you see them they will tell you more details.

She was about to move under his body but he held her tightly by the waist as he deposited some of his sturdy weight on top of hers to immobilize her.

-Brin... everything is perfectly all right, that man confessed, Jane has nothing but a scratch, Suraj is free and I want you... -he said, raising his body on his elbows and looking at her with devout need.

-I don't believe you." He replied without thinking as he recalled the hours in which they had barely rested.

-You think so? -he said, pushing his hardened manhood into her belly.

The doctor forgot about the problems and accepted that even if it hadn't been the way she would have liked to have the information for the moment it would be enough. It was clear that her spirit of inveterate curiosity would need a full afternoon with Jane and a good cup of late macchiato, but for the moment she would settle for the terse version of Akim and his insurmountable passion.

"Men...", was the last thing she thought of as she felt the hard, hot body penetrating her insides and making her forget all curiosity.

Soft, moist lips were placed on her forehead to wake her up and she smiled even without opening her eyes.

-Did I fall asleep again?

-It seems so.

-Mmm, what time is it? -He asked, not knowing if it was day or night. They had been cooped up all day. She wasn't sure if it was lunch or dinner time.

-Six o'clock. I'm going to order something to eat, I'm starving. He said as he placed a second kiss on her forehead and left.

Brenda would have liked to order him a coffee, a double slice of cake and a juice but she lay back on the softness of the sheets enjoying the scent of her boy still permeating the fabrics.

-Mmmm," she commented in the solitude of the room as she stretched one last time to get dressed. Akim would bring the tray at any moment and to tell the truth she felt famished. "Blessed youth," she thought as she remembered the intense moments spent in the arms of her hungry man.

Satiated in all respects, she found a T-shirt and looked for some of Akim's pants that would serve her to get to her room in a more or less decent way since her clothes were totally stained with Jane's blood.

-What are you supposed to do? -He asked as he looked at her with narrowed eyes.

Brenda loved it when she felt responsible for his unhinging. To tell the truth she loved to drive him crazy in every way. It made her feel alive, radiant, adored and very much a woman.

-I'll give it back to you when I'm in my room.

-I brought food and it wasn't exactly for you to leave the room," he said, putting the tray on a table and approaching her stealthily like a leopard after its prey. Brenda watched him walk with slow movements and laughed in amusement at his attitude.

-I have to go, I have an engagement, I have a date.... No!

Brenda tried to escape his grip and run, but the room was not big enough and Akim's long arms caught her very quickly.

-You're dating? -Another man? No honey, those times of blue knights and strangers are over for you.

-Yes? -He answered with a small pout on his lips. I used to love that sexy turban....

-If you're good, I might invite him home sometime. He said as he laid her down on the bed.

Akim tried to remove her shirt but she refused as she giggled under his body.

-No, no, I'm serious. I'm expected for dinner. Lina is waiting for me.

-There are still a few hours before dinner. He said with his voice cracking and desisting from taking off his shirt to pull down his pants, which fell without the slightest effort.

-You're not the least bit tired?

Akim lifted his face from his belly to laugh mischievously.

-You went away, you left me alone, I came for you and had to endure your constant insinuations to a stranger and unable to confess that I was dying for you, and you ask me if I am tired? No, I'm not. What I am is jealous and I want to make you pay for it," he replied, nibbling at her waist. Never again will you want to replace me with an idiot with a face covered in cloth.

-But that idiot was you! -He laughed out loud as he tickled his incipient beard on his belly.

-Yes, and I'm jealous of myself and don't even think of telling me what a jerk I am.

Akim positioned himself above her and penetrated her with apparent fury but his caresses were tenderness personified. Absorbed by a sea of sensations she let herself be taken to that place where he showed her the way. Madly she clawed at his body begging for mercy but he did not offer it, he was willing to break one by one the chains that once bound her and forced her to separate from his side. She was the breath of his life and every movement of her body would remind him of that.

Brenda stretched her head back dizzy from what she never thought possible to experience as her body surrendered to a reality with a man's name. Sweaty with need, Akim abandoned loving affection, to possess her with the passion of a man who no longer wished to wait a second longer.

I am this

He was disgusted, very disgusted. Why were they there when they could be frolicking their last night in Morocco under delicious cotton sheets? Akim drank of that concoction called Arak and it tasted increasingly bitter to him as he continued to wonder. "Why are we here!"

Would he always be like this, would Brenda never tire of helping people, and who was this Lina? For heaven's sake, if before he met her he barely accepted that there were more human beings than his father, Lucien and Nikola, yet now, after meeting her, one day he was being shot, another attacked from behind and another he was fighting with a jealous ex-husband and a terribly sharp razor. He swallowed another sip and leaned against the bar doing the only thing he knew how to do when it came to Dr. Klein: wait. He tried to look angry but he himself was surprised at the idiot's grin that settled on him at the mere thought of her. Yes, she may have been a magnet for calamity, but what would life be without a little pepper?

-Not again... -He mumbled as he heard the music and saw the female silhouettes in front of the warm flames of the torches.

He was dazzled. Her figure attracted him like a snake before his piper. She dazzled him and he ate her up with his eyes. A few simple steps and a few silk scarves and he was drooling, wishing to have her under his warmth again.

He wanted her like the first day. "No, no way!" he thought rabidly, more, much more. Today he knew the scent of her body vibrating with desire, the sound of her moans as he penetrated her, the taste of her fleshy lips moist with need, no, today it was much worse. "If I lost her..." Distressed he halted the course of his negative thoughts, he couldn't even imagine losing her again.

She approached with a smile so radiant it lit up the room, as with one, two, three movements, her hips slammed back and forth driving his heated senses wild. His hungry wolf gaze bored into her gorgeous chocolate eyes and he felt himself tremble as he recognized the depth of feeling that nestled in her heart. Twice she had left his side and twice it was that he felt like he was dying in life.

Proud of her Arabian dancing skills, she pressed her small body to his and he held her like a hunter to his prey.

-Don't leave me... -He implored her with his lips pressed to hers. Mine..... -he murmured against her lips before kissing her with rapturous possession.

She stopped moving to stretch her arms and hang around his neck, receiving his undivided attention. Her burly hunter cared little that the music continued, this prey was his and no one else's. Intoxicated by the moment, he pulled her away just a few inches to plead with his forehead resting on hers.

-Let's go to the hotel...

Before answering, Brenda noticed one of the young women at the other end of the room winking at her as she was led by the hand of an attentive Mohamed.

-We can. She replied mischievously.

-I imagine that's Lina and that's the poor man trapped by your macabre stratagems.

-Poor man? -He answered, laughing happily. Not at all, I only helped him to open his eyes.

-Well, honey, my eyes are wide open. He said raising an eyebrow and making his intentions very clear.

Brenda stood on her toes and kissed him with barely a brush of her lips. The good stuff was coming. She smiled and turned away as she hurriedly replied.

-I'll get my shoes and we'll leave.

-Don't change, I'd like to see some more of that dance.

Brenda smiled and nodded enthusiastically. Akim turned to pay for the drink when a shriek chilled his blood.

-Bitch! -Max insulted with all his might as he held her by the elbow.

-Max? -What are you doing here? Max, please... -Brenda wanted to die of embarrassment once she came out of her astonishment to find him. Max reproached her dress and her behavior as a whore caught in the middle of the act.

-I can't believe it. I'm embarrassed just looking at you. You look like a...

He did not finish the sentence when a closed fist hit him squarely in the jaw. Staggering, he leaned one knee on the ground so as not to fall.

-No!" Brenda shouted, holding an Akim who was shooting flames of fire from his eyes.

-You bastard. Insult me if you have the courage!

Akim screamed madly without looking at Brenda who was leaning her hands on his torso to stop him. She had heard him call her a whore and would have killed him but for the fact that he was now kneeling on the floor. He would offer her a chance to defend herself, but then he would rip her teeth out one at a time.

-I should have known better," Max said as he stood up and tugged on his impeccable linen shirt. So you're the one behind all this.

-Max, what are you doing here? -Brenda asked with a trembling voice.

-Apparently saving you from this... What do I call him? -He said, looking disgustedly at the tattoo peeking out from under his shirt, "Whore pimp?

At those words Brenda could do nothing. Akim moved with extreme speed and threw himself on the architect who this time, prepared for the attack, answered with a few punches straight to the face. Both bodies rolled on the ground and Brenda screamed in fear but also furious at the pitiful spectacle.

Some guards of the local interposed themselves and managed to separate them. Both were hot-blooded and continued to insult each other but this time they were restrained by the strong arms of the bodyguards.

-You bastard! You've turned her into a slut.

-Son of a bitch, insult her again and I'll rip your head out of its place," Akim replied angrily.

-How could you! Did you see yourself? -Max focused all his verbal attacks on her and Brenda shivered in embarrassment.

Minutes before she had felt attractive, sensual, but now... now she was a simple whore without dignity. Max's continued insults brought her back to a forgotten reality. She was no wild young girl, let alone any exotic dancer. Surely everyone would be laughing at her right now.

-What has he done with you? How can you be here with him after all his shams? He lied to you, he took my money, what more proof do you want!

-That's not true! -Akim shouted, restrained by the strong arms of the two guards, who did not cease their grip.

-Yes, she is. You took my money, you lied to her and now you turn her into... into.... -he said with disgust, causing Brenda to cover her barely covered body with her hands, "Do you want more money? I'll give it to you.

-Max, please..." She said with barely a voice trying to get out of there as soon as possible, dead embarrassed.

-Have you forgiven him?

Akim took a deep breath and the custodians released him as they accepted his promise not to hit the stupid Englishman again. Determined he walked beside her showing her that she was not alone and Brenda seemed grateful for his gesture, which set Max off.

-Did he tell you he has another woman? -Brenda froze in place and Akim growled loudly.

-That's a lie!

-Just as much of a lie as the money, or that the same day you got on a plane to Ibiza, you went without sleep? -Akim didn't answer and Brenda looked at him doubtfully.

-What do you mean? -She asked, looking him in the eye.

-Don't listen to him... -He asked pleadingly, "Just try to separate us.

-No, Brenda, don't listen to me, lest I tell you that he was fucking his girlfriend all night and then you went after my wife.

-Fucking bastard. Akim was heading towards Max when small, feminine fingers stopped him by the elbow.

-Tell me he's lying," she pleaded, almost in tears, waiting for an answer.

-He wants to separate us, don't listen to him.... You knew about the check. He answered with the sweat of fear running down his body.

-You know what I'm asking. Tell me it's a lie and I'll believe you.

-Brin...

-Say it!

Akim dragged his fingers through her dark hair. He looked at her begging for forgiveness and she felt herself breaking inside as Max's words begged for a denial that did not come.

-That girl and he had it all planned out. They've been together for two years.

-No!" Brenda replied angrily and Akim held her by the shoulders trying to calm her down.

-I've told you everything. I'm not lying, you know I'm not. What he says is a lie, I never wanted your money.

-And did you sleep with that woman the same day you were crying for my wife? yes or no? -Max shouted angrily.

-Brin...

Angry, sad, embarrassed and a thousand other things, she started walking towards the restrooms. She didn't want to hear another word. At this point the truth and the lie were two sides of the same coin, but she didn't know which was the good and which was the bad.

-We need to talk. Akim followed her but she raised her hand to stop him.

-I'm going to get my clothes.

-I'll wait for you," he replied nervously. We'll talk at the hotel.

Brenda did not respond and he felt himself dying inside.

-You're not going to disappear again. You hear me! I will not allow it.

Akim shouted after her but his threats didn't bother her in the least. She was stunned. She needed to pull herself together and come to her senses, and to do that the first step was to dress like a woman her age and take off those damn rags. "Who was I kidding?" she said to herself angrily.

I am who I am

Her attitude was not that of a brave woman but to hell with what was expected of her, she was sad and hurt, she was not qualified to argue with those two, she said to herself as she fled through the back door of the store. She was mentally exhausted. When she decided to start a new life with Akim, the lies would hit her full on, when she tried to distance herself, Max would appear as always with the sensible words to bring her back into the fold.

God, it would explode at any moment.

Whether Akim was lying was something she would have to find out for herself without Max's interventions. He considered himself her savior and that was the first problem she would have to solve as soon as possible. The man would have to accept that between them there was no longer anything to be rescued. Their relationship was over long before Akim came into their lives, and with respect to that one, with him she would have a few words to say. He hated the very thought of Lola and him.... Imagining them together was more painful than bearable, but feelings couldn't cloud his reason, not anymore. Akim showed him his feelings too many times to continue doubting, maybe in the past that girl was in his life, but now they had a future together, a career start with a new starting line and they would both decide their path.

Brenda continued down the dark street and couldn't believe she could find her way to the hotel without help. Content in her musings she climbed the first step of the hotel when Max's piercing voice left her frozen in place. He was sitting on the curb, his hair disheveled, his shirt outside his pants and looking disheveled, which was quite unusual for him.

-I was waiting for you," he said with his face focused on the ground as he moved an ant with a toothpick.

So focused on her own thoughts, she didn't notice him at first, but now, seeing him sitting there looking defeated, she felt very guilty. Saddened by a past that was writing its last lines, she sat down beside him by the curb of the step.

-I came here thinking that... -Max didn't finish speaking and she didn't need him to understand what he was trying to explain. I thought that after all the evidence I gave you... Why? Why did you do it? Why, why did you do it, why behave like a...?

-I am not going to justify my clothing or my actions, you have no right to claim anything from me. We are separated.

-I'm talking about him," she said, her voice breaking with pain. You had decided to forget him. You managed to open your eyes in spite of his lies, yet here he is, once again by your side, like a hateful plague that we can't get rid of.

-That is not true.

-And why did you cash my check? For charity?

-I'm not going to discuss Akim with you.

-Because of him we are here! Don't you see? He has interrupted our lives by breaking what we had. Without him we would still be together.

Brenda could not answer. Maybe Max was right, maybe Akim's bursting in precipitated a decision that had not yet been made but that didn't mean much. She tried to be the woman she was expected to be but she didn't succeed. She was neither the decorous society woman, nor the stuffy one at private cocktail parties, her character was much more than those worldly frivolities. Max always tried to take her to his field, he tried to mold her in his tastes and decisions and she always bowed her head. That time was past.

-He's lying," he said with conviction.

-You can. He answered without explaining himself. He didn't need it anymore.

-How can you forgive that stupid man and not me? Don't I mean anything in your life? Haven't all these years been nothing to you? -Max caught his head in his hands and Brenda stroked his hair as broken as he was by the pain.

-I have nothing to forgive you for.

-Then come back to me," she said, raising her hand to clasp his and bring it to her lips. I need you by my side. You are my other half. We can put it back together. We deserve a chance.

Brenda looked into his eyes and felt her heart break into a thousand pieces. For a moment she doubted his safety, what if he tried, what if they gave each other a second chance? All might not be lost. Max understood her mistakes and she knew his, maybe he was right and with a little effort? -she thought sadly as the past crumbled before her eyes.

But the doctor shook her head, recognizing the follies that the heart out of pity makes you commit. She loved Max very much and would offer him a hundred chances if it would free him from his suffering, but it was no longer possible, his heart was in other arms.

-I can't... -I'm sorry...

Both remained for long and sad minutes in silence, without moving from their places. With a broken soul, she wiped away tears that ran down her face, erasing years of a love that had gone to ashes.

Lacking courage and dead with grief, she got up from the step and tried to walk towards the entrance, but as she took the second step she stopped and looked back wanting to say something that could alleviate Max's suffering.

-I wish you the best... -she said with tears breaking her voice.

-It will break you into a thousand pieces," Max said and Brenda felt the cold freeze in her veins.

Broken by grief and frustrated at not being able to offer the slightest comfort to the one she loved so much, she arrived at the doors of her room, entered without turning on the lights and threw herself on her pillow to cry without comfort. Months ago she had decided to separate from Max, but that night, at the door of that hotel, the chains were being broken for good. The feeling of freedom should be gratifying but it wasn't. Her hands ached, her body ached. Her hands ached, her body did not respond and sadness overwhelmed her. Deep sorrow crawled under her skin and the pain for her abandoned companion tore her apart. She cried for what she thought was hours until calmness came to her breathing. The points and endings were not easy but it was not possible to extend what would be nothing more than a lie. Shaken and puffy-eyed she jumped out of bed and sped off to the one place she really wanted to be. She knocked on the door but no one opened. She knocked a second and a third time when she finally got up the courage to open it without permission. He was there, sitting, smoking a cigarette and looking out the window. She approached slowly thinking he hadn't heard her but his thick voice made her skin crawl.

-Are you coming to say goodbye?

-Farewell? -Displaced, she approached and could see that from her window she could see perfectly the step where hours before she and Max had been talking. Happy for the new future ahead of her, she approached him from behind and caressed his shoulders.

-Is that what you want?

-Don't play with me," he replied angrily.

Akim lifted that gaze, as deep as the deepest of oceans, and she lost herself in them without remembering the reason for her life or the reason for her destiny. Without a second thought she sat on his legs and embraced him by the neck while her mouth sought him determined and indiscreet. He received her as thirsty before a night in front of the desert and delighted in her taste.

-I saw you," he whispered against her lips.

-We were saying goodbye.

-That means... - Akim hesitated tensely not knowing what to expect and she understood his hesitation.

The evidence may have always been against her, but she didn't usually expect explanations either. The last few times, she had decided to leave the fighting territory before the combat began, and he had always gone for her, showing how strong his feelings were. He tenderly rested his face on her torso and caressed the warmth of her body, awakening a new dawn in their lives. This was a new Brenda, a new woman and she wished she could make every dream that started in her mind come true.

-I'm not much fun, I'm recently divorced, I have a complicated job, sometimes I get in where I'm not wanted, and I may be a few years older than you, but only a few," he smiled and winked, "Would you like to be my partner?

Akim looked at her as if she was a freak or at least that's what it seemed to him in the first instance because the next second he let out a loud laugh, lifted her up in his arms and kissed her with the greatest of passions as he laid her down on the bed.

-You still haven't answered me. She said cheerfully as she watched him take off his shirt, leaving his torso bare.

-That's because I'm not sure." He replied smiling as he unbuttoned his pants and dropped them to the floor to climb up his body.

-If you're not sure, I have to leave anyway. He replied threateningly.

Akim nibbled at her mouth and ran his tongue along the contours of her full lips. Supporting the weight of his body on his elbows he looked into her eyes and rested his forehead on hers. He took a deep breath, once, twice, three times before saying in a soft voice the most heartfelt words she'd ever heard him say.

-I swear I will never betray you. Since I've been by your side I've never been with another woman, I swear. She didn't mean anything. Not like you, I promise.

Brenda brought her lips to his and accepted his statement as a new beginning. She had no desire to talk about Lola, the money or any of the myriad reasons that were fighting to keep them apart. She wanted to be happy and tonight she would get to work. The new Brenda did not listen, she acted. The new woman did not obey but decided.

Part II
Clouds in paradise

The morning still covered by the thick fog had no intention of giving free rein to a sun that refused to appear. Brenda drank from her steaming cup of coffee still wearing her silk nightgown. Last night she had stayed up until the wee hours of the morning but he never showed up. Standing up she looked out the window and took her first sip of the morning. The picture outside was no sharper than the one inside. Dampness covered the red bricks of the street and the facade of the house across the street showed a decaying peeling paint. A green moss timidly appeared on the lower part of the neighboring walls indicating that autumn was soon to appear and the winds were cold.

Leaning his elbows on the small countertop, he took his second and third sips, watching the morning cars rush by on their way to jobs that were unforgiving of tardiness. He glanced at the toast on the counter but dismissed the idea of eating it. He had no appetite. It wasn't that he didn't like the new house, he even thought it was charming at first. Yes. It didn't have the wonderful views or gardens of her previous home and it wasn't in the wonderful residential neighborhood she had enjoyed for so many years with Max, but that didn't matter because new memories would come, or so she imagined when she bought it.

Distracted in her thoughts she recalled the changes that had taken place in the last six months and a deep shiver ran through every little furrow of her skin. Max, who always claimed to love her more than anyone else, turned out to be a vengeful angel. First it was the house and the car, and she wanted to imagine that his pain would stay there but it didn't. The deep love he supposedly had for her turned into a need to see her destroyed. Her ex's lawyers squeezed her to such an extent that she barely had enough money to buy a small house, which although very modest, from the very first moment she decided to give him a chance. Everything in order to put an end to that unhappy divorce that fed her ex with hatred and undermined her hopes for a better future.

She took another sip of her already lukewarm drink as she acknowledged that nothing came out as she expected. Max had kicked her out of his practice on the grounds that he owned the building and didn't want to rent it, and that wouldn't be the worst of her problems. The patients were decreasing month by month and all thanks to her beloved Max, who did not skimp when it came to airing his dishonorable qualities as an unfaithful woman.

Friends were also not unaffected by her defamation. Horrified by the lascivious behavior of a lady who abandoned everything for an unsuitable man, they decided to judge her without pleadings or defense lawyers. The phone stopped ringing, patients became suspicious and invitations to luxurious events stopped coming.

The doorbell began to ring insistently, snapping her out of her thoughts, and she hurried across the room to the door. A floorboard was about to blow up and she told herself that the parquet would be one of the first things she would have to fix. The house was quite old and needed a few repairs, but of course, the divorce had not yet been finalized and she was only able to live on her income, which was being cut sharply month by month. Nervously, she opened the door, eager to see Akim. She hadn't seen him for two days and it seemed like an eternity.

-Hello. He said stepping aside to make way.

-Hello. Connor responded a little tense. They had both forgiven each other but the tension was still palpable between them.

The artist had long supported Max, but his belligerent attitude and Brenda's ex's recent underhanded actions caused Connor to come to his senses and arrive one morning to apologize. Brenda welcomed him with open arms and hoped that someday Akim would win her trust, because at the moment, they barely tolerated each other.

-I bring Latte macchiato," he said lifting the two plastic cups with lids and she smiled gratefully.

-God bless you. He replied as he closed the door.

-And since when did you become such a believer? -he answered just as amused.

-Since friends bring Starbucks to your home.

-Then this is out of the question. He said, holding up a small box with what he knew instantly was a delicious slice of cake. One of those with a little more than a thousand calories, but irresistible in the morning.

-Have I told you how much I love you?

Connor smiled as she went to her room to change into one of those plush, unglamorous robes. It was too late and there was no point in waiting seductively for someone who clearly wasn't coming. The message on her cell phone rang and she read it anxiously.

-A maddening night. Fallen in battle ☺ I call you when I wake up. Always yours.

She wanted to smile and think it didn't matter but she didn't succeed or at least not well enough to fool Connor who watched her carefully before speaking.

-Problems?

-Not at all. Akim has just finished work.

-Work... -Connor said, stretching out the last letter as he searched for a couple of dishes in the small kitchen.

Brenda decided not to answer, after all she didn't like that job either but what could she do, Max had put him out on the street and had given his details to every major construction company in town.

She hated knowing that almost every night she was heading to that venue with hundreds of young, insinuating women willing to do anything for a free drink, but she wasn't foolish enough to object to her taking a paycheck home. Rachel came in at that moment, opening the door with her copy of the keys and poking her nose through the door.

-You can come in, I'm with Connor. Rachel breathed a sigh of relief and Brenda smiled and shook her head. If you rang the doorbell you wouldn't be afraid of running into embarrassing situations. She said, making her friend blush probably remembering the little incident of her and Akim cuddling on the couch and Rachel coming in with a tea box in her hand.

-Sweet, if I rang the doorbell it wouldn't be me," she said, smiling and giving two kisses to Connor and then to her friend.

-You beat me to it," she said annoyed, looking at Connor and showing the tray with two more coffees that she placed on the small table.

The two friends smiled and passed out the cakes. The three of them began to chatter about hundreds of silly things and she felt grateful to have their friendship. The days had not been very sunny lately, and despite their differences, they were still by her side like sturdy posts willing to do anything to support her.

-Thank you. She commented with feeling but those two did not pay any attention to her, they were too busy discussing the gossip of the last cocktail party, which of course she could not attend due to lack of invitation.

-And did you see the cockatoo on his head?

-As if not to see it. Connor responded in a sea of laughter in front of a Rachel who was squirming in two from laughing so hard.

Brenda walked over to her phone and answered an incoming call, taking a step away from those two judgmental wives.

-Hello... yes, I received it. I'm meeting them in a couple of hours... yes, my friend Rachel is coming with me... I'm very grateful... that's done but this time let's make it a Mexican that uses less spice...

Brenda laughed her lungs out as she cut the call short when she discovered that her friends were no longer laughing and just staring at her trying to figure out who she was talking to.

-Murray spoke to confirm the visit with the tenant.

-Murray? Isn't that the politician?

-Yes, and very concerned about the welfare of our friend. Rachel replied, raising her eyebrows while hiding her mischievous smile behind her coffee cup.

-Don't be a shrew. Brenda sat down next to him and swung her legs over the couch to cover her cold feet with a blanket. He has an acquaintance who rents offices and he thought one of them might be a good new practice for me.

-Ahem... and he won't charge you.... -he said, coughing as if he had a throat clearing.

Connor looked at her raising an eyebrow and Rachel again clarified without any prompting.

-He is very kind. He invited her to dinner to offer her his help.... -Rachel said at length and Connor nodded as if it was all very clear.

-If you bite your tongue, you would die in less than five seconds, you know?

-Three seconds would be enough. Rachel replied confidently and Brenda could do nothing but laugh along with them.

They finished breakfast and Connor left to allow them to change and go to the famous new office.

-You know that in my studio we could adjust. He commented as he gave her two kisses.

-I appreciate it," Brenda replied apologetically. Max's last expulsion had been her own. He now had a new studio, but it was too small to be shared. I'm sorry he kicked you out, too.

-I would have left anyway. I never agreed to lie to you or to hurt you.... -He commented with his arms dropped to his sides.

-I know.

They both hugged excitedly and Rachel squealed from the couch.

-We are running late!

Both friends smiled and Connor placed a kiss on his dear doctor's forehead.

-Good luck. Let me know.

-I will. He said before closing the door and running to change his clothes so he wouldn't be late for his appointment.

-It's not so bad. She mused half-heartedly in front of Rachel who sat on her couch without responding. The neighborhood is the only thing different.

-You're right there, sweet, the neighborhood is one of the most... the most... simple?

-Yes, maybe, but I think my new patients will like it better. Don't forget that the previous practice was too ostentatious.

-And that's bad?

Rachel commented intrigued and the doctor didn't know what to say. Of course it wasn't even a tenth of what her previous practice was like, let alone after the changes Max had made, but what could she say? It was the only thing she could afford.

-You don't have to worry. He said while simulating a huge yawn.

-Are you tired? -Rachel narrowed her eyes suspiciously.

-Ugh yes, we've been out all day and I think I'll turn in early.

-And you want me to leave? -He confirmed with a sideways face.

-I'm not kicking you out," he said with a second fake yawn.

-Of course not," Rachel picked up her purse in mock indignation, "but next time try a little harder because you won't win the Oscar.

-I haven't seen him for days and he's not working tonight. She answered like a sorry little girl trying to justify herself.

-Don't be silly, you don't have to justify anything. A good fuck with your boy or a movie with your friend, we both know very well who wins.

Brenda didn't answer. She was red with embarrassment but she needed to find herself in his arms and feel a little bit of that security that she had been losing unavoidably. Knowing it every night in that place fed all her insecurities.

She ran to the shower to get ready. She would put on a pretty dress, a few drops of her delicious perfume, black lace lingerie and a cleavage indecent enough to take his breath away. Nervously she finalized every detail. She climbed into her heels, lit the candles and put lasagna in the oven.

The hours on the clock moved relentlessly and the book with which she passed the time fell to the floor as she closed her eyes, promising herself not to sleep more than five minutes. The sound of a chime made her jump from the sofa to open her eyes and read the message.

-I had to work. Don't wait up for me. ☹

PS: Always yours.

Brenda walked to the bedroom, tore off her clothes, washed her face to remove her makeup and lay down on her cold bed. At another time she might even have cried but this time she didn't, she just thought and thought. She remembered her past days, the patients she no longer had, the professional future she no longer had and the friends she had lost, okay, it wasn't all gold but it glittered a lot more than what she had now.

Akim opened the street door carefully so as not to wake her. It was still early morning and with luck he would find her in bed. Glad to imagine her a warm ball under the blankets he walked over, kicking off his shoes on the way. He hated that he hadn't been able to share more than simple messages with her for so many days but the hateful job didn't allow him much more. When she woke up, he went to bed and what should have been only a few days a week turned out to be seven full days a week. That job stank, his clothes smelled of smoke and cheap perfume. He didn't like it there but he needed the paycheck and Max had taken it upon himself all too well to contact every damn construction company to tell them not to take him on. He didn't know exactly what that asshole had said but it was clear it would be something convincing enough because some of them were even trembling as they slammed doors in his face.

Tenderly he looked at her from the bedroom doorway and saw how her shiny hair covered part of her delicious face. She was adorable. In absolute silence he removed his shirt and unbuttoned his pants. He was ready to jump into her bed and devour her. He needed her. He hadn't possessed her for days and if he added to that the more than willing young girls who kept tempting him, the abstinence seemed most painful. Altered and with erect need, he approached his girl to watch her breathe. He loved to do so. Brenda in her sleep was fragile and that feeling was sublime. To feel like her savior, her man, her refuge, her future, her blue knight...it was the best of rewards.

Without holding back he began to kiss her face, careful not to frighten her, but Brenda sleepily jumped on the spot to discover the owner of her caresses curled up under the sheets.

-I'm here... -he said hoarsely as he pushed her shoulders against the mattress and gently pulled her up so as not to crush her.

I should slow down, he told himself thinking of being a delicate lover but it was impossible. Too many days apart, too many nights without her in the company of overly willing women, he had to love her or he would die right there. Brenda turned her face away but Akim thought she was doing it to give him room to kiss that little corner of her neck that he adored so much, so he continued his attack barely listening to her verbiage.

-Akim... today... I went... to see a doctor... -He commented, trying to hide the passion that gripped his senses.

"Talk? Did she really want to talk?" He said to himself in confusion.

-Later my love... Later...

-But we have been so long without.... -He wanted to say the word, but Akim didn't let him finish.

-Too much... -He answered hoarsely as he positioned himself between her legs, which opened eagerly and accepting sweet defeat.

Perfect days

She got up carefully so as not to wake him and headed for the kitchen. Sad? content? She didn't quite know how she felt. She was delighted with the night spent with Akim, or rather the morning, but she wasn't entirely sure it was exactly what she expected. She would have liked to talk to him, to tell him how she felt but he not only didn't understand her but slept with her with an overwhelming, almost maddening need, and although she should feel flattered, she wasn't entirely. That night she had felt like a spring to a thirsty man in the desert and although it might have seemed most romantic it was not.

"Were you looking for me or were you on fire for a woman, whichever one it was?"

She stroked her forehead trying not to be so incoherent in her thoughts. Akim was by her side and kept showing her his feelings but she kept thinking about Lola and many others that crossed her path. Young girls with small waists and tits defying the law of gravity.

She felt insecure and did not like it. She recognized better than anyone that this was not the way to build a solid future. Confused, she prepared juice and toast when two strong arms grabbed her from behind to lift her up and carry her away. At first she was startled by the suddenness of their arrival but the next second she let herself be swept away.

-Toast. Akim ordered seriously and she obediently brought a piece of bread to his lips. He smiled with that look of rogue and fire and Brenda forgot all her doubts.

He bit into almost all of the toast as he carried his body in his arms as he made his way to the bedroom.

-It's still early," he said, nibbling her ear from behind and leading her into the bedroom. Brenda might have said it was quite late, but she wanted the same thing he did.

Her body was thrown without any delicacy on the mattress and the hungry young man threw himself on her with a look that any mortal would have been frightened but Brenda knew too well that wolf with tattoos to know perfectly well that she was not in danger in his arms. Or at least not that kind of danger, she thought as she felt imprisoned between his weight and a mattress that gave way under his passionate lunges.

-Wake up, sleepyhead. A smile that illuminated her mornings woke her up with so much joy that she didn't hold back and grabbed him by the neck to keep him by her side forever.

It seemed unbelievable that someone you didn't know a year ago, today became the person you felt like possessing every morning. With a smile identical to hers she smiled at him and replied in mock amazement.

-Sleepyhead? If I remember correctly I was the one who got up to prepare breakfast and was dragged back to bed without any consent, by the way.

-Are you telling me I abused you? -He feigned offense.

-Basically yes.

Akim breathed hard trying to show his deep indignation and sat up on her body threatening to tickle her to death. Just when she thought she would faint, he stopped and raised a threatening eyebrow.

-You haven't met my most fearsome side yet....

-Oops, scary," she said moving under his body provoking him by raising her hips to bump into his.

-I am dead... -he declared, defeated by the evidence. Let's get up before they find us stuffed on top of each other.

-What's the rush? -she asked disappointed.

-I promised Lucien that we would spend the afternoon with him. What's wrong? -she asked when she saw his unhappy face.

-I'm so sorry. Today is my practice move," she said in disgust. I made arrangements to have everything ready this afternoon. It's a shame because I would have loved to spend the afternoon with you.

-I didn't know it would be today. Akim replied with a frown.

-You've been so busy I didn't want to worry you. I got a really good place. It will be the perfect practice for my patients. The few I still have left. He thought without saying it out loud.

Akim had no knowledge of Max's machinations and planned to continue to keep it from him.

-I work, I don't think I can help you.... -He commented between angry and embarrassed.

-It's okay, Rachel and Connor will help me.

They both cuddled naked on the bed when Brenda jumped as if the light bulb of ideas had suddenly turned on for her.

-I'm dumb.

Akim looked at her lifting his shoulders in a "I'm not going to argue with that" sign and she threw a pillow at him as he headed to the restroom.

-You have chosen me, what other explanation than nonsense explains it? -he replied, smiling mischievously.

-Come on, get those muscles up and let's get in the shower. If we hurry we can spend some time together until I start the move. The boys won't be here until four o'clock. I have plenty of time to enjoy Lucien and talk to the little one for a while.

-And what would I have to tell you? My father told me that he spends all day texting you on your cell phone.

-It's lovely. She replied, stepping into the shower and watching in amusement as he stood behind her back without waiting for an invitation.

-Just as adorable as his father.... -He replied affectionately, kissing her back.

His lips began to nibble her neck under the stream of warm water as she resisted the inevitable pleasure. Sighing she released herself from the prison of his embrace and handed him the bath gel trying to interrupt the moment or they would never leave his house. Akim's passion when aroused proved tireless.

-We must hurry. It's for Lucien." Her voice sounded like a plea as she tried to reject his embrace with little result.

-For Lucien... -He answered hoarsely and carelessly as he pressed her against the cold tiles. Akim had no intention of freeing her, not for Lucien or anyone else.

After a perfect day Brenda had to break up such a magnificent moment. Lucien laughed with the freshness of innocence and her father lavished her with an affection that melted her just by looking at her. That clear and penetrating gaze was always the beginning and end of all her ravings.

-I have to go." He whispered to the father who was waiting for his son to bring the ball.

They both tried to show a touch of serenity even though they were well aware of the storm that was coming their way. Every time Brenda said goodbye to the child, it was not a good time for their ears. Meanwhile, the little boy, who apparently had a special radar, looked up at the adults like a distrustful poodle and listened with narrowed eyes.

-Lucien, I have to go.... -Brenda said with some trepidation to which Akim responded with equal trepidation.

-He has work to do, but we can play with the ball for a while longer.

-Sereno watched them carefully and raised his head as he answered like a resigned dwarf.

-Is he all right? -Akim asked, looking up at the sky to see when the thunder and lightning would strike their heads.

-If she doesn't want me, I can't stop her. The boy's little feet kicked each other as he looked down at the grass.

-And here we are again... -The father muttered, holding the ball tightly and Brenda bent down to get close to his side and look at him face to face.

-That's not true and you know it. Life brought you into my life and I am the happiest woman on the planet.

The little boy began to grin as he hung on tightly to his neck knocking them both to the ground from the momentum.

-I have been very busy but I promise to come very soon.

-Friday? -he asked enthusiastically.

-What happens on Friday? -she answered uncertainly.

-It's the autumn festival at school. I'm one of the main trees and.... -The little boy stopped talking and Brenda waited for him to take his time although his father was not as patient.

-¿Y? -Akim asked.

-All the moms are coming, and I said you were coming.... -He answered as he tapped one slipper against the other.

Akim turned his head to the side so as not to show the depth of his emotion. She, for her part, gathered the little boy's hands into hers and caressed them with delicious tenderness.

-I am the main tree. The little boy clarified as if he needed to explain himself but it wasn't necessary, she would go to that party even if the end of the world was coming.

-I'll be there. I wouldn't miss it for the world.

The boy smiled from side to side and Brenda stretched out her arms to wrap her warmth around him. Lucien was the unanticipated but terribly wanted son. She kissed him on both cheeks before watching him run into the house to tell his grandfather the good news.

-You've got him crazy for your bones. Strong arms wrapped around her from behind.

-And he to me. Brenda replied, caressing the rough hands that crossed over her belly, "Ugh, it's so late, I have to go.

He spoke quickly so as not to show the tears that caught in his throat as he watched the little boy leave so happily.

Full of dust but laughing their heads off, in the company of Connor, Rachel and Murray, they entered the house with a few boxes of pizzas and a few cans of beer as they lounged exhausted on the couch. What they thought would be a couple of hours turned into the whole afternoon and they were exhausted.

-And when that guy saw us running down the sidewalk and thought we were thieves? -Murray said amused, and the others responded with loud laughter, remembering the poor janitor's confusion.

Murray leaned back on the couch with those perfectly lined manly airs and Brenda felt even more amused. In his new jeans and freshly branded T-shirt, he was trying to look casual but the evidence gave him away. Smiling and grateful for his solidarity, she sat down next to him.

They began eating directly from the box and laughing at any nonsense when she discovered a shadow in the entrance frame that covered almost the entire door and that was looking at them in a way that she did not understand. He looked disgusted, but why?

-Akim?

Don't walk away from me

-I thought you were working. He commented, approaching Akim to greet him with a kiss on the cheek and trying to bring him closer to the group by pushing him by the hand.

-I managed to escape. He answered with few words and staring at his friends. Hello everyone," to which they responded with the same dryness.

-We were able to move all my stuff. You don't know how hard it was. Brenda was explaining the past events, but to tell the truth, they didn't make her laugh at all.

He had escaped from work knowing that even though it was already late he could share a few moments with her, but he never expected to see her come in so happy, so smiling, so well... without him. Let alone with an unexpected guest.

She didn't mention Murray's collaboration, he was sure of it, if she had, he would remember it perfectly, he thought, getting angrier by the minute. That was a detail she would not forget. For some time now that new friend had been very, very present in their lives. Excessively present for his taste.

He pulled up a chair and sat down next to Brenda containing a bad mood that grew exponentially with every smile from those amusing transporters. They had dinner and continued with their adventures, but he couldn't have a say because of course he had missed them, like everything else lately. He cursed himself for his absence, for the demonic job that was distancing him more and more from his side and for the odious Murray who seemed to have too much free time.

Annoyed but restrained, he grabbed a can of beer and nodded when he should have even looked civilized, though he wished he had kicked the damn widower out. With tense muscles he drank two gulps of beer in a row and ignored the smirks that asshole was throwing at his wife.

-But you owe it all to Murray. Connor commented still smiling at the previous comment as he looked at Akim absentmindedly.

Damn son of a bitch. He pretended in front of Brenda but he knew perfectly well that it was all a hoax. Neither of them could stand each other, but it was all because of how much they loved her.

-That's not true. The person involved replied with apparent humility and Akim would have thrown rotten tomatoes at him for being a bad actor.

-Yes, that's true. You rented the van and that saved us a lot of trips. I can't thank you enough," Brenda replied with a smile. You rented a huge van and showed up without telling us anything. It was great, so we were able to load all my stuff in one trip. He said as if he cared anything about that stiff's heroics.

-That's good... -The coarse voice came out as he swallowed the third sip of beer that dragged down the bitterness that settled in the center of his throat.

"Always so thoughtful," he said to himself finishing the can with one last sip and squeezing the can in his hand.

-Well, I guess it's late." Murray spoke, rising from his seat, and Akim thought it was the first intelligent sentence she had heard him say all night.

-Will you need the van tomorrow? I think driving that wagon is my thing." He commented with another one of those little smiles that got on his nerves.

-You can give it back. Brenda replied with amusement.

-All right, then, I promise not to take her to the Carrington dinner. He said smiling as he kissed her twice goodbye.

-Dinner? -Akim didn't hide his displeasure as he asked his girl curiously.

-Yes, the Carringtons are hosting a humanitarian fundraising dinner and it seemed like a good opportunity for Brenda to get back into her social environment and win back clients.

"Winning back clients." He looked at her intrigued but she didn't answer.

-I imagine you won't be able to attend, but don't worry, I won't leave his side.

"I'm sure of it." Either they would open the door and all leave before he finished counting to ten or he would throw them out the exit himself. Luckily for world peace, the said guests left and he was able to restrain himself until the door closed.

-Recovering customers?

Brenda closed her eyes as she squeezed her brow with her hands.

-I didn't want to tell you.

-That's for sure." I snarl furiously with a burning look in my eyes.

-I didn't want you to worry. Max's comments...

He didn't finish the sentence, it wasn't necessary, he knew perfectly well what that wretch had done.

-I guess you didn't want to "worry" me either, so you didn't tell me about Murray helping you move. More white lies?

He didn't have a mirror in front of him but he knew himself well enough to know that his eyes were on fire. His arms were so stiff from the tension that he was sure the tattoos would jump off his shoulders.

-Your ironies don't scare me. She replied annoyed as she picked up the empty pizza boxes to take them to the trash can.

-So what's the truth? You wanted his company and didn't know how to tell me? Is that it? The perfect politician, educated, widowed, well-to-do. The perfect man.

-What are you talking about? Brenda stopped in mid-stride and turned to face him, and he regretted the horrible comment.

God, he knew perfectly well she wasn't the type, she wouldn't cheat on him so viciously, but seeing that guy trying to win her over made him unhinged. That man was everything he wasn't and he hated to compete with a second Max. Just thinking about it made his nerves stand on end.

The demons of the fear of losing her were taking hold of him and driving him mad. Did he not yet know his fear of losing her?

-I didn't tell you because I was afraid of just that," he replied with his arms up in the air. Every time Murray offers himself graciously, you get mad as a mad dog.

-Gently? Did you say gently? You think I'm stupid not to guess that guy's intentions. If he could, he'd step on me like a cockroach. He can't stand me.

-That's not true. She commented with weariness in her voice but he didn't care. He was launched and would continue.

-I don't want to see him or you again, I don't want to have to endure his gentle company ever again. And I forbid you to go to that dinner.

"There, I'd said it." She'd go to dinner with that scoundrel over his dead body.

-You what? You forbid me? You forbid me what exactly? -Brenda stretched out her whole body to meet him face to face despite her twenty centimeters less. You forbid me to talk to someone willing to help me get more patients and who selflessly helped me move?

Akim gulped. That said the scoundrel seemed to be him but she didn't back down. If he gave in that guy would get closer and closer to her and that meant danger of losing her. No, he wasn't willing to give in.

-Yes, that's what I'm saying," he answered sharply.

-And this from the same man who walks around every night with scantily clad women smiling cheekily at him and who has a woman he slept with until two days ago attached to his back?

Akim swallowed again. This time he was in deep trouble. How did she manage to twist everything around?

-We weren't talking about that just now. He commented unconvinced when he heard how stupid his defense was.

Brenda threw the boxes in the trash and spoke with a coldness that froze her heart.

-Close on your way out.

She stormed into the room slamming the door. In a rage he kicked the coffee table in the living room choking with anger. Damn it, that wasn't what he had expected when he went there. He just wanted to spend some time together and hear how his new practice had been going, but like everything else that was going on between them lately, every step he took drove them further apart. Furious remembering Connor's smiles, Murray's approach and his disgusting night job, he stormed off in rage and bewilderment.

He would have liked to break down the bedroom door and argue with her until he could make things clear and finally tell her how much he loved her and the fear of losing her, but he preferred to leave. That was not a night to continue arguing, the door Brenda had slammed when she closed her bedroom had made that clear enough and his blood was still boiling from the fire of jealousy to be able to calm down.

Burdened by the weight of a future he did not know how to assume, he walked under the cold night. The icy air hit his face freezing his skin and he was grateful for the sensation. He needed to cool his heated spirit. He walked and walked thinking of a solution soon or one day he would find he had lost her.

"But what can I do?" she thought as she walked. She was losing patients because of her ex but also because of him. He belonged to another social stratum and that same society reminded her of it every moment, he may have been Murray today but tomorrow he would be someone else. He had to find something to unite them and fewer jobs to separate them, he told himself as he entered the subway station, concentrating on his ideas.

Desperate solutions

-I don't want you to look for me again. I'm not willing to continue your charade. Connor replied to Max with disgust.

-Are you going to tell me that you are now on the side of that dirty bricklayer?

The artist continued leaning on the frame of his last work waiting for the architect to leave, but nothing. He was not leaving.

-I am on her side.

-But what a bug has bitten you! Everything I've done has been for us. I've always wanted the best for her.

Connor glared at him angrily, his fists clenched on his lectern.

-You lied to him. All that story about the photos was a vile lie, nothing was real.

-That's what he says, but you know I checked him out and that bastard took my money," he commented, walking nervously. I have no idea what his new lies were to convince everyone, but I assure you he's with Brenda for the interest. I really love her.

-And so you have defamed her and bankrupted her? -Connor felt like he was spitting venom in every sentence. She had originally bet on Max and she had been wrong. She thought he really loved her, but now she doubted his good intentions. You talk trash about her, you denied her what was rightfully hers, you took away her practice, and you say you love her? Allow me to doubt your praiseworthy feelings. He said, throwing the stained brush on the briefcase.

-You just don't understand...

-No one understands Max. Now do me a favor and leave.

-If he sees her destroyed he will abandon her. Don't you see! With no money and no future she is worthless to him and then she will come back to me.

-Connor shook his head, not wanting to hear another word, and waved his arm in the direction of the exit.

-You'll see how right I am. He will forget about her. He will see her without a future and will abandon her.

Connor in two quick strides approached the ex-husband and squeezed him by the knot of his tie as he grunted in startlement.

-If you hurt him, you'll have to deal with me! You don't know what you're saying. You've lost your mind.

Connor sentenced each sentence and then pushed and shoved him off balance. Max twitched on the verge of falling but within a second he was repositioning his impeccable suit.

-I'm right, you'll see. Everyone will see." And he left the way he came in.

Connor began to put the materials away. His mind was not now on the art but on the number of mistakes he had made. He thought Max was the best choice for Brenda and now he understood his big mistake. She had needed him and he had opted for the safer choice. He thought Max was the best and participated in that charade when in reality he should have always supported his friend. She was free to choose who she wanted and he shouldn't have bet on anyone but her. Not even a thousand years would be enough time for him to apologize.

The door sounded very faintly as a tall, sturdy body asked for permission.

"Bingo," he said to himself as he saw his new visitor at the studio entrance.

Willing to completely change his attitude towards a young man whose only mistake was to feel in love with someone everyone said he shouldn't, he decided to give him a quota of trust. A small one, but a quota nonetheless.

-I need to talk to you about something very personal. If you are not willing I will understand," Akim was tense, his jaw was stiff and his eyes were glittering nervously.

Connor looked down and began to arrange his brushes, ashamed of his past attitude. This young man felt defensive of the world, but much of the blame lay with people like him who had judged him without offering him a choice. What an idiot he had been! He, who in the past had been condemned by his parents for his sexual choice. Could one be more foolish?

-Come in. He replied dryly. Akim closed the door and leaned against the wall. He heard you.

The young man took a deep breath or at least that's what it seemed to her as he began to speak with a poise that Connor fully understood the immediate interest that had subjugated her friend. This young man might be strong and handsome but it was that intriguing, secretive touch that incited discovery.

She talked and talked and he just listened. This time he did not judge, he did not want to. When Akim finished his speech, his gaze no longer reflected the rebelliousness of the misunderstood. His shoulders were slumped and the tension was gone. Connor was sure that if he sharpened his ears he would be able to hear the strong beating of her heart when the young man named her.

"He's madly in love, how could I be so blind?" He thought regretfully for a past he wished to start erasing as of today.

-You know it's dangerous," Connor analyzed aloud.

-I know, but what choice do I have?

-Not many. The artist answered sincerely.

-You've noticed it too. Akim reflected as he slowly approached the window.

-Partridges are scarce in most royal finals.

-And in mine there weren't many..." he reflected sadly. Akim nodded as he covered his hard face with his palm. I love her." He said as if needing to justify his past and future actions and Connor cursed himself for his past blindness. What would have happened if he had supported them from the beginning?

-I think you may be right, or at least you should try.
-Does that mean yes?
-Yes, and I think the sooner the better. He answered confidently.
-I don't know if you're doing it for our sake or to bring me down even further, but either way, I appreciate it. Akim replied with calm coolness.

Connor accepted the harshness of her words. He deserved them.

The young man in love walked out the door and Connor watched him carefully. He didn't look happy but he couldn't blame him, if he were in his place he would be scared to death.

He was still angry, even though he had been climbing the walls for two days. Who did he think he was to tell him who he should or should not talk to? God, just remembering it made his blood boil like teapot water. She was beside herself. She would do as she pleased, she thought as she parked the car in front of Lucien's school. Oh yes, because she would go to the boy's party no matter who he liked. Little did she care that he hadn't apologized. If what Akim was looking for when he talked about a relationship with her was submission, he was terribly mistaken. He didn't plan to dialogue over her decisions, not anymore. In the past he had bargained with Max and was only able to get a personality trampled for the sake of someone else's interest. No sir, that would not happen to him again.

With a firm step, and wearing a very nice suit of pants and jacket, she walked to the celebration of her adopted son, after all Lucien was the main tree! She entered the hall and saw him on the stage. She raised her hand enthusiastically indicating to him that she was there and that she was terribly proud despite her broken branch. Grandpa came to her side smiling and showed her a free place next to him. Delighted she accepted deciding that for the child she would raise the white flag.

Akim was not in the chair and with the air of a distracted and uninterested woman, she looked for him with her eyes. She was still annoyed with him but when she discovered him talking to a smiling young woman who was nodding her head as if he was offering her the magic formula of youth, the rage was born again from her guts.

"Please, there are women who don't have a shred of dignity," she said to herself without acknowledging that jealousy was beginning to eat away at her again as it always did whenever she saw him talking to someone younger. Trying to hide her nerves she listened to the words the proud grandfather whispered in her ear as the autumn music began to play. The warmth of a body pressed to his right informed him that the seat had been taken but he didn't move his head. He knew perfectly well who it was. "How quickly male hearts heal!" she thought through teeth clenched in jealousy.

Lucien began to narrate his poetry and pride leapt from his every pore squealing at the top of his lungs. "That's my boy!" The little boy recited the poem to perfection and she lip-synced along to it recalling the hundreds of rehearsals they had done via cell phone. When the 1stA performance was over and Lucien came down from the stage to sit next to his classmates, he looked up to smile at her with all his might and she responded with a kiss in the air which he accepted with a face flushed with shyness.

His chest heaving with pride, he waited for the other courses to perform, when a large, rough, seemingly lost hand reached up to his leg to intertwine its fingers with his own. Her heart skipped a beat at the feel of his touch and a current ran through her from the tips of her hair to the last toe. She was angry, that was true, but she did not wish to find herself like this, she could not stand the distance between them. The absence of his touch was too much to bear. That man awakened in her a need she didn't want to feel, but even if she wanted to deny it, it didn't make it any more bearable. She did not look at him, she could not. The feelings of seeing him, feeling him and touching him were too strong to hide.

"Why didn't you come to see me?" Ruefully she ducked her head and fixed her eyes on the hand that intertwined with his wanting to say what she had not yet said. Courageously and somewhat shyly, she lifted her face to meet that gaze that had won her from the first day it collided with his.

His lips curled into a little boy's pout of apology and happiness instantly settled in his heart. That was the way things were, a few apologies and her world came to its senses. The event came to an end and the attendees began to rise from their seats. She did too, along with Akim who was still holding her hand tightly. She could have tried to wriggle out of his grip and have an adult conversation before giving in to the temptation of a body that aroused every fiber of her womanly body, but she did not. Everyone moved down the rows to leave the room and she waited for Akim to do so but as always happened with him, he did the opposite of what was expected. Not caring about the huge number of parents there, he tugged her hand until he slapped it against his body. Startled by the act and somewhat uncomfortable feeling the center of attention of some mothers who murmured in scandal, she opened her mouth to tell Akim that this time he was out of line, when his wet tongue penetrated her silencing her with a possessive and hungry kiss.

Lucien appeared at full speed and threw himself upon them with a smile on his face, ending such a sweet caress. Her father released her from his grip to lift the small tree that no longer held any branches in place and she staggered confused and with a burning heat reborn from her loins.

-Did you like it? -The boy, still in his father's arms, turned to ask him hopefully.

-You were magnificent," she replied proudly.

-I got a few sentences mixed up. Her little blue eyes sparkled with sorrow.

-I didn't notice. She said confidently.

-Really?

-You were perfect," his father replied, trying to put his doubts to rest.

-Lucien, you must come with the rest of the class. Said the young brunette girl with an announcing smile and who was talking so interestedly with her father before.

-Teacher," the little boy quickly got out of his father's arms to pull her hand closer to the young girl. This is Brenda, my new mom.

The doctor felt her body begin to tremble. Of course she adored the little boy and loved being that important woman in his life, but to hear him call her that word in front of everyone was something very hard to digest. Embarrassed and without looking at her father or grandfather, she greeted the teacher as best she could, who kept smiling at her all the time.

-Lucien keeps talking about you. I'm very happy to meet you. He said with amused politeness and Brenda wanted to die. "For heaven's sake, she's lovely." She thought regretfully of her murderous jealousy.

In a state of shock and extreme embarrassment he accepted the very cordial greeting and watched as his new son walked away with the young woman by the hand.

-I think I'll go home. It's still more than an hour before it's time to leave. Grandpa commented as he rubbed his hands together.

-If you want, I can give you a ride home," Brenda offered gladly.

-He prefers to walk. Akim answered for his grandfather and his father gave a loud laugh.

-Birthday for your children to answer for you. I'll expect you for lunch and don't be late or I'm afraid the tree won't forgive you.

-We will be there, won't we? -Akim answered, waiting for his confirmation.

-Yes. He said nodding his head.

-Good. By the way Brenda... -he commented with a smile on his face- do me the favor of forgiving my stubborn son before Lucien and I have to ask for political asylum in another country.

Akim snorted loudly and his father spoke stretching his neck and widening his smile.

-You see? An unbearable beast.

She nodded trying to hide her face and the father walked away towards the exit.

-Do you think it's fun to make me suffer? -He said, moving closer to her breasts, which felt his touch and bristled despite the layers of clothing that separated them.

-I sympathize with those who, like me, have to put up with your bad mood. She replied amused.

-And all because of you.

-My fault? -She answered, bewildered and with her eyes wide open like saucers.

-Yes," he replied, nodding his head and hugging her around the waist, "If you were able to understand that I am an idiot whom you must forgive, it would save us a lot of unpleasantness.

-You're not an idiot. He replied, lengthening the last letter and resting his hands on his torso.

-I am, but in my defense I have to say that's your fault too.

-And may I ask why?

-Because I'm so in love with you that I no longer think or reason. Brin... I'm afraid of losing you.

-Akim...

-No, let me continue. I did terrible and I know I make stupid mistakes every time I put three words together, but I swear I'm trying, I'm trying to be a better person for you but I can't help but feel threatened. No matter where I look, I think out there there will always be someone willing to tear us apart and I don't want to accept it, I can't accept it. You are everything.

-You have to trust me.... -she said, choking with emotion.

-And I trust. It is in the world that I do not.

Brenda accepted his embrace and rested her face against the warmth of his chest. She was unable to answer a reality that also gripped her day by day. She was unable to recognize that those same doubts also assailed her on her lonely nights. They both walked a path too swampy to ignore.

Let's write together

He should go home but Lucien was so happy that he did not want to disappoint him. The little boy kept recounting over and over again his autumn performance and they did not stop laughing along with the great performer. Akim left for work but she agreed to have hamburgers for dinner while they watched an episode of a series with many spaceships and many colored lasers, but she didn't understand what world they lived in or if the blue ones were the good guys or the bad guys.

After listening for the tenth time to Lucien's explanations that those in red used to be the good guys but now they were bad guys because the star government had been overthrown, her grandfather settled the discussion and she thanked him with an intense look of relief.

-It's bedtime. Grandpa said as he turned off the television.

-Will you stay and read me the story?

Brenda forgot that it was late and that she was opening her new practice the next day, agreeing without a second thought. They both went to the bedroom and Lucien quickly changed into his pajamas to get into bed while she chose a story from the bookshelf. When she turned to approach the little boy, he opened the sheets to make room for her. Delighted with the invitation, she kicked off her shoes and pulled the blanket over herself as she leaned against the backrest and the little boy laid his little head on her shoulder to look at the colorful pictures. What at first would be one story, ended up being five, until the little chatterbox stopped commenting.

With the utmost tenderness of a new mother she stroked his silky hair wishing him good night and smiled as she listened to him murmur in his sleep. She watched him ecstatically. She had always wanted to be a mother but her dreams were interrupted when a doctor, in a cold consultation room, confirmed that her body would never carry a baby. Saddened, she decided to face her fate but now, with Lucien resting on her chest, the feelings of being more than just a good psychologist surfaced with hope. Happy, she lay back, enjoying one more moment of such sweet company until she felt tiredness seizing her strength. A few more minutes, she said to herself before closing her eyes and letting herself be enveloped by the scent of a small child.

It was almost four o'clock in the morning when Akim entered his home ready to throw himself head first into bed. He was exhausted but that situation would soon change. He stripped off his T-shirt that smelled of smoke and night lounge, when he saw under the door, a trickle of light. That rascal would have left it on.

He walked smilingly remembering the star tree when the image he found in front of him hit him like a bull's eye in the center of his heart. Both were sleeping happily in each other's arms. The little boy rested his head on his girl's body and she intertwined her fingers in his thick hair. Dressed only in jeans, he leaned his long body against the wall and remained in that position for long minutes, enraptured by the dreamlike view.

When he saw her for the first time, there in that office hallway, his heart pounded with unknown force, but today it was much more than a feeling. Brenda was a madness impossible to explain. Some might call it love at first sight, others instant crush, some Buddhists even say it's that delicate invisible red thread that binds soul mates, those destined to be together. Who knows which explanation was more accurate, the only reality was that he was totally and madly in love.

That woman represented so much that any words would be poor in the face of the immensity of his feelings. He could not lose her, he could not conceive of losing her, not after seeing what was before him. "There are two of us men pining for her love," he thought as he noticed how the boy clung to his waist trying to hold on to the one he considered his mother. Akim shook his head as he reached beside him to caress them both, his two most precious treasures. He could not give up the fight. They would be happy together, and if there was a God, he had better be on their side because he was willing to fight. He had a chance to escape a disturbed ex-husband, a stalker Lola, a nightlife she was jealous of and a society that insisted on separating them and he would get to work. He only hoped she would be able to understand.

Tenderly he spread his rough fingers across the angelic face of the little one and then brought it almost trembling over the tender countenance of his beloved. Her skin was as soft as his eyes and as tender as his heart. He did not deserve her, he knew perfectly well that there was no cord of destiny that united them, nor love from other lives that returned to this reality, but how nice it would be to believe it.

She opened her sleepy eyes and he bent his face to kiss her gently. She seemed to respond with a smile but instantly closed them again. She was asleep. Carefully his strong arms picked her up from under her knees until he lifted her up and settled her on his chest to abduct her to his room. Whispering in her sleep she moved closer to his warmth and he held her with extreme strength making it clear that he would never let go. He walked to her bed and deposited her inside on the blankets and quickly removed his jeans to settle in beside her. Very carefully and without waking her, he removed her pants leaving her with only her shirt and covered her with the sheets. She settled on her side like a small child with her legs curled up and he hugged her from behind, breathing in the scent of jasmine, vanilla and the sweetness of his own skin. With a tight embrace he wrapped her in his warmth and fell asleep enchanted with life.

-Brenda! Will you take me to school?

Lucien's screams as he threw the bedroom door wide open caused them to wake up in alarm. The little boy jumped on the bed as Brenda covered herself trying to recognize where she was and Akim smiled in amusement. His Brin should get used to such morning outbursts.

-What did we say about knocking before entering? -The father said in a deep voice and winking at his girl, who began to clear her head and smile as she recognized where she was.

Lucien rushed out and closed the door at full speed. Brenda looked at him quizzically and he merely raised his shoulders in surrender.

-Knock, knock, can we?

Brenda burst out laughing and Akim nodded closing his eyes somewhat embarrassed by his son's nonsense.

-You can. He replied, sitting on the back of the bed.

The boy again launched himself at them but this time the couple was waiting for him. Pushing this way and that he began to make a place for himself in the center and asked again excitedly.

-Will you walk me to school? I've already had breakfast and we leave in ten minutes.

-Of course.

-Of course not." Akim answered flatly and the boy frowned as she watched him in intrigue.

-It's early and I need to... talk to you," he commented with a mischievousness that even he thought sounded a bit depraved.

Lucien threw himself into the arms of his new protector and kissed her full cheek.

-But you choose me?

The father's eyes widened in indignation at the bad arts used by his son to take the girl away.

-I saw her first." Akim replied threateningly amused face to face, to which the little boy responded with equal ferocity but with a slightly deeper blue in his eyes.

-But he will come to school with me.

The men pretended to snort and growl like lions and Brenda took the opportunity to cover herself with a sheet and escape from the ring amused at being the center of such handsome savages.

Lucien -Lucien go get the backpack ready. I'll be ready in five minutes.

The little boy jumped out of bed as he stuck his tongue out at his father from the doorway in victory.

-He loves me more. He answered his father and ran away.

-But... -Akim answered, supposedly angry, and waited for the door to close before jumping on the woman who was holding the pants and trying to get a foot inside. No way. You were asleep last night and I didn't even have you for five minutes. He replied, pulling her back onto the bed.

The woman bounced on the mattress with one leg covered by her pants and one not. She tried to wiggle out of his grip but he was too heavy to push away with a simple push.

-Enough... enough already... -She shrieked trying to get out from under that body. I have to prepare a consultation. She answered amused and unconvinced to leave when she felt the humidity of his kisses on her neck. I have... to... leave". I have to go," she spelled, her voice thick with desire.

-And I need you," he said, reaching under her shirt and caressing her belly, which burned under his touch.

-We slept together... -He replied, closing his eyes and stretching his body to give her better access.

-Exactly... asleep... Now I don't want to sleep.

Akim rested his weight on his forearms and looked at her with fire in his eyes when the door burst open and a little voice shouted excitedly.

-I'm ready now," he said and left with the same speed he entered. Akim dropped his body on top of his own defeated before his son.

-Come on, it's no big deal," she replied amused.

-You think so? -. He asked rubbing his hardness against her to make her feel the gravity of the situation and Brenda wrapped her arms around his broad neck and kissed him fleetingly before slipping away to the side.

-Today is my first appointment at the new practice and I want everything to be perfect. Brenda was getting dressed and he admired her leaning sideways.

Sunrise by her side was blessed glory, despite the interruptions of her son and the pain of unfulfilled desire. He got up to approach her and tell her to wait for him for lunch but as always when he had her near he pounced on her mouth agitated and needy to possess her. He wanted to mark her until her body recognized that there was not an inch of her skin that did not bear his name.

-Akim... -She said, enraptured in his kisses and he enjoyed knowing that he managed to confuse her as much as she did him.

-I'll pick you up at lunchtime. I have something to tell you. Brenda looked at him curiously but he pushed her towards the door with a slap on her buttocks. I'll tell you later.

-Anything good? -She asked fearfully and he took pity on her fears. Since they had been together they had only passed test after test and not the good kind.

-Yes.

She kissed him quickly and left with Lucien waiting for her with his little hand raised. Although she tried to lie down and rest a little longer, she could not fall asleep. His question rumbled in her head like a marble in an empty box. "Anything good?" He hoped so because he could no longer think of ways to keep her by his side. Disturbed he lay looking up at the ceiling and talked to a God he barely believed in. He had abandoned him too many times.

"But if you're there, if you'll help me this time..." He said pleading to a ceiling with peeling paint.

Unresolved frontiers

The practice was perfect and her first visit could not have gone better. He was happy, he felt that his life, although different, was falling into place. Time to time, she thought, sorting through the files and waiting for Akim eager to have lunch together. He remembered the morning in his bed and it seemed perfect. They both fit together perfectly and together they were beginning to be a family, an idea that sounded like music in her thoughts.

-With such a beautiful smile on her face, I hope it's for me. Akim's voice entering the office made her turn and approach with a sensual gait.

She knew how he liked that game of woman on the prowl and enjoyed making him suffer. She brazenly swayed her hips and walked slowly. Boldly, she moistened her lips hoping to capture the fullness of his desire and reached out to rest her hand on his chest and feel his heartbeat as it pounded in agitation.

-We are not going to eat. He said in a thick voice as he pushed her against the desk.

Wedged against the furniture Akim interlaced her fingers over the hand that rested on her enamored heart.

-It's written... right here... -He commented with an air of suspense.

-Here?

-Yes, right here. Right here. He said squeezing his hand over hers.

-And what does it say? -He whispered, playing along.

-Eternally yours. Always yours. He answered without hesitation.

She did not answer, she could not. Emotion knotted her senses. Since his return from Morocco, Akim had not hidden any of his feelings. It was as clear as it was overwhelming.

-I love you... -He whispered on her lips and she opened her lips accepting this madness called love.

With teary eyes she discovered that true love was not a person, a moment or a place, as she had believed before, love was much more than all that. True love was to wake up in white sheets feeling happy to breathe. It was smiling in the morning for no reason or discovering madness in the simplicity of life. Eternally yours, how many times she would have read it in a book but how much it meant when it flowed from her lips?

-I love you too.

Akim opened his eyes and closed them as if he was unable to react and she glued her forehead to his, enjoying the most wonderful moment she had ever lived. She never used to tell him in words but that had to change. She was completely devoted to him and she knew it. She would never feel anything like this for anyone.

-I will always love you. From the first moment I saw you I loved you and I will always love you. Always. Akim sentenced with fire in his eyes while his strong arms wrapped around her and kissed her passionately.

Enveloped in his warmth she felt herself being drawn into the red divan as his kisses savored her tenderly.

-We're not going to have sex," he said hoarsely as he nibbled on the contour of her ear.

-No? -. She replied somewhat disappointed as she pulled his shirt up so she could caress his hard naked torso. Are you sure?

-I am. I'm going to make love to you. She said as she wrapped her body against his. And love was what they did.

They ate in a restaurant that could not be awarded but she thought it was the best salad and the best steak. They laughed, enjoyed and talked in complicity. They walked down the sidewalk hand in hand, looking at each other in complicity. Something had happened that afternoon that made it different, special. Excited, she sat down on the park bench and asked anxiously.

-I can't wait. What's the good news? -At first she thought he tensed up but it couldn't be possible. It was good news, he had sworn.

Cheerfully she let herself be guided to a bench and waited smiling. Maybe a trip? A new beginning? The big lottery prize? Thousands of crazy ideas boiled through her brain but she didn't want to anticipate. He deserved his moment of glory.

Akim began her story and her first reaction was to look around to make sure she was awake. When she discovered that neither the sound of cars rushing by nor the loud screeching of children in the park could wake her up, she realized that she was not in a nightmare.

Could he be so macabre to have deceived her in such a way? She wanted to scream, to insult him, to leave offended, but the enthusiastic smile on his face made her wait perplexed in her place. It couldn't be a joke, but then why was he hurting her with such a dagger? When Akim reached the middle of his tale, the anger and offense left to be replaced by painful understanding. He, in truth, believed hopefully in a happy ending. He talked about the perfect opportunity before him and she felt defeated.

He spoke enthusiastically about working in an art studio and she understood his illusions, but in Barcelona? thousands of miles away from her? did she really believe that theirs could continue? From second to second the man's euphoria increased in proportion to the bleeding of his silent heart.

-... it would be for Connor's studio and I could resume my studies in the arts. I'd have a career and a job, isn't that perfect?

Her head tilted up and down without being able to speak. If she did she would start crying like a child abandoned in a doorway. Of course it was a great opportunity.

-Lucien will be able to travel in a couple of months. The school will prepare all the documentation for me.

"You've made up your mind." She thought saddened but without uttering a word. The pain was a dagger of disappointment tearing at her chest.

-It's a very good opportunity for you," she tried to say without sounding like a selfish bitch, but she doubted she could pull it off.

-For us," he said, pressing her hands in his. Don't you see? We can start somewhere else. I won't have to be a man of the night anymore. I have a chance to live in your world. I would be up to it. He said hopefully.

-I never considered you any other height. He replied, loosening his grip limply.

-But I do. We're drifting apart day by day and I can't let that happen. This is our chance to start from scratch.

-What exactly are you asking me? -He asked, narrowing his eyes and wondering what part of the conversation he had missed.

-I want you to come with me. I want us to make a life together in Spain.

Brenda shifted nervously on the bench but was unable to stand up. Her knees were shaking too much to support herself.

-The salary is very good and you would not need to work. You can take some time until you find a practice and new patients.

"I already have a new practice." She thought in agony.

-I could support you, you could choose your patients without worrying about everything Max took from you.

-Keep me... -He uttered in a barely audible voice.

Akim went on with the hundreds of arguments why the position in Barcelona was the best for them but he did not quite understand it. Living in Barcelona was a very good opportunity, but only for him. She had no place there. She had just separated, she had a practice that opened its doors that very morning and she was beginning to feel free of action and thought, she could not leave everything and go after a man, not again. Separating from Max was

already a new beginning and she did not wish to live one more.
"Kept..." she repeated again silently.

-And when would you leave? -she asked, holding back tears.

-Connor has booked me a ticket for this Saturday.

-This Saturday! That's in three days... -He said short of breath.

-Yes, I know, it's too soon, but I can get everything ready and when you arrive we'll have a home to live in.

"A home..." She thought confused. She had recently bought that small house because she needed to live alone and find herself again and now Akim was talking about changing countries, living together, leaving her profession and hundreds of changes for which she was not prepared.

-Brin... I need to know that you are in this with me..." He said with a deep voice and that accent that was more pronounced when he was nervous. -He said with a deep voice and that accent that was more pronounced when he was nervous. If you don't agree or if you don't see it clearly I will tell Connor not to count on me. I think this is the best thing for both of us but if for some reason it is going to separate us I am willing to resign the position. I will not undertake any start without you.

Brenda felt the weight of responsibility crushing her back and hunching her into the seat. No, she couldn't do something like this. Akim had struggled a lot in his life and lived through many misfortunes, today he had a chance and he couldn't miss it.

The art world was not easy and the train of possibilities did not often pass that way. From what little she understood about art she knew she had talent, otherwise Connor would never have offered her such an opportunity. She couldn't be so selfish with him, but she wasn't ready for a leap into the void. With her fists clenched and the lie on her lips she answered as truthfully as she could.

-This is great news.

Akim hugged her enthusiastically and happily talking about the magnificent future that awaited them together and she shed a single, imperceptible tear on her sweater as she enjoyed the warmth of arms that in a few days she would have to let go.

Saying goodbye

-If you keep looking at me like that, I won't get on the plane.

He wanted to answer their jokes, but how to get it when your soul escapes to farther places? The plane would erase in the clouds what he once believed to be real and would take with it a trunk of memories he should never have allowed. Grief, like a dagger stuck in the center of his heart, hurt so much that it didn't even hurt anymore.

People walked through the airport with their dreams waiting to be discovered, and wondered if any of the hundreds of passersby marching in haste would be able to notice the sorrow that was born inside her belly and ran coldly over every millimeter of her skin.

-I'll find a house and I promise you'll like it," he said enthusiastically as he hugged her lovingly.

-He whispered in her ear as if he knew a truth that he did not want to assume.

He hugged her tightly, kissing her hair while describing the thousands of dreams that would never come true. Broken by grief she sighed, drowning her sorrows in a corner that Akim could not reach.

The airport microphones announced flight 7848 and her heart stopped beating. A chime, a sweet voice, a four-digit number and what could have been would no longer be. Instinctively she clutched at her waist, she had to let him go but how much it hurt. Tears were held back in eyes that shone brighter and brighter.

-See you soon. Don't delay... -He said, choked by the sadness of saying goodbye but unaware of the end that was looming over them.

Akim let go of his arms for a moment to say a cheerful goodbye to Lucien and his father who promised to have everything ready before Christmas. He shouldered his backpack and determinedly held her hand to escort him to the security grinders.

The two walked quietly until a watchman who, kindly, indicated that the damn countdown had reached its end. With a forced smile she tried to conceal a hope she did not possess. Her fingernails clung desperately to his leather belt as she kissed him with the wetness of tears bathing her lips.

-Shh, I'll see you soon. I'll be waiting for you... -He said, wrapping his fingers around her and bringing her close to his heart. I'm yours, remember? Here, I have it tattooed.

Brenda couldn't hold in her sadness a second longer. Tears welled up like an uncontrolled spring. The sorrow broke her in two and let a love that would never come back to life escape. With trembling knees she stretched her body on tiptoe and kissed him for the last time. There was goodbye.

-I wish you well. He stammered, his voice choked with pain.

Akim nodded without responding. His gaze was lightening with a glow much like her own. For the last time he wrapped his large hands around her face and kissed her passionately. A passion he would never feel again.

Sighing he released her and set out to walk down the desolate hallway. He did not look back and she thanked him. With sorrow and millions of tears streaming down her face she watched him walk off to a happy destination without her.

-You're not planning to meet with him, are you? -Akim's father spoke with regret.

-I can't." She replied without turning around. "I can't... I can't... I can't...

Lucien reached over holding her little hand in his and Dr. Klein, the most controlled woman of all, the confident and courageous, the polite and responsible, broke down hugging a child who comforted her without understanding the background of her pain.

The days passed in shades of dark grays and blacks. No morning seemed to dawn sunny but that mattered little to him. Akim was settled in, he had a perfect house next to the painting studio and when he spoke she could tell he was happy. He kept asking her how her business was going and she had always avoided him, but that afternoon was the moment of truth. He was consolidated in Barcelona, Lucien and his father were by his side and she had to break his ties and allow him to fly. In Barcelona he had a promising future and who knows if even a new love.

-Hello. Akim answered angry with her. He did not understand her delay.

-Hello. She said, grateful that the phone allowed her to hide her tears.

-Do you have something to tell me? -he sentenced as an ultimatum.

He was waiting for the date and time of her flight to Barcelona. He had been demanding it in recent conversations and in every conversation he asked it in a firmer and angrier voice.

-I don't... -Silence settled on the phone line and for a minute he would have thought he had been cut off but for the heavy breathing on the other end that told him he had not. With supernatural courage he spoke as if he were making a speech. I've thought it over and I think it's better for both of us if I stay in London. Here is my work and there...

-You have me. He said as if he had figured out what I was going to tell him.

-You don't understand, to give it all up and start all over again, to lose everything I have achieved with so much effort.

-Damn you, you promised. I told you if you didn't agree I wouldn't leave, you could have said so, you could have been honest with me.

-Akim...

-But no, you preferred to keep me fooled," he growled through his teeth.

-It is not a deception, it is a reality. You have a world ahead of you. A more appropriate one... -She said, choked with grief.
-No! Not this time. I can't fight your own prejudices anymore.
-Please try to understand me.
-I will not forgive you! I'm not going to look for you, not again. I can't be the only one who believes in us anymore. Twice I thought I lost you and ran after you, but not this time, either you accept what we have and face the world for our love or this is over.

Brenda on the other side bit her lips not to answer, what could she say?
-Brin... please... -He whispered behind the line and she thought she felt the wetness of his pleas.
-This is for the best. He said with mock serenity.
-Is it better? Is it better to split up? Is it better to forget me?
-Try to understand me...
- Answer me...!
-Goodbye." He whispered curtly with all the letters before feeling the absolute silence on the other side.

Brenda lay down on the bed with a feeling of cold so deep that nothing could warm her. She didn't cry, she had no more tears to shed. She curled up on the blanket and waited and waited. If the hours passed, if the days were over, maybe this way, that emptiness in her chest would be filled with something other than more pain.

A not so distant future

The leaves fell, the cold winter departed and the sun's strong rays signaled that summer would come with hot afternoons of sandy beaches and refreshing lemonades.

She hurriedly closed the office and stood in the middle of the street ready to hail the first cab that came along. Rachel's call had sounded so concerned that the doctor feared the worst.

Without counting any of the bills he threw them on the cab driver's tray and went downstairs without listening to the man's shouts that he had money left over. She ran to the entrance of the house and with barely a breath she rang the doorbell several times hoping that someone would open the door. She was ready to knock it down with blows or kicks, it didn't matter. If Rachel was in danger she would throw herself at the assailant.

-Hello. Connor smiled and Brenda was trying to figure out what the hell was going on as she caught her breath, leaning against the wall. Are you being chased?

No, if what he needed was to be laughed at his expense.

-Rachel... -he commented, taking a breath and walking through the door. She said it was urgent. Life or death. Total crazy! Those were his words. He replied as he sat down on the couch.

-I may have exaggerated a little bit. She commented amused.

-A little bit? You almost scared me to death. I almost pushed the last patient out of the office, I ran five blocks until I decided to stand in the middle of the avenue and stop every damn cab with my hand in the air like a madwoman just out of the madhouse and you say "a little bit?

-Yes, yes, well sweet, the patients at some point must return to their homes and we haven't spent a night of very friends in a while.

Connor approached with a can of beer and extended it to her while holding back laughter.

-You don't laugh! I almost had a heart attack. It may have been his words or the way he said them that made Connor's heart go wild and he could no longer contain himself.

-Your fault for listening to him. She also began to laugh, recognizing the wisdom in his words.

The three of them ate dinner, laughed and talked as they had not done in a long time. Since Akim's arrival in their lives, she thought saddened as she realized that not a day went by without remembering him. Nine months had passed, if it were childbirth the discomfort would have passed by now but, in her case, and even though the tears had stopped, the emptiness was still there, in her heart, as deep and as profound as the first day.

-What are you thinking about? -Connor asked, observing her gestures in detail, trying to guess her deepest secrets.

-Nothing...

-He still remembers him. He nodded as he pecked a Dim-Sum from the tray.

-What are you talking about?

Rachel didn't answer, she just asked him interested.

-Why did you do it? Why did you let him go?

Both she and Connor looked at her expectantly and Brenda answered bluntly.

-It was not the time. Since I met him my world was a continuous action and repair. It was as if one act led to another without being able to think, without having the ability to choose. First discovering feelings I couldn't accept, then the divorce, the loss of my house, my practice.... I couldn't keep rolling through life without being the one to decide. When Max and I broke up I wanted to find myself again, to be me and not a simulacrum of myself.

-Keep rolling and bouncing like a tire without a rim. Connor spoke seriously and she looked up feeling understood.

-And now? If I asked you now, what would you answer today? -Rachel asked with great interest.

-I'm not sure. She answered doubtfully while holding her glass of red wine tightly.

-Come on, don't be a coward. Our Brenda is not. Connor spoke, stinging her in the center of her pride.

-Yes, I might have said yes. I've matured, I've reflected and I've stood up for myself. Now I no longer pretend, I am what I am and I am happy to be what I am. I have recovered my patients and now I understand that here or there I would always be Brenda Klein.

-Good, very good. Super Well! - Rachel shouted, clapping her hands and making Connor laugh.

-Can you tell me what this is all about? Why so much interest?

-Honey," Connor cleared his throat, "We're going to Spain.

-What? What!" she shouted trying to stand up but her friend grabbed her shoulder to hold her back on the sofa. No! Don't even think about it. She threatened loudly but those two didn't listen to her. Connor took out of his jacket something that seemed to be a private invitation card and Rachel three cards with the Iberia Airlines logo on the front.

-No, no, please don't do this to me... I can't... I'd probably have a partner and I'd die of shame. I can't, I don't have the courage, with what face do I show up there? and what do I say? Oh, mother, I'm thinking about it... -She said fearfully to the amused laughter of those two madmen who rubbed their hands together, enthusiastic about their plans.

In less than thirty days, her house was rented, the patients were referred to a colleague and she was landing at El Prat airport in the wonderful city of Barcelona.

-Wow, it's beautiful. Rachel commented, stepping on the burning asphalt of the city, "You scoundrel! How come you've never brought me with you so many times?

-Honey, you have enough money to visit her on your own.

Rachel smiled in acceptance of his reasoning as Brenda held her hands herself to stop shaking. "What am I doing here," she said to herself over and over again, scared to death. I'm going to die of embarrassment. How could I even think of coming here after almost a year apart?

-I'm leaving. She said turning around and trying to get back into the airport but her friends each held her by a different arm and lifted her off the ground.

-Not at all, sweet. We are here for our future," Rachel said with the firmness of a respected actress.

-Ours? -Connor asked interested.

Brenda stroked her forehead, thinking her head was splitting like a ripe melon. Maybe that was a manageable problem, hopefully she would die at the airport and Akim would never find out that she had ever set foot on Spanish soil.

-Let's go to the hotel. I got one that is only two blocks from the studio.

-Two streets? -Only two?

-Yes, only two, and now move one foot and the other like a good girl and get into the cab.

Brenda would have liked to insult her friends who were pushing her by both arms to make her walk as if she were a raving lunatic but for that she would have to be able to speak and at the moment her ovaries were knotted around her neck.

Looking for you

The great night illuminated the dazzling exhibition. The room by the harbor represented the perfect place for the grand presentation of someone like Connor. Everything was prepared, everything except him, who found himself shaking like a leaf in autumn. He went over and over every detail of the room, rearranging even the smallest of details.

The lights were perfect and the layout of the works magnificent, he said to himself as he walked through the three rooms and greeted the first guests with a gentlemanly greeting. Connor had placed all his trust in him and he could not let him down. On the artist's success depended his own success. The painter had offered him the possibility of exhibiting some of his recent creations and he had not hesitated. The third room, the most secluded, out of respect for Connor, had been his choice for the presence of his four works. Walking nervously he checked the time again and again. It was still early.

-Akim. Iuju... Akim. Paula's honeyed voice roused him from his reverie. She was raising her hands with two cups halfway up and wiggling her hips from side to side as if she was dodging an obstacle course.

With a fake smile, the one he used to wear lately, he received her while he kindly accepted the refreshing Catalan cava. He took a sip and looked at her trying to find out why this woman could not catch his attention as she should. She was a magnificent model. Blonde hair almost to her waist, wide lips, long legs like roads and brown eyes, just brown.... No chocolate.

She looked at him hungry for a repeat of what had happened in his studio one hot afternoon, and he... he wasn't sure of anything anymore. He thought this woman would offer him comfort but that never happened. Damn his doctor who took away his will to live.

He had to forget her and maybe Paula was that woman, maybe if she offered him a chance....

-You look so handsome, you dazzle. He said as he fixed the collar of his shirt.

Grateful for the gesture, he decided to mingle with the people who were beginning to fill the room and explain the artist's works to the visitors. He would think about Paula later, today he had one of his greatest opportunities and he would take advantage of it. He would get ahead even though she hadn't trusted him or supported him or taken a chance on their relationship or believed in him or.... "Shit, enough of remembering her, you must sleep with Paula urgently," he thought scolding himself.

It's the day, she told herself, fixing her hair for the tenth time in a half updo on the side. The cream-colored dress seemed just right but despite Rachel's continued flattery, she couldn't help but look in the mirror and see that she looked terrible. Her skin color hovered between pale and deep red from sunburn. In just three days on the beach she had managed to go from dead pale to shameless shrimp.

-You look beautiful. Rachel said as she adjusted the plunge of the immense cleavage she wore on her back.

-If you say so. She answered suspiciously while observing the intensity of the red on his shoulders.

-He'll be breathless when he sees you, you'll see.

Remembering Akim caused the tachycardia she was trying to control to start again. Nerves surfaced and she had to breathe heavily like a pregnant woman in the face of impending childbirth.

-Rachel, I'm just asking you for a favor," her friend looked at her with interest, and she spoke with her throat pierced with grief. If he doesn't want to see me, if he refuses to talk to me, or if he's..." she couldn't say with another woman, "I'm asking you not to intervene.

-I ask you not to intervene. We will let him go and leave without disturbing.

Rachel began to look at her nail polish and Brenda cursed with desire.

-Rachel! Either you promise me or I won't go.

-Promise what?

Connor appeared looking simply spectacular. His misaligned fire-red knight counterbalanced the perfection of his lead gray suit.

-You look great. She commented excited to see how her teenage friend had become a successful international artist.

-You look beautiful. Let me look at you.

Enthusiastic at the compliments of her friends she turned around with her finger held high by Connor the dancer in a musical box. Thin straps held up a discreet neckline that when turned was counterbalanced by the huge opening in the back.

-Magnificent. You will leave him shocked.

-That's what I said," Rachel assured him as she rearranged a loop of his hair.

-Guys, I'm not sure, maybe it's too much. She commented, studying herself sideways in front of the mirror.

-We have to go all out, and you, my dear, you're a sweetheart.

-Conquering beautiful women in front of me? I can't believe it.

A man just as tall as he was but with hair as black as night and eyes as black as a mischievous cat, spoke amused as he held the artist by the waist.

-Mother of God. Rachel was the only one able to speak.

-Girls, meet Manuel.

Rachel shook her head wordlessly.

-Honey, this is Brenda. Connor said proudly pointing at her. The god of all sins smiled so brightly before giving her two resounding kisses and the doctor thought she was starting to hyperventilate. For heaven's sake, was he really gay? Maybe if he knew a woman...

she thought amused, remembering the phrases of a former patient. Politely she merely greeted him enthusiastically, but Rachel, when she awoke from her shock, pounced on his neck and squealed with delight.

-Mine, I'll keep it.

Connor smiled in amusement and her boyfriend held her around the waist as she replied just as smiling.

-If Connor abandons me, I promise to change my appetite for you.

They all laughed out loud and marched enthusiastically towards the exhibition. They talked non-stop, commenting on one funny anecdote after another, well, everyone except her, who kept squeezing one hand with the other to get courage and shake off the icy cold of fear that was freezing her fingers.

-Manuel, I will be very busy, will you do me the favor of accompanying my two sisters? I wouldn't want them to get lost or be kidnapped by any naughty little Spaniards," he said, winking at her.

-Leave them to me. I'll take care of them. Those Latinos are the worst. He replied with a smile that would have illuminated the very passage of terror.

-If all Spaniards are like you, I'll let myself be kidnapped. Rachel commented amused and everyone followed her with intense laughter.

The cab took them to a bar that, according to Manuel, was the last hit on the promenade so they could have a few drinks before going to the venue. According to those in the know, Connor was the headliner and was due to arrive a little later. She would have liked to end that agony as soon as possible but she also wished that the moment would never come. She was about to see him. They hadn't seen each other for almost a year, but her heart was still beating with the same intensity. How was he? How was he? Did he still remember her? Did he think of her as much as she did of him?

The time had come and the countdown was over, she thought as she stepped onto the first step of the hall. With her nerves on edge and her knees trembling, she walked with fear of falling when Manuel's hand grabbed her elbow and gave her confidence.

-Thank you, I'm a little nervous.

-Relax, Connor has told me everything.

Brenda looked at him with a touch of shyness and asked with some embarrassment.

-But everything, everything?

-Yes," he replied sympathetically. He replied sympathetically, "And let me tell you that if that man doesn't realize what's in front of him, it's because he's a complete fool.

-Thank you. Do you know him? -She asked enthusiastically. Maybe he told you about me sometime.

-I'm sorry, I don't usually go to Connor's studio, I don't like to interfere with his work. Tonight is my first public performance. I'm afraid you'll have to help me too because I'm scared to death.

Brenda smiled as she held onto his arm.

-We will support each other so we don't fall.

Manuel smiled and the four of them walked through the door hoping the night would not be too hard.

Where would Connor be? He wondered, looking at his watch for the umpteenth time. He should be there by now. People were asking about him and Akim didn't know what to say anymore. It was one thing to be the main star but quite another to show up crashed. If he didn't arrive soon he would call him on the phone and tell him to get there as soon as possible.

In the distance he discovered Lucien and his father looking at his work and for the first time his heart swelled with self-pride. His son was smiling in front of his paintings. Ready to go to his family's side, he stopped on the spot when two fans and friends of the artist applauded as they saw him enter. He would have smiled at such a scene were it not for the fact that his eyes had just popped out of their sockets. She was there, in the same city, in the same room, a few meters away.

His heart stopped and instantly began to beat wildly. The air escaped from her lungs and the people disappeared from the room. She smiled as she stepped over the threshold leaving the full limelight to her friend even though he was unable to look at anyone but her. Her doctor, her Brin.... Without realizing it she found herself murmuring his name as if time had not passed, as if the sorrows had been forgotten and as if an imbecilic and radiant Spaniard was not holding her by the arm.

Trying to look calm he asked himself upset, should he keep walking towards his family as if he hadn't seen her, should he ignore her, should he continue with the guests as if it was the right thing to do? What was the right thing to do! Nervous and trying to rearrange a picture that was perfect he was stuck to the floor when Paula grabbed him by one arm as she shouted excitedly.

-Come on, Connor is here.

Damn it, he said to himself as he was dragged by the woman towards the artist.

Good, thank you

Brenda looked from side to side but was unable to fix her eyes on anyone in particular. Her scrambled brain tried to locate him but there were too many people, either that or nerves blinded her, either excuse was valid. She greeted the guests Connor introduced to her attentively when as she turned to make room for Rachel her eyes collided with the reason for her trip.

As soon as their gazes met she felt the winter chill of fear and shame transform into an intense warmth, one that emanated directly from her sky blue. She had been remembering that blue for so long, and comparing it to so many things, that she was not surprised to find that she still remembered even that tiny speck of more intense indigo at the left edge just below her pupil.

She would have jumped into his arms and told him in a thousand different ways how many things she regretted, but she couldn't. He barely looked at her for a few seconds.

-Connor, I need to take you to some people. They are very interested in seeing you and I think they would be in your best interest. Akim's thick voice sounded much more serious than she remembered.

-Of course. Akim, I don't know if you've noticed but Rachel and Brenda are here.

Of course she had seen them, she thought nervously. He politely greeted Rachel before turning his attention to her. Brenda prepared to start talking to him so she could explain herself as soon as possible.

-Hello. She said nervously and trying to get closer to give him a couple of kisses but he just nodded at her.

-Hello. He replied dryly, "I see Connor has managed to bring you in.

"And you don't." He thought as he realized the ironic tone of her words. Okay, I get it, you're not going to make it easy on me. Brenda accepted the first blow with sporting dignity and willed herself to relax to speak normally.

-Things always come at the right time," she replied confidently and hoping that the double meaning was understood, but Akim turned his head away as if the answer did not go with him.

-Connor. He said in a thick voice and something she interpreted as authoritative.

-Yes, yes, I will, but first I'll go to Julia, look, I just saw her and it's urgent that I tell her some details.

Connor left there so fast that she wasn't even able to ask who this Julia was and Akim had no choice but to stay in front of her. It was clear that he looked uncomfortable but she smiled eagerly trying to show some reassurance. She wanted to speak but it was Rachel who broke the icy ice.

-I have been told that some of the works are yours.

-Yes, a few. Nothing important. He replied flatly and with that strong foreign sound he got when he was nervous. Well, she thought, you're as affected as I am.

-That's great. Brenda said, trying not to shake her voice as she spoke to him. I always knew you had a future in art.

He watched her and would have even thought his eyes lit up for a few seconds if it weren't for a slender blonde hanging on his right arm answering in a honeyed voice.

-I always tell him, but he's so humble. Honey, there's that friend of mine I wanted to introduce you to. Akim nodded as he excused himself to leave.

Brenda felt the ground sinking beneath her feet and taking her straight to the center of the earth. Honey? Her worst fears were confirmed. She had been replaced, and so soon. You loved me so much and so soon you forgot about me? Anger, jealousy and intense pain settled in the center of her heart to break what little she thought was healed. With inner trembling she watched him leave on the arm of what she thought was the perfect woman. Heart-stopping body, mermaid hair and a silly girl's voice, everything any man would want in a woman. Her eyes misted over and hopes fell from the sky to hit her square in the face. There was no future, she had traveled for nothing. "No! Worse," she thought rabidly, she had traveled to feel like an idiot, a humiliated one who had been forgotten and replaced. Saliva choked in her throat.

-Manuel spoke almost in a whisper in her ear but she did not answer him. With a little embarrassment and a lot of humiliation he turned to Rachel who immediately stroked his arm showing understanding.

-I have to go.

They were about to leave when Manuel stopped right in front of them, with his almost two meters tall and as many centimeters wide.

-If you're thinking of leaving the war field for a mere broom then you're not the woman Connor told me so much about.

-You don't understand.

-Oh, no? And what part is it that I don't understand?

-Manuel, this doesn't make sense. He is with someone else. She answered hurt.

-And does that mean you're going to abandon him at the first stone you come across?

-And what do you want me to do? -She answered grumpily and mumbling, "Should I pull her by the hair and throw her to the ground?

The god of gods smiled and she could only throw her head back in wonder.

-That would be nice but I don't see you as that kind. For heaven's sake Brenda, I saw you for the first time today but Connor talks about you so much that it's like he's known you for a long time. Are you really going to give up on that little model? Didn't you see how speechless he was when he saw you?

-That's true... -Rachel answered hopefully and switched to Manuel's side.

-You're crazy. Of course I was surprised, I wasn't expecting it, but that doesn't take away from the fact that I'm in love with someone else.

-For heaven's sake! It's a good thing I'm gay. You've just seen him for five minutes with a woman and you assume he's in love? You see him for an hour and you even make him the father of her children.

-She called him honey." he growled through his teeth.

-And Connor calls you that and I'm totally convinced he's not sleeping with you. Stay. Just for a while, just long enough to see if he's still interested in you. If he's not interested in you, I'll walk you back to the hotel myself and we'll get drunk together.

-I agree," Rachel replied enthusiastically.

-Which side are you on?

-Sweet, I think he's right. We got carried away but what have you got to lose? Besides, what would he think if we left? I'm sure he'd think you were a coward.

The truth is that even though she was hurt, wounded and in deepest sorrow, her feminine pride screamed fight!

-Maybe a few minutes. He said as his determination to leave began to waver.

She was sure that Manuel would try to finish convincing her when a little voice calling out to her in the middle of the room made her smile with excitement.

-Brin! -The little boy called her using the diminutive that his father used to use and that he had also appropriated. She bent down and thought she would fall as she felt the momentum the boy brought as he rushed into her arms. She squatted down to be at his height and they both kissed with the sincere affection of mother and son who had been separated for some time.

Don't listen to your heart

No matter how hard I tried not to look for her, I couldn't. She was there, just a few meters away. She was there, just a few meters away. If he breathed hard he could smell her scent of jasmine and vanilla, which was making him so upset. What was it about that blessed woman that her mere presence tormented him to the point of leaving him lost and aimless? Since his body had passed through the entrance gate, he had not been able to focus. He tried to ignore her and get on with his work but with her in the same room and after almost a year without seeing her, it proved to be too complicated a task. When she extended her face to greet him, he thought the whole body would receive her like a lapdog, luckily he was able to refuse or who knows what would have happened if he felt her skin caress his face again. "Impossible to hold back," she thought dragging her fingers through her hair trying to relax.

Everything seemed to be running smoothly. Everything except her, who was still chatting happily with Lucien as if they had never been separated. She could still hear the shriek the boy gave when he saw her. Trying to disguise it, he turned and focused his gaze like a distracted man to see that the two of them were still talking happily, a conversation now joined by his father. "Great." he thought in annoyance.

-Honey, in half an hour we have to leave for the cocktail party. Paula said approaching seductively and he thought the woman was starting to tease him.

"No!" he scolded himself. Brenda couldn't get away with this. She hadn't come for him but for Connor, his endearing little soul mate. He wasn't about to let the mere sight of her send his ideas to the dustbin. She was there for a man other than him, and though he was dying of rage and jealousy he would not show it to her. He would rather die than acknowledge the power she still held over him.

-Why don't you go ahead...? -and let me breathe while you're at it?

-It's ok... Don't be long. She commented with a kiss on the cheek, which he accepted, closing his eyes so as not to send her and anyone else he met along the way to hell. He was getting grumpier and grumpier and it had nothing to do with that asshole who was approaching Brenda again as if he thought she was his property.

Taking a few deep breaths she tried to calm herself as she approached where she didn't want to but where she should. Lucien and his father were standing next to Brenda and they were to leave for the party in Connor's honor. "Fuck, that's what was missing," she said to herself as she watched her son lead her into the small adjoining room and show her his only four works. "Fucking hell, you can have worse luck! No, you sure can't... And on top of that that dress that looks like it's about to fall down her bare back."

-And this is Dad's exhibition. Do you like it?

The boy commented with a proud smile and Brenda would have eaten him with kisses right there and then.

-They are beautiful. He said almost without looking at them.

With enthusiasm, the little boy guided her, showing her one by one the paintings, which she began to analyze with her face transformed. If the first one, whose only base was a pair of dark eyes looking into the distance and whose name was "Chocolate Look", had managed to surprise her, the other three left her speechless.

The second painting was a poem he knew perfectly well because Akim had dedicated it to him. The third, a bow made with a rope that he called eternally yours and the last one, and the icing on the cake, was a perfect interpretation of a spice market that he titled, "The Blue Knight".

Brenda swallowed a couple of times until she felt hope begin to reborn like a fruit germ in spring. Those paintings represented hours of work, hours in which he showed that he had not yet forgotten her.

-Brenda! What a pleasure to see you again.

Akim's father came over smiling and she hugged him with equal effusion. That little family had become her little family and she missed them dearly, particularly the stubborn one, she told herself amused.

-When Lucien told me you were coming, I didn't believe him at first, but now I'm happy.

-Thank you very much. He replied as the boy pushed his hand down to look at him.

-You're not angry? I just told grandpa. I swear.

-I'm not angry. Brenda replied, tousling her tousled hair.

-Yes, and because I insisted," he replied amused. Your secrets and weekly chats are safe with me. He said knowingly and Brenda felt she needed to explain.

-We both needed to keep in touch. We missed each other very much and I was afraid I didn't have permission to do so.

-I understand perfectly, but next time I would like you to trust me.

-I didn't want more people to be involved. I needed that time... -She commented, hoping that her father would understand her.

-I know, just as I know the stupid things we men say out of love.

-For love? -He answered, watching the gorgeous, blonde model walk out the door.

-If you don't risk it, you'll never know. Grandfather said with such a broad smile that it only added to his confidence.

Akim approached them and again ignored her. He addressed his father and Lucien as if she did not exist, but this time he would not fall into their trap, not in front of those four works that indicated how much he still remembered her.

-We must leave. He said in a thick, authoritative voice.

-We're going to the burger, will you come with us? -asked the boy looking at her hopefully.

-No." Akim answered decisively, but she was not intimidated.

-Brenda just told me she was going, didn't she? -Akim's father winked at her and she accepted the challenge.

-I can't today, but I think I'd love to see you tomorrow. What do you say? The sky-blue gaze, just as intense as her father's, shone with enthusiasm.

-And could we go to the beach?

-We could. He answered in front of Akim's withering look.

-We'd better go to the cocktail party. If you'll excuse us. Connor's boyfriend appeared as if by magic to lead her by the arm.

Akim glared at him, and Brenda sensed from the tension in his arms that he wished he could have hung him. Why was he acting with such poorly disguised tension in front of Connor's boyfriend? It didn't make sense. Everyone politely walked out the front door without a word.

Nothing was turning out as I had planned. The blissful cocktail was spreading more than he expected. It was either that or her blessed presence was tantalizing and attracting him in a superhuman way. What did she have over anyone else? Impossible to describe, he was only able to comprehend that his heart fluttered at the sound of her smile and that his hands burned just to caress her. No matter Paula's efforts to focus his attention, Brenda was there, after the most horrible of years,. She was there. Although his reason would have wanted to expel her from his side with insults and thousands of expletives, no sentence left his lips, "and better this way", he thought when he realized that the only thing he wanted was to hold her by the shoulders, scream at her why she caused him such suffering and then kiss her until they both fainted with pleasure.

Nervously he drank from the glass in his hand and squeezed the delicate glass, fearing to break it as he watched the man approach him and talk with the utmost abandon. Could it be that he cared so little about his feelings as to have introduced himself to his new boyfriend? Akim drank, trying to calm the accumulation of sensations that stirred his insides until they burned the center of his heart. Without being able to help himself he went back to look for them to find that the unpleasant man was no longer there and neither was she.

Curious, he looked for her trying not to get caught. She was walking towards the huge balconies surrounding the hall and in solitary. "Don't go...don't go..." He repeated to himself as he felt her legs take on a life of their own and go where they shouldn't. She had deceived him. She had lied to him. She had plunged him into the worst of his nightmares and now she was coming back to haunt him. Her presence emphasized to him over and over again what he could not have, what he should not aspire to today or in a thousand lifetimes.

Furious with her, with destiny and with the opportunities that had never come his way, he walked angrily. It didn't matter if he was in another country, with a new job and hundreds of possibilities ahead of him, that meant nothing in the face of the fact that he was seeing her again. Buried feelings surfaced and invaded his tormented heart. Resentment replaced all the love he once gave her. She said she loved him, she said it was him she wanted to be with but she abandoned him. Her prejudices were stronger than her desires. He would have given it all. Yet she thought of nothing but her own damnable age and the years that separated them. Wrapped in his own rancor he found himself watching her.

Leaning on the railing she enjoyed the sea that could be seen in the distance and he lit a cigarette leaning his hard body against the wall. There, in a dark corner, he studied her shamelessly, like a stalker who didn't want to be discovered. It was funny, but with Brenda he had always felt that way. An intruder waiting for his blessed opportunity. One where her chocolate gaze would awaken him from his nightmares and envelop him in her sweetness. A gaze he would obey with his heart in his hands. One that was still engraved in fire. Always yours, he thought caressing himself over his shirt in a reflex action. Called by the sigh she emitted towards the landscape or maybe, perhaps, by the scent of her body that he remembered perfectly, he walked to her with slow steps while drinking in every little detail of her hair swaying in the soft Mediterranean breeze.

His body crept up behind her back and he breathed in her perfume closing his eyes and remembering the mornings when he caressed her after making love to her. "My home... ", he thought as he breathed in the fragrance of her skin.

With the rancor forgotten, with the fury gone and with love boiling through her veins, and in a completely unconscious act, his right hand rested on the railing and his left hand followed her, leaving her imprisoned in his arms. The woman's breathing was heavy, she could feel her body tense but she did not flee or scream. She knew perfectly well who he was. She didn't need to look at him to know who was behind her back enveloping her in his warmth.

-It's beautiful...

She spoke observing the landscape as if no time had passed and he did not have her imprisoned in his arms and with her chest now resting fully on that small bare back.

-Beautiful." He answered without taking his eyes off the profile of her face almost glued to his.

It wasn't logical, he shouldn't have her like this. They were nothing anymore, but what a wonderful ache it was to feel her in his arms again.

-Your works have been sold this very night. I am proud of you. You don't know how happy I am.

She continued to look straight ahead. She didn't move her face a millimeter and he had to thank her for it. If she moved just a few millimeters she would be met directly with lips that yearned for her too much to hold back. Ignoring his flattery, she spoke for the first time.

-What are you doing here, Brin? -He whispered so close to her ear that she could feel the wetness of his own words.

She sighed and he waited confidently for her.

-I wanted to be here. He replied confidently.

What did it mean, was it for him, was it for Connor, for whom, he wondered desperately? Turning in his arms she faced him face to face and he wouldn't let go.

-I am proud of what you have achieved.

Her soft, smooth, delicate hand stroked his chin and he had to hold on tighter to the hard, cold bars of the railing so as not to show weakness. She had abandoned him, he must not forget that.

-If you had been here, with me, you could have experienced my progress first hand. His voice betrayed him and came out with a tone of sadness closer to melancholy than anger.

-I needed time. I could not go on without stopping to think. Too many changes, one after another and no decision made of my own free will. I had to take control of my life, to feel that I was in charge of my own changes. Akim, with Max I lost a part of me that I needed to get back.

She spoke appealing to his reason but his heart was galloping too upset to understand her.

-I would have stayed... For you I would have done it. If I had imagined that you would not be by my side I would never have left London.

Foolishly he looked up and knew it was the end of him. She was there, again, disarming him.

-And I couldn't accept that you would miss such an opportunity. I needed you to move on. Now both her hands wrapped around his face and he felt the heat of her fingers burn every fiber of rage he needed to keep alive or he would fall again at her feet.

-And I needed to stay by your side! -She shouted, breaking free from his grip to pull away, but she barely managed to do so by a few inches.

-Akim?

Still breathing heavily and with his fists clenched in tension he cursed for the untimely interruption.

-Tell me. He answered sparingly without ceasing to focus his gaze on Brenda.

-Honey, Connor is looking for you. He says it's time for the main toast and he wants you by his side.

-I'm coming. He said without looking away from Brenda, who didn't look away from him either.

Damn woman who, without permission, stole him and dragged him to her side like a trained puppy. If Paula hadn't interrupted them, he would be at her feet now and he would be the one begging for forgiveness. Why did he feel guilty? Yes, he may not have offered her a chance to explain, but what the hell! She had been the one who had let him go. She was the one who hadn't fought for them. Opportunity? What the hell did he care about opportunity if she wasn't by his side. Traveling to Barcelona was only meant to make him feel like a better man and a better person. But for her. It was all for her.

Without saying goodbye, he walked next to a Paula who, ready to capture his attention, clung tightly to his arm. He cared little about what she spoke or how sweet her words were, his heart remained behind his steps, on a railing next to a woman he did not wish to leave behind. He walked slowly towards the entrance doors to the living room, wondering if he wasn't making one of the worst mistakes of his life.

Back to

He was not tired. You could say he didn't go to bed too late. When Connor finished the obligatory thank you speech, he walked out of there as if the air was choking him. Brenda's blissful companion continued to watch over her and her friend Rachel as if he were the protector among protectors. What stupid things was he saying to her to make her smile so much? What else but nonsense could a long-haired guy with the looks of a washed-up model be capable of talking about?

With an incipient headache he poured himself a cup of coffee for breakfast and prepared to leave. He needed to lock himself away as soon as possible with his canvases and his writings.

-Hi Dad! -Lucien's shouts sounded like a bulldozer in a brain too full of problems.

I couldn't say that I had too much to drink the night before, or at least not enough to keep watching her smile at another man, one who surely didn't deserve her. Luckily she would be returning to London today and everything would be back to normal. The thought of knowing she might be taking a plane caused an emptiness in her chest that she tried to deny with the first sip of bitter coffee.

-Please don't shout. The little boy paid little attention and dropped his backpack full of things on the dining table. -Are you going somewhere? -He asked, looking at his grandfather who was entering the kitchen at that moment.

-I'm going to the beach with Brin. The little boy threw out the information as if it were nothing and the father felt that he was choking on his drink and running out of air.

-With Brenda? -He thought he saw his grandfather smiling as he looked for the carton of milk in the refrigerator, but he paid no attention.

-Don't you remember? You promised yesterday. He replied while carrying two bottles of water.

-No, I don't remember, and I don't think so. You can't go. The little boy and the grandfather stopped on the spot without giving credence to his orders and Akim felt like the worst of parents.

-But Dad!

-Brenda can't come and decide about you. She should have asked my permission. He replied angrily.

-He invited him in front of you and you consented to it, and so did I." Grandfather replied sharply, "We both did.

Fuck, I didn't remember any of that. Akim lowered his shoulders and stroked his forehead disturbed at his own incoherence.

-Maybe he said it out of compromise or he didn't realize how many days, he might be boarding the plane back to London right now," he commented in a daze.

-No, Brenda will be by.... -The little boy was pushed by the strong hands of his grandfather who guided him from above to the door and cut off his verbiage.

-Don't forget the ball. Remember how much Brenda likes it.

The little boy ran off to the bedroom and Grandpa smiled behind the cup of his milk tea as he sat down to spread a piece of toast.

-I haven't said that I can go yet.... -Akim commented, trying to retain some authority.

-You did it last night and I reaffirmed it this morning when she texted me.

-Did he call you? -He asked, trying not to sound so interested.

-Yes, they will spend the day together on the beach. He'll be here in fifteen minutes. The doorbell rang and Grandpa answered amused. Or maybe less.

The little boy ran to the door without realizing that his father was following him closely. He opened the door and threw himself into Brenda's arms who welcomed him with a warm hug and he felt stupid jealousy of his own son. He wanted to be in those arms, even though he wouldn't offer her the same kind of kiss.

-Lucien said they were going to the beach. He asked with the authority of a father involved in his son's life, resting his hands on the little boy's shoulders.

-Yes, it's a beautiful day," she replied with something that if he didn't know any better, he'd say it was shyness.

-Which one?

-The truth is that I don't know.... -she answered uncomfortably. I was hoping Lucien would guide me.

-Across the street from the studio and just five minutes from here is a good place to spend the afternoon. Akim suggested in a most interested manner.

-They have an ice cream stand. Lucien completed the information with a mischievous look and she smiled at him.

-Then let's not talk about it anymore, we will go to that beach.

The two laughed merrily as they walked away and he followed them with his eyes when his father's voice brought back his headache.

-So a beach in front of the studio..." He said with the tea cup in his hand hiding the sarcastic smile.

-Shut up. Akim walked a few steps and stopped short. -Shit. - He said to himself when he realized his mistake. His father was laughing his ass off and with the door still open, he couldn't contain himself.

-If you're looking for your room, it's inside the house, not outside. Akim came in, cursing loudly and angrily, while his father laughed heartily. And don't forget to wear shoes, lest you catch a cold.

With all the strength he had he closed the door to his room, but even then he could not hear his father's tearful laughter.

-It's so hot. He said, approaching the window and looking out.

-Horrible. Paula answered by opening her shirt even more trying to get his attention but he kept looking outside.

Had they moved? Lucien mentioned the ice cream stand and that was the one just a few meters from his studio. From the second floor he had a perfect view of the sand, the sea, and every couple that passed by but nothing. They did not appear. For the umpteenth time he looked again before picking up the brush from the palette when he finally spotted them. Yes, that was them. They were running after a ball. Lucien was throwing it to Brenda and she was throwing it back with very little grace, he thought amused. The woman at one point missed the shot and tripped over herself falling face first into the sand. The little boy jumped up and started throwing sand at her and she hid her face behind her hands. With infectious joy she found herself smiling with them in the distance as she said without a second thought.

-It's too hot. I'm going to the beach.

He began to put away the brushes urgently when the model replied happily.

-That's a great idea. Let's go.

"Shall we? At what exact moment had I invited her?"

-I'm exhausted and you owe me a soda." Akim remembered that she had offered to pose without charging him a cent and felt guilty.

-All right, let's go. He said, arranging the last utensils.

-I know a great place. It's not too far. In twenty minutes by car...

-No!" He answered with such a forcefulness that he noticed the fright in the malnourished model's eyes. I prefer it right here. It's too hot to travel by car -. He finished answering with a smile that although he wanted to seem enthusiastic turned out to be dark, or that was what he thought when he saw the face of the young woman who nodded without speaking.

They went into the beach and he searched and searched but those two were lost again. Now where the hell had they gone? The shrieks of an amused woman trying to enter the water and being splashed by an imp told him they were there. He sat down on the sand just in front so he could watch them play in the water when Paula commented a little angrily.

-So here?

Akim answered seriously, thinking the woman would think he was crazy. They had been searching for fifteen minutes for what was supposed to be the right place.

The young woman sat down and began to talk, but the truth is that I had not managed to glean much from her talk. He was too focused on watching those two having fun in the water. The smile came to his face without thinking and that seemed to excite the model who thought that such joy was due to his company.

-...honey, I'm so glad you finally took the plunge!

Akim listened to those words somewhat distractedly and looked at her as if trying to understand. What step forward was she talking about? And why did this woman insist on calling him sweetheart? In England a romp in an art studio didn't mean something to be called a sweetheart. He was about to ask which step she was referring to but the image of Brenda coming out dead laughing squeezing her long hair and smiling at the little boy left him dumbfounded. They both represented the perfect image. Their two loves united showing the world the happiness of being together. His heart swelled with satisfaction. Without listening to the reason that told him that this was madness, and that she would leave him again, he approached leaving Paula standing on the spot. Brenda was the first to see him but Lucien was the first to jump into her arms.

-Dad! -The little boy shouted enthusiastically and he picked him up high without taking his eyes off his body.

She may not have been the most model among models, nor the most beautiful among the beautiful, but what did it matter if, just by having her in front of him, he would lose his pants.

-Brin is going to buy me an ice cream, are you coming, Dad?

-He answered with his eyes fixed on her and talking about something very different from ice cream.

Paula's squeal as she hopped across the hot sand made him curse loudly.

-Oops... hello, Lucien, isn't it? -He said, regaining his composure and showing off his great figure.

-Hello. He replied with the typical children's angry mouth.

The three of them looked at each other uncomfortably until Brenda herself was the one who, acting with more head, at least more than his, greeted her politely and spoke serenely.

-Hello, my name is Brenda. We are going to buy some ice cream, if you want you can join us.

-Oh, no, no. It's a lot of calories and I have to maintain this great body," she commented with an artificial smile. We models have to look impeccable to please our artists, don't we, darling?

Brenda tensed but did not respond. She accepted Lucien's hand as he guided her towards the ice cream stand as if he didn't care about her explanations.

-I'm coming with you. Akim proposed running a few steps behind them and followed by a protesting model who was beginning to make him more and more uncomfortable.

They bought three ice creams and sat down on the sand. He swallowed more and more annoyed and begging for that woman to stop once and for all telling her supermodel experiences and calling him sweetheart. "If she ever calls me that again," he thought, chewing like an angry lion on the cone that was shattering between his teeth.

-Ugh, yes, and it's very hard, sometimes men chase you and don't realize that you are more than just a pretty body.... Well, more than beautiful, perfect," she said, smiling humbly.

-Brenda answered without taking her eyes off the horizon and Akim without taking his eyes off her.

-And you Lucien, are you going to be a painter like dad?

-No. The boy answered seriously, showing how little he liked the woman.

-You are as handsome as your father. He commented, smiling from ear to ear and making Akim want to bury himself in the sand. You could be a model. Be like me.

-How could you not! -Akim was about to scold him but it was Brenda who stepped forward speaking with a tenderness that made him melt at her magnificence.

-Lucien, modeling is a most interesting and attractive profession. She spoke sweetly and the little boy answered regretfully.

-I will be like you. He said, surprising his father, who did not bleed if he was pricked. Until that moment he had not understood how important Brenda's presence had been, not only in his life but also in his son's life.

Dizzy with information, he understood what he had so far seemed not to want to. It was her. It was Brenda he wanted. Father and son wanted her in his life. Akim thought and thought. She was there, with them, and he had to play all the cards on a winning horse or at least die trying. He couldn't let her go, not proving that his life had no smiles when she wasn't by his side. What the hell! Even the pictures he painted or the writings he put on paper longed for her. There was no color palette that didn't remember her or words that didn't seek her out. He had to try, but this time with much more determination than before. She told him that it had taken time to find her again but now she was there, that meant something, it had to mean something.

-This time I'm going to score a goal straight from the goal. Lucien looked at her with a quizzical look in his eyes and then smiled at her with the biggest of smiles.

-You don't believe that yourself.

-The goal on the right is mine," shouted Brenda as she ran to take her place.

-It's not fair. In the other one the sun shines in front of us. He replied, running with the ball in his hands and kicking up so much sand right in the model's face that she snorted indignantly.

-Oops, it's filled me with sand. I hope it doesn't scratch my skin. My skin is very delicate.

She continued to protest as he smiled at the pair throwing balls at each other with the worst technique he had ever seen.

-We're leaving. You owe me a soda," he replied, stroking his chest over his shirt.

-I am not thirsty.

-Honey, but I'm thirsty.

Paula spoke sensuously as she gently scratched his neck with her fingernail and Akim smiled with little humor.

-Paula, I'm sorry to get your hopes up, but I don't think I'm interested in the offer.

-Honey, that's because you haven't listened to her yet," she said, holding him by the neck ready to kiss him.

Trying not to come across as too rude he put his hands over hers and made them open to release him.

-I'm not interested in hearing it.

Akim stood up shaking the sand out of his shirt ready to take part in the most important game of his life.

-Honey, are you sure? -. Paula stretched out her magnificent body covered by a pair of shorts and a barely noticeable T-shirt leaving her ample assets on display.

-I am. He replied with a smile. And by the way Paula. He said before walking towards his final game. I'm not your sweetheart.

She was left grumbling loudly and Akim was amazed that someone who once seemed so sweet was capable of such an immense repertoire of curses. Forgetting Paula, he ran to the ball and took it from his son, who smilingly protested.

-That's no good. Two against one is not legal. Lucien protested indignantly.

-Come on, she's not even worth half a player. He said with a laugh and Lucien nodded with the same impudence.

-Hey, I heard you! -She replied amused as she was unable to remove the ball Akim was hiding between her legs.

You and I

-Brenda spoke, caressing the little boy's head as he lay on her lap.

-I'll drop you off at the hotel first. I'll drop you off at the hotel first," he commented, looking for the car keys and somewhat annoyed to realize that after a wonderful afternoon together and an excellent dinner of hot dogs and chips the day was coming to an end. She was resting on a park bench and Lucien, exhausted from so much enjoyment, had fallen asleep with his head in her lap.

-It's not necessary, I can call a cab. Manuel gave me a radio cab card, I think I have it in my purse," he said, looking for it and picking it up to show it to her.

"Manuel, of course, I had forgotten about him."

-Those two are protective and think they're going to lose me. I may be a mess, but I'm not that much of a mess." She commented with a smile so radiant that it left him wanting so much more.

"Wait a minute. Two?"-Two?

-Yes, Connor and his boyfriend. They are horrible. She said, gently taking the little boy's body into her arms and handing it to him.

-Boyfriend? -Manuel and Connor are... a couple?

-Yes, isn't it great. Manuel is charming and Connor needed to settle down for once.

"Couple. Couple? Connor's? God thank you!"

-Any problems?

-None." He replied with a smile too obvious to be ignored.

-Well, I'm leaving," she said, somewhat puzzled, and Akim understood her perfectly. Lately he didn't seem to be a very sane man.

-I said I'll give you a ride," he confirmed with a deeper seriousness than he had intended.

-Akim, I don't want you to have any more problems because of me. Your friend left upset and I'm partly to blame. I'd better go... -She answered with her face down, and Akim wished he didn't have her son's body in his arms to hold her and tell her that he wouldn't let her go. That was no longer possible.

The first drops began to threaten heavy rain and the two ran to the car. In a drive too short for his liking, they arrived at his hotel and he had to say goodbye without being able to express everything he was holding in his heart. Smiling, he heard a little snore from the little boy in the back seat and sped off towards his home just a few minutes away. With Lucien's fainted body in his arms he entered the house and was greeted by his father who was watching a movie in the living room.

-So you found them on the beach. What a surprise..." he muttered between his teeth with a touch of amusement.

-It seems so. He said without explaining himself too much.

She may have been told everything she had bottled up inside but that didn't mean she liked to open her heart to everyone and among that world was her father's heavy one.

-He did not answer. He just took off the child's clothes and laid him on the bed, covering him with a sheet.

-So it's all settled?

-I don't know what you mean. -He replied, sprawling out on the couch.

-You know exactly what I mean. What do you plan to do?

-I'm not sure," he said with some concern. I want to, but if she's not willing, will I be able to bear it?

-I see you haven't talked much.

-What do you mean? -he asked curiously.

-I mean, if she had told you about her new job, you wouldn't be sitting there like a fool asking silly questions. Her father spoke as if he were advising rather than scolding her.

-I don't understand.

-Brenda has agreed to be a psychologist for the Amazon group here in Barcelona.

Akim leaned back in his seat trying to digest the information. Completely bewildered he spoke again in fear of being the butt of a practical joke.

-Here? -You mean here?

-God son, everything you're big about you're slow. Yes, here. She plans to stay in Barcelona, or at least that's what she thought. I imagine you'll have a lot to do with it.

Akim jumped off the couch as he paced nervously around the room. Confusion was mixed with full happiness. She was there. For him. For him!

-Why didn't she tell me?" he wondered, scratching his forehead nervously as he smiled, unable to hide his happiness.

-Because you are a fool and you wanted to make him jealous with that little model. Her father spoke admonishing her behavior, "And don't even think of denying it to me," she threatened, narrowing her eyes.

Akim was scratching his head and pacing back and forth like a penned-up dog trying to clear his head when his father said confidently, "It's early. If you go to the hotel you'll find her having dinner," his eyes rose mischievously. And if you walk you'll get there faster than by car.

He had not finished commenting on his idea when Akim was already rushing out the door.

-What would he be without his father. You'd have no future," he remarked, looking out the window at his son scurrying about in the downpour. That's if he doesn't catch a good flu.

Grandpa laughed out loud and sat down to finish watching his movie.

I want to be...

Brenda dried her hair with a soft towel as she pondered her past, her present, and her increasingly unclear future. The doubts had her too confused. She pulled and squeezed her long hair as if it were her brain she had to squeeze. She tried to understand something of what had happened that day but logic was not on her side.

"Why did he show up at the beach?" Remembering the long-legged model, he got a lump in his throat. He didn't need to be a fortune teller to realize that he wasn't interested at all in that girl. But why did he take her? Did he want to show her that he could have anyone he wanted by his side? He already knew that, he didn't need to throw it in her face, she thought angrily. She sat on the bed and unwrapped the bag of chocolates Lucien had forgotten in her purse and set out to taste them all. Today she needed them more than the little one.

"Tomorrow, what will become of me tomorrow?" The fear of making new mistakes gripped his nerves. Life is a game of chance, so they say, where if you don't bet you don't win, but how much pain can a bad game cause? The door rang with loud knocks and Brenda licked her chocolate-stained finger and wondered who it was. It was pouring outside. She put the bag of goodies aside and got out of bed looking for something to cover herself with but the knocking was so insistent that she opened the door without asking.

Akim was dripping water down the bottom of his jeans, his T-shirt and his unkempt hair. His hair was plastered to his forehead, his cheeks were flushed and his breathing was labored. He didn't speak and she shivered at the sight of him. His chest was heaving and heaving and she was immediately frightened. His gaze never left her but words would not come and confusion gripped her mind. The blue fire of his gaze pierced her but she did not move. After what seemed like an eternity he held her with his strong hands by her elbows speaking in a deep voice. Water ran down her hands and wet her body but she didn't care. Akim's tension paralyzed her on the spot.

-Tell me that you are not here for me, tell me that you don't love me anymore, that you have forgotten me," he ordered, agitated, without taking his intense gaze from hers. Tell me something, a phrase, a simple word and I will leave.

Brenda was completely silent. She would not open her mouth. There would be no more hesitation between them, not on her part. Seconds passed and the smile began to appear on her hard face as she brought her soaked forehead close to his and spoke in a husky voice.

-But if you tell me that you are here for me, if you tell me that you still love me, then let me make it clear to you that I have never stopped loving you. Never.

Their foreheads rested on each other and Brenda's hands wrapped around his waist to pull him closer as she lifted her face to speak to his lips and answer him with all the love she had been hiding since the first moment their gazes met.

-I love you. I have always loved you but it is today that I accept it.

They kissed each other tenderly, madly and resignedly. They loved each other in spite of everything and everyone. Passionately he held her tightly and pulled her into the room as she tugged her wet T-shirt upwards trying to caress him skin against skin.

He was too tall and helped her remove it over her head when she froze. With tears in her eyes her finger skirted one by one the letters of her new tattoo next to her heart.

-Always yours... -He mumbled slowly outlining the skin.

Akim rested his hand on hers to accompany her on her journey as she spoke tenderly.

-Always. Eternally.

They both kissed lovingly but without urgency. It was no longer necessary. A life together awaited them from today until eternity.

Epilogue

-I'm fine, you don't have to worry.

Brenda spoke as Akim covered her legs with a blanket. It was a delightful autumn evening and she enjoyed watching the sunset from her garden. At first she thought he would refuse but he didn't and the woman was grateful. Sitting on her beautiful wooden deck chair, she enjoyed the coolness of the air hitting her cheeks and smiled gratefully at life. He sat down on the floor and rested his face in her lap. Lovingly he scratched her mane whitish with gray hair as his fingers were raptured taking them straight to her heart. There where her tattoo throbbed loudly despite the years.

-Don't leave me... -He pleaded, choked with grief. I won't be able to....

-You can. He said with the calmness of those who know.

Akim silently began to moisten her lap with tears and she tenderly caressed his face.

-I will love you always. Eternally yours... -He raised his wet face and ordered angrily. You will wait for me. You are not going to marry anyone, do you understand?

Brenda smiled lovingly to promise solemnly.

-I promise.

-I will look for you. I swear.

Akim's silent tears ran down his face relentlessly as his eyes closed for the last time. A little girl barely two years old arrived hand in hand with her father who, seeing him kneeling on the ground, ran to her side.

-Mom... -Lucien said with grief choking his throat. To call Brenda Mom was an understatement. That woman represented everything a child could wish to have and he had had it.

Akim looked at his son and granddaughter with a heart broken with grief. He wanted to speak but his lower lip trembled and he preferred to keep silent. The young man helped him up from the ground but he would not let go of his love's hand, as if by parting from her touch, he would lose her forever. He was not ready. Not yet. He needed at least another lifetime to love her as she deserved.

-Dad, she's gone. You must let her go.

Akim refused and Lucien feared for his mental integrity.

-Dad," she said with tears choking her heart. Her mother had just abandoned them, but that seemed like little sadness when she saw her father's hopelessness. When she thought she needed to scream for help to separate them, the girl, as if she understood her grandfather's immense sorrow, tugged his shirt down to speak tenderly to him.

-Grandfather, come with me.

Akim seemed to react and stood up with as much integrity as he could. He wiped his face but did not let go of her hand.

-Go get help. I'll wait here. He said to his son. Lucien accepted the order and headed into the house.

-Do you want to go to Grandma? -The little girl asked, stroking her adored grandfather's free hand.

-Yes, honey, I want to go with her. But I can't now.

-And when will you go?

-Soon.

-How do you know? -he asked with childish curiosity.

-I just know.

And Akim kept his promise, his eyes closed six months after his wife's departure. Everyone said it was out of grief, but his son knew it was out of love. His father said goodbye with a smile on his lips assuring him that his Brin was there, by his side, that he had come for him and Lucien believed him, for as his father said, he would belong to him in this life and into eternity.

...*Our bodies seek each other, our gazes meet and love is unleashed. Two bodies found by destiny.* Burning with need we fight unsatisfied in front of our hearts, which tired of waiting, surrender against each other before a reality they can no longer hide. Together we lose control. The burning of our skin burns us and with anxiety we break the limits of a modesty that, ashamed in front of the sweet awakening of kisses and caresses, fades in the silence of your room. Loving each other, we become entangled in an uncontrolled possession in which legs and arms are inflamed with need. My nervous hands tug at your crumpled garments. Proudly I scatter them on the carpeted floor of a hotel that, accomplice of our sin, is the only one incapable of judging us. My rough fingertips tremble as they brush against the warmth of your skin and my lips, hungry with need, impatiently roam every little nook and cranny of your body. You lie back, watch me, I melt into your gaze and beg for it to never end.

The moans, fruits of our passion, break the silence of secrecy while awakening to passion you rise with sweetness inviting me into the intimacy of your secrets. I kiss you, my tongue tastes your nooks and crannies and my possessive fingers cling to your rounded hips. I tremble, writhe and moan accompanying you to a destination where only with you I can reach. Agitated I clutch your wet body beneath mine. My unbridled heart beats furiously at the awakening of the tastiest of dreams and my arms take hold of a love that I will not give up. In the darkness of the night we embrace and my body surrounds you protectively imagining to be all that you seek, because you are all that I need.

Always yours. Eternally yours.
Akim

Other books by Diana Scott

Infidelity Series
    After you
    It's for you
    The custody of your heart
    Game of Passions
    Sorry I fell in love
    Tied to a feeling
    Stonebridge Series
    Hidden treasure
    The days we are missing
    Until you came along

All rights reserved
Copyright
© 2020 Diana Scott
@dianascottromance